PRAISE FOR
Red Hawk's Woman

"I would love to be Red Hawk's Woman . . . This is a great rainy-weather book. Grab a cup of hot chocolate and cuddle up."
—*Fallen Angel Reviews*

"[Karen Kay] hooks readers with a paranormal element but also delivers a solid Native American romance that's everything fans of the genre want."
—*Romantic Times* (4 Stars)

"Karen Kay has created a gripping story that reaches through time . . . *Red Hawk's Woman* is Native American writing that will leave you wanting more."
—CataRomance.com

"*Red Hawk's Woman* is a tenderly told tale of adventure, of honor, of forgiveness. It's also a story of love, survival and peace. This heartfelt story is the latest gift from Karen Kay, who never disappoints her readers. It's a treasure not to be missed."
—*The Best Reviews*

D0950602

continued . . .

THE LAST WARRIOR

KAREN KAY

BERKLEY SENSATION, NEW YORK

THE BERKLEY PUBLISHING GROUP
Published by the Penguin Group
Penguin Group (USA) Inc.
375 Hudson Street, New York, New York 10014, USA
Penguin Group (Canada), 90 Eglinton Avenue East, Suite 700, Toronto, Ontario M4P 2Y3, Canada
(a division of Pearson Penguin Canada Inc.)
Penguin Books Ltd., 80 Strand, London WC2R 0RL, England
Penguin Group Ireland, 25 St. Stephen's Green, Dublin 2, Ireland (a division of Penguin Books Ltd.)
Penguin Group (Australia), 250 Camberwell Road, Camberwell, Victoria 3124, Australia
(a division of Pearson Australia Group Pty. Ltd.)
Penguin Books India Pvt. Ltd., 11 Community Centre, Panchsheel Park, New Delhi—110 017, India
Penguin Group (NZ), 67 Apollo Drive, Rosedale, North Shore 0632, New Zealand
(a division of Pearson New Zealand Ltd.)
Penguin Books (South Africa) (Pty.) Ltd., 24 Sturdee Avenue, Rosebank, Johannesburg 2196,
South Africa

Penguin Books Ltd., Registered Offices: 80 Strand, London WC2R 0RL, England

This is a work of fiction. Names, characters, places, and incidents either are the product of the author's
imagination or are used fictitiously, and any resemblance to actual persons, living or dead, business
establishments, events, or locales is entirely coincidental. The publisher does not have any control over
and does not assume any responsibility for author or third-party websites or their content.

THE LAST WARRIOR

A Berkley Sensation Book / published by arrangement with the author

PRINTING HISTORY
Berkley Sensation mass-market edition / March 2008

Copyright © 2008 by Karen Kay Elstner-Bailey.
Cover art by Robert Papp.
Cover design by George Long.
Hand lettering by Ron Zinn.

ISBN: 978-0-425-22100-6

BERKLEY® SENSATION
Berkley Sensation Books are published by The Berkley Publishing Group,
a division of Penguin Group (USA) Inc.,
375 Hudson Street, New York, New York 10014.
BERKLEY SENSATION and the "B" design are trademarks of Penguin Group (USA) Inc.

PRINTED IN THE UNITED STATES OF AMERICA

10 9 8 7 6 5 4 3 2 1

*This book is dedicated with love to
my very dear friend, Sue Swift Friedman.*

To my wonderful agent, Roberta Brown.

*To Caroline Veach.
Thank you for your care
and your help with the music,
and for introducing me to
the magic of André Rieu.*

*To friend and fan Velma Boren.
Thank you for your years of support.*

*And to my husband, Paul Bailey,
whom I love with all my heart.*

THE LAST WARRIOR

In a time long ago, a Northwest Indian tribe betrayed the god of thunder. When the men of the tribe sought to kill more game than was needed, the children of the Thunder god thought to intercede on the animals' behalf. Because the tribe's greed had turned to lust, the men—who were cheered on by the women—killed the Thunderer's children, every one.

In retaliation, the Thunderer sought to destroy every member of the clan, all bands. It would have been accomplished, too, if not for the Creator, who intervened.

"Nay, these people shall not die," the Creator decreed. Instead He sent the people into the "mist." There, they would live a half existence, neither alive, nor dead.

But once a generation, each tribal band would be charged with the responsibility to summons a boy to become their champion. Armed only with the knowledge that he must show kindness to an enemy, this boy would become real and would go out into the world, entrusted with the duty to break the spell.

In 1875, there is but one tribal band left imprisoned

in the mist. Black Lion, a lad of twelve, has been chosen by the medicine man, White Claw, to represent this last band, the Black Fire band.

Venturing forth into the world, Black Lion has grown to full manhood within the Hunkpapa band of the Lakota Sioux. Many times he has confronted the enemy, and in each instance, he has shown kindness and understanding. Yet, the spell remains intact. Because of this, Black Lion has become desperate.

Meanwhile, the Thunderer's heart has become harsher, blacker. In his possession are now four stone nuggets, each containing the image of one of his children. However, owning these stones has not healed the Thunderer's thirst for revenge. In fact, it is the opposite; now, he can see his children, but never can he be with them.

Thus, he has sworn eternal revenge, making it his task to prevent this last of the tribes from ever going free. To this end, the Thunderer follows Black Lion, not intruding on him, at least not yet, but always is the Thunderer awaiting the right time and the right place to work his evil deed . . .

PROLOGUE

Aboriginal people in the United States have been closely involved with circuses, staged buffalo hunts, Wild West performances, and other forms of public entertainment for more than 150 years. As early as 1843, P.T. Barnum included Native dancers as part of his "Grand Buffalo Hunt."

Morgan Baillargeon & Leslie Tepper
LEGENDS OF OUR TIMES: NATIVE COWBOY LIFE

**The Hunkpapa Reservation
South Dakota
1890**

"You must go in my place." Two Bears clutched at Black Lion's hand. Two Bears lay on the floor, atop a bed of soft buffalo robes. His one-room shack was shabby, dark and decorated with scarce furniture. In a corner of the room, Two Bears's wife, Rabbit Leggings, lingered. But she made no attempt at conversation. Perhaps she was too worried.

Black Lion squatted next to Two Bears; he held a cloth in his hand to wipe the sweat from Two Bears's face. Said Black Lion, "*Ho*, I cannot go. Though I would do most anything for you, in this, I must stand firm. Surely you realize this."

Two Bears groaned.

"Wait and see," continued Black Lion. "You will get well. You will be able to travel with the Long-haired Show Man."

"*Hiya!* No! My brother, the white man's disease has me in its grip—it eats at me. I need rest if I am to recover. And if I go, I fear I will not get well, for I have heard rumors that the ride across the great water is treacherous."

Black Lion hesitated for a long, long moment. At last, choosing his words with care, he said, "My brother, can you not ask me for some other favor? I will give you most anything else, if it is within my power to command it. But I cannot travel with the Long-haired Show Man in your place. Though you are my *kola*, my brother, you know that I come from another tribe, and that I am sworn with a trust to help my people. If I go to this England, a land that is far from here, it would be as to give up all hope for what I must accomplish. And if I fail in my task, as others before me have done, forever would I have to live with the knowledge that I let my people down in their time of need."

Two Bears shut his eyes, pressing his lips together. He drew in a shaky breath. "*Waste.* I understand. You are right. It is not my place to ask you to do this."

Black Lion remained silent.

"But," said Two Bears, "you would only be gone for one full journey of the sun, for this is what it says in my contract with the Long-haired Show Man. Only a year, as the white man calls it. When you return here, you would still have time to end the curse that plagues you. Perhaps I might even be able to aid you in doing so once I have recovered."

Black Lion swallowed hard, his throat constricted with anguish. In the distance Two Bears's wife dropped a pot over the fire, the flames rising up to sizzle around its bottom. Though she never intervened in their conversation, Black Lion was more than aware that she, too, pinned her hopes on Black Lion taking her husband's place.

Black Lion said, "Tell the Long-haired Show Man you cannot go."

"It is impossible."

"It is *not* impossible," countered Black Lion. "He is still in our camp. Simply tell him of your problem and promise to become a part of the show in the next full season."

"*Hiya*, you don't understand. The Long-haired Show Man has already paid me a portion of the money I will make, for I have needed to buy things before I go. He and I made a pact, one that he calls an advance on my work."

"Then give the money back to him."

Two Bears looked sheepish. "I have already spent it on food and farming tools for my family."

Black Lion gritted his teeth.

"I have no way to pay him back that money," Two Bears added.

"*Tula*, it would never work," Black Lion said in defense, as though he knew he were trapped. "Except for our hair and eye color, we look nothing alike. The Long-haired Show Man will surely see the difference between the two of us."

"He will not make the connection," said Two Bears. "I have heard him say that all Indians look alike. He will not presume to know the difference."

"But there are other Hunkpapas going with the show. They know you; they know me. They will tell him of the deception, for they cannot lie."

"But," said Two Bears, "as long as the Long-haired Show Man does not ask them if you are who you say you are, no one need lie—not even you."

Black Lion exhaled a very deep, a very drawn out sigh.

Said Two Bears, "Think on it, my *kola*. Think on it."

Black Lion hesitated. Inwardly, he wanted nothing to do with it. If he left here, it would, indeed, place him at a disadvantage. But, Black Lion also knew that if Two Bears were in his place, his *kola* would do this for him, and more. Was that not the very meaning of a man's *kola*? Was it not a friendship that placed honor to each other above all things, including one's life, one's vow to another?

At last, Black Lion nodded. "I have no need to think on it further; of course I will do as you ask. You are right, I will have two years left when the show is ended, and were our places reversed, I know that you would do this for me. Therefore, I will do it."

Two Bears breathed out slowly, and across the room could be heard a feminine sigh of relief. Two Bears nodded. "I ask much of you, my brother. This I will admit. Know that if I were not so ill, I would never presume to impinge on you, on our vow of friendship. But I promise you that when you return, I will help you in your quest in any way that I can."

As though the mere speaking of these words taxed him, Two Bears lay back upon his bed of soft and warm buffalo robes, pulling a white man's trade blanket up around his neck. "But," continued Two Bears, "have you considered that perhaps what you seek may not be in this country? The white man is a cunning enemy, to be sure, and he lives in many different places. Perhaps what you hope to find is not here. Maybe this is the best chance that you could ever have."

Black Lion nodded. "*Sece*, perhaps. It could be." Although personally, thought Black Lion, he didn't think it was so. "But come, my friend," said Black Lion, "you need your rest. And I think your wife, Rabbit Leggings, is happy about our talk. But she is also waiting to serve you dinner."

"Stay and partake your meal with us," said Two Bears. "It would honor me if you would do so."

In the not-so-long-ago past, Black Lion would have accepted the invitation without hesitation. But not now. Food was too scarce here on the "rez." He shook his head. "I thank you for asking, but I must decline. If I am to leave with the Long-haired Show Man, I must find a spot where I might seek out the Great Spirit, for I would not go on this journey without His guidance."

Two Bears nodded. "*Hau*, yes. Go. Seek your vision as the old ones used to do before the white man came and forbade us to speak to the Creator as our fathers thought was right."

Black Lion frowned; what his friend said was true. No longer could the Lakota worship the Creator as they had always done. Indeed, so many things had changed since the people had been forced onto these small reservations that the Lakota were almost a different people.

In due time, Black Lion said, "This is good advice. But I fear that the Indian agent will never let me leave the reservation to seek this vision."

"Then perhaps you could slip away undetected for a day or two without the Indian agent being the wiser. Certainly, our old scouts would have been able to do so. Seek out their advice."

"*Hau, hau.* You give me good counsel. This I will do."

"*Waste.* Good. It is good." Two Bears lay back, inhaling an unsteady breath.

"And now I will leave you, *kola*," said Black Lion. "I will let you rest. I only ask that once I go with this Long-haired Show Man, you will promise me that if it is in your power to do so, you will be well when I return."

"I will give it all my best attention." He grinned slightly.

"Then I can ask no more than that from you."

The two men clutched arms, and with a slight nod of his head, Black Lion came up to his feet. Without another word, he let himself out of the Two Bears's shabby cabin.

Naked, Black Lion sat in a circle of the smoking, fragrant herbs, those of sage and sweetgrass. As the Lost Clan's medicine man, White Claw, had directed so long ago, Black Lion had cleansed his body in the herbs' sacred smoke. Alert, Black Lion watched the morning sun rise into the eastern sky, and even though his spirits were low, he rejoiced in the new day set out before him.

On his knees, and from his position atop a lonely butte, he raised his arms to the heavens. Lifting his voice so that the Great Spirit heard it, he sang:

> "*Wakantanka, Great Spirit, I come to you to ask advice. What must I do to end this curse for my people?*
> *Wakantanka, I leave this country to go with the Long-haired Show Man across the great water, for I am honor bound to defend my friend.*

Wakantanka, *help me. I do not know what I am
doing wrong. Have I not shown my enemy
mercy; have I not bestowed kindness? Why does
the curse still remain?*

Wakantanka, *I go because I must help my friend. I
only ask that you understand.*

Wakantanka, *I will return when the show is ended
for this season, and when I come back, I
promise that I will not rest until I discover how
to end this enchantment that binds my people.*

Wakantanka, *to show you that my heart is in the
right place, I offer you not only my flesh, I
proffer you the best possessions that I have. My
robe, given to me by my Lakota grandfather, is
now yours. My arrows, bestowed upon me by
my father, who is still imprisoned in the mist,
I give to you.*"

Black Lion placed the robe and the arrows on the
ground before him. Then, as he had been guided to do
by his elder, White Claw, he cut off sections of his flesh
on both of his arms, offering the gift to He who stands
above all others. Then returning to his knees, there
amidst the aromatic herbs, he continued:

"Wakantanka, *hear my plea. If you accept these
gifts, I would ask your guidance.*
Wakantanka, *I have said it. My prayer is done.*"

Black Lion sat back on his heels. Fanning the gentle
smoke onto his body, he closed his eyes, and inhaled
deeply. And that's when he heard it.

A song. A beautiful yet strange song wafted to him
on the wind. It was unlike any other melody he had ever

heard; it was also sung in a language he did not understand. The structure of its refrains was different than those he was accustomed to, and he wondered at it, for it had a strong beat, and then two small ones; then again, a strong beat, and then two small ones, over and over. Gradually, he began to hum along with the strain, finding it pleasing, soothing.

But who was singing this melody to him? he wondered. He glanced to his right, to his left, behind him, all around him. There was no bird here, no other person to be found on this butte, which itself was stuck out in the middle of the prairie. Then came the words:

"Human!"

Who was talking to him?

"Human, hear me," said a voice. Looking in the direction from which the words came, Black Lion recognized his namesake, the mountain lion, or perhaps more correctly, lioness.

"You must seek this song, and the singer of it. Look for it in a place far from here. Seek it wherever you may go. It is a white man's song, it is true, but its heart is Indian, and will always be so. Once you find this most sacred melody, and the person who owns it, you must sing it with a brave heart, and not one word must be missing from its verse. If you do this, you will pierce the Thunderer's heart. The melody will heal his anger as well as his need for revenge, and he will cease to be your enemy. When this happens, your people will be freed from their entrapment. I will sing the song one more time. Listen well, for when that moment comes, remember that not one word must be misplaced."

Black Lion nodded. "I am listening. Will you chant it more than once so that I may learn it well?"

But the lioness didn't answer. Instead, she sang the

song one more time, and Black Lion, attending to it well, memorized every word.

From high up in a cloud, the Thunderer watched the mountain lioness and this last champion. He grumbled, and the skies echoed the sound. *So*, thought he, *this last champion means to find a song*. Did the mountain lioness possess some magic that was unknown to him, a god?

A song? To heal his heart?

The very notion was impossible. Glancing toward the golden effigies of his four children, the Thunderer knew true rage, for while his children were caught in stone, in image only, most of the clan now roamed free upon the earth.

"Never will my heart heal!" he exclaimed, and thunder tossed through the heavens. "Never! Only when my children are free will I ever think to forgive. So sing all you desire, you, who are the last champion. It will do you little good. In sooth, it will do you no good. None!"

He laughed, the sound of it echoing down to the mountaintop below. And Black Lion, hearing it, felt his spirits sink.

CHAPTER 1

London
Summer, 1892

The sun was high, the day was sultry, warm and muggy, and despite the fact that the exhibition's seating provided a canvas roof for protection, nineteen-year-old Suzette Joselyn was hot. Daintily, she pressed a handkerchief to her forehead.

What, she wondered, had possessed her to accompany her grandmother, Irena, to this rather crude display of American culture? Even though people from all over London had flocked here—especially after the Prince of Wales's endorsement of the show—it still seemed to her that the show would be crude indeed.

Irritated, Suzette thought of the old saying about a cat and its dire curiosity. Perhaps next time she would heed the cliché's warning before agreeing to one of Irena's schemes.

In truth, Suzette was embarrassed . . . and with good

reason. The smell of horseflesh—and perhaps unwashed bodies—wafted through the air . . . And she, sitting here so primly beside her fiancé, who was a fine young man, wondered what she was to do. A proper young lady, especially one who was to become the wife of the Earl of Lankersheim, was not supposed to acknowledge the rank odor of horse manure, stables and worse, was she?

Suzette frowned. Leave it to Irena to put her granddaughter in such a position. Alas, Suzette feared that Irena did not approve of her granddaughter's engagement. Although why this was so was a mystery to Suzette.

But Suzette ignored her grandmother's opinion. It was a wonderful piece of luck that the earl wanted to marry her rather than use her in return for furthering her career, which was the fate of most opera singers.

Suzette, the daughter of opera stars John and Beatrice Joselyn, had always looked upon the practice of "entertaining" rich young men as . . . well, as distasteful. Of course she realized it was sometimes a necessary part of the "business." No doubt she knew that very few prima donnas attained their position without compromising their virtue. But having grown up with such things, having witnessed the sordidness that attached itself to the business in general, she had long ago decided that this sort of life was not for her.

She craved love, she craved position and respect within British society, she craved a family, she craved . . .

Blare-e-e-e!

What was that sound? Looking around, she recognized the problem at once. She rolled her eyes and sighed.

A twenty-piece brass band had materialized across the arena. Complete with trumpets, trombones, bass and drums, the band was only beginning to bellow out the strains of a very loud marching song.

Dear Lord, could their music be any more vulgar?

"I say." William Blair, Earl of Lankersheim and Suzette's fiancé, leaned in toward her. "It's not exactly operatic music, now, is it?"

"Indeed not!" Suzette wrinkled her nose.

When Suzette turned to speak to Irena, she discovered that her grandmother was gone.

Spinning back toward her fiancé, Suzette asked, "Pray, did you see when Irena left?"

"Indeed, I did," replied the earl. Taking hold of Suzette's gloved hand, he patted it as a parent might do when scolding a child. "I do wish you would call your grandmother by her proper title, darling. She is, after all, your grandmother."

"Yes, yes, of course," Suzette said, though she frowned at her fiancé and retrieved her white-gloved hand.

"Oh, and now I've upset you," said the earl.

"Indeed, you have not," Suzette lied. "I am simply wondering where Iren—where she went."

"Darling, I know she raised you under unconventional circumstances, and the two of you like to call one another by your given names. It's not for me that I mind. It's only that when we are in public, to address her as . . . and then, there is my mother . . ."

"Yes, yes, you are right, of course," said Suzette. "Heaven forbid someone think the wrong thing."

"Now, now, Suzette. Let's not be sarcastic. I must think of my position, after all."

Suzette smiled. "I know you must, William, and I am not annoyed with you for reminding me of it." Again, she lied. "It is only that Iren—my grandmother should not be roaming around this Wild West Show alone. You know how she is, what might happen."

"She is a grown woman, Suzette."

"Yes, but . . . Have you never noticed that trouble seems to seek her out?"

"No, indeed, I have not."

She stared at William for some moments, admiring his handsome face, which was alight with tolerance. And in his eyes was a gleam of admiration for her.

At last Suzette smiled. "You are right," she said. "It is wrong of me to worry about her. She is a grown woman and capable of handling herself, and yet . . ."

"Oh, look there! Is that Buffalo Bill, himself?"

Dutifully, Suzette gazed down into the arena. "It does look as though it is he."

"And who is that off to the side, there? I daresay, is that—"

Suzette gasped. "Irena! Oh, William, I must go down there."

"Calm down, darling, I'm certain she is fine. Maybe she will sing the first song of the season so that the performance can begin."

Suzette closed her eyes and prayed.

As it turned out, William was right. Apparently, Irena *was* going to sing.

After a short introduction by Buffalo Bill himself, Irena stepped up to the platform, which was set out in front of the band. She even opened her mouth as though to sing the American National Anthem, but instead of a melody, her speaking voice rang out loud and strong. She said, "I would like to dedicate this beautiful work I am about to sing to my granddaughter, Suzette Joselyn, and to her fiancé, William Blair, the Earl of Lankersheim."

And to Suzette's complete mortification, Irena began to sing the opening stanza of Henry Purcell's "Dido's Lament," an aria of death and of love, betrayed. She might as well have been singing a funeral march.

William's complexion turned pink. However, he laughed. Suzette, on the other hand, knew her face had to be a bright shade of red.

Oh, to find a hole and sink into it . . .

"Darling, be fair," said William. "Your grandmother is older, she's eccentric. She has a right to live her life as she has always lived it."

"But not when it influences me . . . and you. And she's not really that old."

"Suzette, I, for one, am not upset."

"But I am."

William placed his hand over hers. "There, there, darling. I am certain she will come to like me in time."

"That is very kind of you," said Suzette. But truth be told, Suzette was too annoyed to take pleasure in William's comfort.

"I must go down there, for I *am* going to talk to her," Suzette said. "Now. Would you like to accompany me?"

William gazed at the arena, where the Indians were only beginning to enter. In single file they came. All were dancing. All were dressed in the most colorful display of feathers, buckskins and beads that Suzette had ever seen.

"Of course I will accompany you."

But Suzette sensed William's reluctance. He wanted to stay and watch the show.

She smiled at him. "No, you needn't come with me, William," she said. "I understand. When is the next time you will be able to witness a spectacle like this? Pray, be at your ease. I will go and find Irena, and we will both be back here soon."

"Yes, darling." William smiled and patted her hand.

"Do not scold her overly much, though. Remember, she is older."

"I will consider it." Suzette accepted William's hand to help her up, and clasping hold of her skirts, she picked her way through the crowd.

CHAPTER 2

Black Lion awoke with a start. Had he overslept?

It appeared he had; the signs were not good. Sunlight poured in overhead from the ear-flaps of the canvas tepee, and glancing up through the lodge poles, Black Lion caught sight of the sun, which was already positioned mid sky.

What had caused him to oversleep? And this on a day when he had been cautioned to arrive for the performance in a timely manner. Pulling his jeans on over his naked body, he had no more than stepped foot into them, when he remembered that he was supposed to be attired in traditional dress.

"Damn," he uttered the white man's word.

Tossing his jeans to the side, Black Lion grabbed hold of a breechcloth lying on the floor, pulling the softened leather through his legs and tying the long string securely around his waist. Stepping quickly into his moccasins, he decided he wouldn't bother with leggings today—the kind of riding he was doing was traditionally done naked anyway.

The Long-haired Show Man, or Buffalo Bill, might have things to say to him later, but Black Lion couldn't think of that now.

He grabbed hold of his quiver full of arrows—mere sticks with rubber tips, since they were now minus the traditional bone arrowhead—and his bow. Then he heard it . . . feminine laughter outside the tepee.

Black Lion shook his head as though the simple action might serve to enlighten him. *What was wrong with these European women that they followed him? Why did they wait for him? Touch him? Ask for his autograph?*

Sighing, he realized he was doomed; not only would he be unable to hurry to the arena as was needed, he was going to have to humor these females. That or face a dressing down if one of them complained.

And this would never do, not when he acted in his friend's stead.

Accepting his fate, Black Lion grabbed his headdress, as well as his shield, and stepped out of the lodge. Frowning, he inhaled the moisture-laden air as he quickly counted the number of women in his audience. At least there were only fifteen this time. Last night there had been more than fifty.

Giggles sounded around him. "May I have your autograph?" asked one of them.

He smiled at the girl. "For twenty-five bucks," he said, his voice deep and baritone. He uttered the words good-humoredly, however, for he accepted the young lady's pen and paper without further argument.

"My parents have given me permission to ask you if you would like to join us for dinner this evening," said another one of the women as Black Lion attempted to scribble out his name—although it wasn't *his* name; it was his friend Two Bears's name.

Black Lion nodded at the golden-haired, pretty and

immaculately dressed girl. In truth, if duty were not so
heavy on his shoulders, he would have liked nothing
better than to spend more time in this young lady's presence. But he could not. Not only was he a man haunted
by a duty to his people, he was also here representing
his friend Two Bears, who was married.

"Stop it, Sadie, I wanted to ask him!" The owner of
that voice pushed in toward him. "Maybe you could
come to see me tomorrow?"

He breathed out another deep breath. Here before
him was yet another beauty. Black Lion jerked his chin
to the left—a typical Lakota gentleman's gesture—and
grinned first at one of them, then at the other woman. "I
would like nothing better than to get to know you all,"
he admitted. "But alas, I cannot."

"Why can you not?" came several voices all at once.

"Because I have work to do and because—"

"I . . . be jealous." The voice was low, feminine and
came from behind him.

Looking around, Black Lion recognized the wife
of Running Fox, a fellow Hunkpapa tribal member. He
smiled at this woman whom he knew to be called Little
Star.

Meanwhile, the giggling of those surrounding him
had stopped. Each of the beautiful young women was
staring at the speaker.

"I . . . often jealous of . . . women," Little Star said,
"who ask . . . husband to dinner." It did not escape
Black Lion's notice that Little Star omitted to say exactly *who* her husband was.

"I didn't know you were married," said one young
lady.

"I didn't, either," chipped in another.

"Nor I."

"Sorry," said Black Lion simply. "But Buffalo Bill

rarely hires an American Indian man who is not married." He cast Little Star a quick wink, as well as a grateful smile. Little Star nodded.

"And now," said Black Lion to the girls at large, "I must leave you. I am late for my performance."

Without a backward glance, he struck off toward the livery.

Once he was far enough away from the women, he didn't waste another moment, but ran as though he were in a race, bolting over anything in his way, which included a rather large hitching post, as well as several mud holes.

"Where's Ranckles?" he asked Old Doc, the man who attended to the animals.

"Son, you're late," the old-timer remarked.

"I know," said Black Lion, barely catching his breath. "I must hurry."

"He's over there in the stall. He's saddled." Old Doc winked.

"Thank you, Grandfather," said Black Lion. "I will honor you for this."

"Honor? Forget about the honor, and just get in there. He's come down here twice to check on ya."

Black Lion had no need to ask who "he" was. Shoving a gift—a pouch of tobacco—into the old-timer's hand, Black Lion adjusted his headdress over his hair, grabbed hold of Ranckles's reins and hurriedly headed toward the arena.

It had rained the day before the show was to open. This was both good and bad. The good was that the air was clear, fresh and invigorating, if a little humid. The bad was that there was muddy water everywhere.

Black Lion had no choice but to leap over the many

mud holes, as he pulled Ranckles, an Appaloosa, after him.

In an effort to determine the time, Black Lion glanced upward toward the sun, not the best action to take when one is also running. Momentarily blinded, he ran straight into an obstacle, sending whatever it was to the ground, and unfortunately for it, directly into the mud. Luckily for Black Lion, Ranckles seemed to have more sense than his owner and stopped quickly enough so as to avert a real disaster.

Looking down to see what it was that he had run into, Black Lion was disconcerted to behold yet another female. Grimacing slightly, he rolled his eyes.

"I saw that," said the female heap on the ground. Her voice was surprisingly beautiful.

Black Lion, however, was not so easily impressed, since it was still a *female* voice. He looked passively at the woman and said, "I am sorry," then he groaned a little as he gave her a closer look.

The woman had raised her eyes, and they were the deepest, the most beautiful blue eyes he had ever seen, and Little Blue Eyes, as he immediately dubbed her, stared back at him. Unwillingly, he found he was not immune to her charm.

"You rolled your eyes at me," she said indignantly.

"Forgive me," he said. "I am late for my performance. I hurry when I should perhaps tarry." He heaved a deep sigh. Then he turned to leave.

"That is all? I get no more apology than that?" she said. "Will you at least help me up?"

Black Lion frowned. Beautiful though this young woman might be, he couldn't help but compare her to the well-brought-up Lakota women with whom he was acquainted. No polite Lakota woman would dare to use a voice on him that, for all that it was pretty, was filled with antagonism. Indeed, in the country of the Lakota, it was considered the height of bad manners to speak to a man with anything but a pleasant demeanor. "Where I come from," he said, "women speak softly and pleasingly. And they do not contradict a man."

Perhaps he should have kept the observation to himself, however. She scoffed at him and said, "I beg your pardon. Do you, an American Indian, seek to lecture me on manners? You, who have not even offered your hand to help me out of this mud? Where were you raised? With wolves?"

He stepped toward her. Obviously, he did not understand what a white man was required to do. He said, "Forgive me. I am not from here. I do not know your customs."

"Pray, is it really that difficult to understand? Look at me."

He did. And that was part of the problem. She was beautiful . . . as well as . . . There was something about her that pulled at him . . .

At the moment, she was a mass of dark hair and sky blue material, except where she had rolled in the mud, of course. And it occurred to him that she wanted him to help her up, something no Lakota woman would ever expect or need. For it was a man's job to protect and to provide, and a Lakota woman knew this. She would never interfere with a man or with his work.

But here in this England, Black Lion was out of his element. With one more apology, he bent over the young lady, and as though she were as lightweight as the headdress he wore, he picked her up.

She was rounded and soft, he noted at once, and she was probably the most shapely young woman he had ever had the good fortune to hold in his arms. However, this embarrassed him. In his country, men and women who were not married did not touch. Rarely did they even speak.

As he grasped hold of her tiny waist, his fingers tingled at the contact. And for a moment, he yearned to hold her closer, to breathe in her sweet scent.

He quickly set her down on her feet. "Sorry," he said again and turned away.

But apparently white women here were more than a little different than Lakota women. "That's it?" she said again. "That's all? You have nothing more to say? You knock me down like some colonial gun-barreling . . . Wild West . . . gunslinger. You ruin my dress and my umbrella. And all you have to say is 'sorry'?"

Spinning back toward her, he spared the delicate creature a quick glance, but for all that it was fast, the look was thorough. Long dark brown hair that cascaded into ringlets over her shoulders; creamy, pale, pinkish complexion; blue eyes that were made bluer by the color of her clothes. In truth, she was more than beautiful . . . she was . . . exquisite.

He said, "I am late."

"Yes? . . ."

"I have to . . . hurry." Was she beautiful, but not very smart?

"Look at me. You have ruined my dress." She held out a muddy piece of the material as evidence. "You slung me into the mud, and then turned away without helping me up."

"I helped you up."

"After I complained."

"I still helped you up."

She sighed impatiently. "That's not the point."

Black Lion realized he probably appeared stupid at the moment, but he could only gape at her. She wanted something else? Wasn't it enough that they had touched, that he was speaking to her when there was no chaperone here to thwart him? Did she not fear for her reputation?

He was not left long to wonder, however, for she continued, "Do you not understand that I will have to pay to have the dress washed and pressed tomorrow?" She blew out a breath. "And that's tomorrow, what about today? How am I supposed to endure the rest of the day with all this guck on me? And look here . . . my jacket is torn, too." She put a hand to her head. "Where's my hat?"

For a moment, Black Lion felt as guilty as a wayward boy. Once, long ago, one of the women from the tribe had scolded him in much the same manner. It had been so demeaning an experience that it had never happened again. He had ensured it.

But this was not then, and he was not a young boy to take offense so easily. What was wrong with her? he wondered. Couldn't she grant him quarter? After all, he was new to this land. He didn't know this town, he hadn't yet learned their rules . . .

"Oh, my hat," she complained. "Where's my hat?"

Looking around, Black Lion noticed an object of similar coloring to the woman's dress. It was probably the object in question.

Letting go of Ranckles's reins, he recovered the article, though the action little aided his cause. Mud had worked its damage on the hat. And a long blue feather, instead of standing straight up, limped to the side. Carefully, he tried to make it stand upright. But the action was useless.

Shrugging, he offered the item to her and said, "Back in my country men and women who are not married, or planning to be married, do not speak, let alone touch one another. I have done both with you this day, and I fear that either I must bring our conversation to an end, or I will be forced to marry you."

And though he smiled a little, she gasped. "Are you trying to insult me?"

"I flatter you. Or I try to. There are many women who would be honored by such a declaration from me."

"Well, I am not one of them."

His smile broadened. "Do not worry. If I am forced to add you to my family, my first wife will tame you."

Her second gasp was even louder than the first. He had known, of course, that the taunt would hit a chord with her, since he had come to understand that white people married only once. But, the Great Spirit be praised, he couldn't seem to help but tease her.

As though to add further insult, in the process of handing the hat to her, their fingers accidentally touched. At once, excitement burst through him. He even swayed a little.

He said, "I will pay for the damage to your dress or I will buy you a new one. People here call me Two Bears. You have only to ask for me, and others will bring you to me."

"I do not want your money. I want you to—" She stopped suddenly. She paused.

Waiting, Black Lion raised an eyebrow at her.

"I want you to go away and leave me alone," she finished, although as she spoke, her hat fell from her fingers, the cap landing in the mud. The feather fell over as though it might drink in the substance. Shame. Her possession was now beyond repair.

Still, he couldn't help but grin at her, and he said, "If all that you require of me is my absence, it will be my pleasure to obey." His smile widened, and without another word, he turned his back on her.

"Wait!" she called. "It is not *my* duty to seek you out. A gentleman should always solicit the lady."

He sighed, saying, "Please, I do not have time for more talk about manners. I am late."

"And you expect me to be sympathetic? Perhaps you should arise earlier if you have trouble arriving in a timely manner. Or better yet, maybe you should watch where you are going."

"I think you are right. I should, and I will," he said, as though agreeing with her. "But at least I have only a change in my schedule to consider."

"A change in . . . ?" She frowned, grasping that she was being insulted. But how? "What's that supposed to mean?" she asked.

"Only this," he said. "Where I was raised, young women do not venture out into the day alone, and if they did . . ." He let the insinuation dangle between them for a moment before finishing. ". . . they are what the white man calls 'fair game.' "

"What? Why, that's as barbaric to a modern woman as—"

"And when they speak," he continued, cutting her off, "only soft words of comfort and pleasure come forth from their lips."

"Meaning that I . . . ? How dare you," she sputtered. "That's the second time you have spoken offensively to me."

"I mean it not as ridicule, but as instruction because you . . ." He shook his head. There seemed little point to explain that it was his duty to protect a young lady's reputation. Besides, such a declaration would hardly be true. He *had* meant to be as forward with her as she was being with him. "If you will stay until after the show, I will seek you out then, and I will make good my obligation to you."

"Pray, do not bother. I will see to the repair of the dress myself."

"If you wish it to be so, then it will be so." He turned to leave.

"Oh!" she exclaimed. "A real gentleman would press his cause."

Once again, he turned back, crossed his arms over his chest and said, "Either I will pay you for the damage or I will not pay. The choice is up to you. Now be clear on this matter. Do I look for you after the show? Or not?"

"You do not. And sir? . . ."

He raised an eyebrow.

"You are no gentleman!" She said it arrogantly, lifted her chin and swung around to stomp off in the opposite direction to his own destination. He might have watched her for a moment. She was certainly pretty enough that he would have liked to memorize her every feature. But he had wasted enough time.

Picking up Ranckles's reins, he hurried off in the direction of the arena.

"Well, Irena," said Suzette. "I hope you're proud of yourself."

"I am." Irena smiled, the action transforming her demeanor so much that she looked forty instead of her fifty-seven years of age. "Did I not offer you the loan of my carriage so that you could rush home and change your dress? And was it not accomplished easily, with little time lost?"

"Yes. However, I am not talking about that. I'm speaking of what you did earlier. You embarrassed me, Irena. You embarrassed William, though he is such a sweet man that he laughed. Really, Irena, can't you learn to curb yourself? Is it too much to ask that you act like a real grandmother?"

"Oh?" Irena raised an eyebrow. "Pray, tell me, how is a real grandmother supposed to act?"

"I am not sure," said Suzette, "since I am rarely presented with a good example. But certainly not like you have today."

"Hmmmm. Let me see. Is it that you want me to be at home cooking, sewing, cleaning? Perhaps you think that I should be teaching your children, when you have them, to sing?"

"Never to sing."

Irena set her head to the side. "Is the opera really so bad?"

"Of course it isn't. It's been my life, it has been . . . it's been the making of me. But I want something more from my life. Certainly the aesthetics of the music are well worth attaining. And if that were all there was to it . . ."

"But that is all there is to it, isn't it, dear?"

"Pray, Irena, do not do this. Do not pretend you don't know of what I speak."

"Oh?"

"There's the jealousy that goes along with the trade, for one; there's also the backbiting, the hypocrisy, the gossiping."

"Oh, I suppose you have a minor point, there."

"Alas, it is a major point, Irena. And it's one I can do without in my life. What I desire is a family, and a man who is not only worthy of me, but who loves me. William is such a man. You will see. William is kind. He is gentle."

"He is ruled by his mother."

"Perhaps. Is that so bad?" Suzette shrugged.

Irena frowned. "It could be . . . if . . . the woman decides she does not care for you."

"She likes me."

"She likes you now. But what is she going to do if you take one false step?"

"Come now, Irena. You know that is all but impossible. Think of the many operettas that I have performed in. Have I ever missed a cue? Have I ever sung an off-key note? Flubbed the music?"

"But that is part of the problem, child," said Irena. "You are from the stage, from the opera. His mother will never forget it, and she will be looking for a chance to take you to task . . . any misstep. And you know as well as I do that when someone is antagonistic toward you, you are more inclined to make mistakes."

"Oh, Irena. It's going to be fine. I love William. He loves me. Even if his mother raises questions about me, he will defend me." Suzette raised her chin. "I know he will."

Suzette looked around. They were talking in the entryway of Buffalo Bill's tent. Across a narrow pathway from this main tent stood the Indian encampment. Suzette knew it was there, but she stood with her back to it, as though by ignoring it, it would go away.

"Irena, let us be on our way. We do not belong here. Besides, William is waiting for us."

"He will keep for a little while. The show is entertaining enough to hold his attention."

"Yes, but why should he *have* to keep? Come, Irena. I know this show may seem exciting to you, but—"

"It is exciting, Suzie. And indeed, when one reaches my age, it is well to find some aspect of life that is . . . enjoyable."

Suzette breathed in deeply. "You are not so old. You know it. And even if you were, which you are not, you don't look your age. Now, please. I miss William. Let us walk back toward our seats."

"I cannot."

Suzette lifted her chin a notch. "Oh? Why can you not?"

"Because," said Irena, "I promised Buffalo Bill that I would sing at his reception tonight. Did you know that the Queen will be attending?"

Suzette closed her eyes, but only for a fraction of a second. "You promised Buffalo Bill? Oh, Irena, no . . ."

Irena placed an arm around her granddaughter's shoulders. "What has happened to you, Suzie?"

"What do you mean?"

"What I mean is . . ." Irena frowned. "Was your upbringing really so bad? You had the best of all worlds, did you not? You had me with you always . . . you had your parents, also, when they weren't busy with an opera. Now, certainly I'll admit that there is jealousy in the trade, as you say. But what field of endeavor excludes jealousy?"

"There are many I can think of."

"After all," Irena continued, as though Suzette hadn't spoken, "your mother never entertained other men, your father never kept other women. They loved each other. They still do, and they love you."

"Yes, but . . ."

"And you and I, we used to have such fun."

Suzette set her lips together. "I have grown up Irena. That's what has happened. And, forgive me, but I think that it's time that you grew up, too."

"Ouch!"

"Tell Buffalo Bill that you made a mistake."

"I will not."

"Shall I tell him for you, then?"

"No, child." Irena's voice was firm. "I'm still your grandmother, Suzie, dear. I know that you are proud of the fact that you are marrying for love instead of using William to further your career. And I am happy that you are proud, and are attaining entrance into the world of your choosing. But do not interfere in *my* life."

Suzette grimaced. "I suppose that's fair. But then, by

the same token, you should not interfere in mine, and especially not in public . . . singing a funeral march . . ."

"I am your grandmother. All good grandmothers interfere in their granddaughter's lives."

Despite herself, Suzette smiled, then she quickly hid it. "You know that's not true."

Irena cocked her head to the side.

"Oh, I give up," said Suzette. "Very well. Have your way. Sing for Buffalo Bill. But I will return here after the show. I will sit and watch as you charm the Queen as easily as you captivate a crowd. But after that, can we then go?"

Irena nodded. "Yes. Then we can go."

Suzette swung her head back and forth, admitting defeat. "Then that is all I have to say. I am going back to William."

"Very well, child."

CHAPTER 3

Night had turned to morning, and still the crew of the
Wild West Show partied. William had long since gone
home, but not so Suzette. She was not leaving without
Irena. She didn't dare. Since Irena was more than a little
inclined to attract trouble, it naturally fell to Suzette to
stay with her, if only to see her home.

So she waited.

As chance would have it, Suzette hadn't been forced
to come face-to-face with the young man, Two Bears,
again. In truth, except for a few of the Indian spokes-
men, none of the Indians were present at the party.

Instead, across the short distance of a small byway, the
Indians celebrated in their own encampment. Their dancing was drawing quite a crowd, and their noise was com-
peting with Buffalo Bill Cody's own party. Even now,
though an orchestra played in the background of Cody's
elegant tent reception, Suzette could hear the beat of those
American Indian drums, as well as the voices raised in
song.

Would *he* be singing along with the others? she

wondered. Would he be dancing? Unfortunately for Suzette, she had no trouble conjuring up his image; she could practically see his near-naked body swaying to the primitive beat of those drums. And try though she might, she could not put the mental image away from her.

She shook her head as though to dislodge the concept, she even wandered as far away from the sound of those drums as Buffalo Bill's tent would allow, but reason seemed to desert her. His handsome countenance seemed etched in her mind.

He was tall, she recalled, perhaps standing six feet in his moccasins. He had been scantily clothed, as well . . . a breechcloth, moccasins, some jewelry and a headdress with eagle feathers had been all that adorned his body. Those feathers had cascaded down his back, almost to the ground, as well . . . an interesting sight.

A looping necklace, similar in construction to a breastplate, had hidden the complete view of a tanned, athletic chest. But the hint of firm muscles and pure masculinity beneath the jewelry had been enough to cause Suzette speculation. Indeed, the mere thought of the man now caused her pulse to race. Why?

Suzette had been reared in an environment of art and drama. There, the changing of clothes often necessitated nudity. So commonplace was it, Suzette took the sight of a near-nude body in stride. Or at least she had done so until today.

Today, the sight of a young man's muscled chest and bare thighs had made her feel more than a little giddy. If she were to be truthful, she would have to admit that when they had first met, she had itched to touch his skin. And *this* made little sense to her.

He was only a man, not unlike any other man. Two eyes, two legs, two arms, a chest, a naked back. Nothing unusual.

Of course, unlike so many opera celebrities, this particular young man was put together rather well, and in all the right places. True, his face was pleasing to the eye . . . rugged without being harsh; perhaps it was this that kept his image haunting her. But it seemed to her that there was more to it than this. There had been a quality about him . . .

Pride. That was what it was. If she had to put a word to his demeanor, she would have to call him dignified—although he was perhaps a little naive as well. At least he had been so about English peculiarities and manners.

Suzette sighed. What wasted thoughts. He was married, and she was betrothed. Betrothed to an earl.

Clearly, the man meant nothing to her, except perhaps a little inconvenience. Where was Irena?

Scanning the crowd for a glimpse of her grandmother, Suzette decided that it was time to bring the evening to a close. Clearly, she and Irena needed to go to the home that Suzette, her parents and Irena all shared. She, for one, yearned for some rest. Certainly, their separate beds awaited them.

Ah, there was her grandmother. Suzette's gaze alighted on a particular dark coiffure, one with delicate curls tied in back that bounced ever so slightly whenever the woman laughed, which was often. With her hourglass figure looking stunning in blue taffeta, and a blue silk handkerchief dangling easily from her gloved hands, she could have easily been a model for a French fashion plate.

From where Suzette stood, she could see that Irena was cuddling up to Buffalo Bill, who was close beside her. Indeed, his face was turned in full toward her, and Suzette could see that he bore the look of . . . What was that? Admiration? Attraction?

Oh dear, that's what it looked like. Worse, was there

a certain sensuality she glimpsed between Irena and the man?

Rumors of Buffalo Bill's reputation with women, and in particular women of the arts, drifted through Suzette's recollections. And Suzette could only wonder if Irena had admitted her real age to the man. Irena had to be at least ten to fifteen years his senior.

Suzette sighed. Perhaps she should have sought out Irena before now. She only hoped that no permanent damage had been done; the last thing she needed was for Irena to believe herself in love.

Gracefully, Suzette made her way through the crowd toward her grandmother. At the moment, Irena was laughing up at Buffalo Bill, and because there was a flirtatious light in Irena's eyes, it was all Suzette could do not to pull her grandmother away from the man. Why did she feel at times as though she were the older of the two of them?

Gently, she touched Irena's hand. "May I speak with you a moment?"

"Of course, darling." Irena turned her gaze on Suzette. "What is it, dear?"

Suzette grimaced. Apparently, she was not to have a private audience with her grandmother. "I am tired and would like to go home."

"Of course, dear, and we shall do so very soon," said Irena. "This is my granddaughter, Mr. Cody."

"A pleasure," said Suzette, nodding toward him but barely sparing him a glance.

"The pleasure is all mine," said Cody, as he bowed slightly from the hip.

After a brief nod at Cody, she asked Irena, "Are you ready to return home?"

"Almost dear. Almost. Mr Cody, might I ask a favor?"

"Of course, Irena. Anything."

"Do you have a private location where my granddaughter might retire until you and I are finished with our business?"

"Naturally, I do," said Cody. "My own quarters are stationed in back of this tent."

"Perfect," said Irena.

"I have no need for privacy," murmured Suzette. "We will be going home soon."

"Yes, yes, dear, of course. But I have a matter of some business with Mr. Cody, and there is no need to bore you with it."

"I do not believe I would be bored," said Suzette. "Please tell me."

Yet Irena was not to be coerced into revealing even the slightest detail of her "business" to Suzette. In fact, with a smooth smile and a quietly muttered "Would you excuse us, please?" Irena took hold of Suzette's arm and smoothly ushered her away.

"By all means," Buffalo Bill said, nodding as they left. "My personal tent is that way, ladies." He pointed out the direction with his arm.

"Thank you, Mr. Cody," said Irena, and the two women took their leave.

"Irena," asked Suzette as soon as they were out of earshot. "What's the meaning of this?"

"A moment, Suzie," said Irena. "Let us attain a more private place. One where we can talk."

"Very well," said Suzette. "Although you must admit that I have a right to be highly suspicious. And though I did wish to speak to you alone, I did not realize that we needed privacy."

"Yes," said Irena. "We do. We need privacy."

"Hmmm," said Suzette. "This sounds as though it might not be to my liking."

"We shall see," said Irena.

Buffalo Bill Cody's quarters, it turned out, were comprised of a rather large tent, which was guarded by a few burly looking cowboys.

"This way," said Irena, as she shot a smile to each cowhand in turn. One of them opened the flap of the tent for the women.

"Do you *know* those men?" asked Suzette.

"Hardly," said Irena.

They had entered a large area with cozy armchairs and a sofa. Although the scent of a gaslight perfumed the place, the air did seem fresher in here than outside the tent, where the atmosphere reeked of horseflesh and smoke. On the floor of the room were lush rugs. And in the room's corners, scattered here and there, were testaments to the Wild West—a buffalo robe, a quiver full of arrows, a wampum belt.

"Come, Suzie. Let us sit and talk."

Suzette nodded, and took her seat on a large, red and rather comfortable-looking chair. Irena sat across from her.

"I am working over some business with Mr. Cody," Irena explained.

"Oh? Pray tell, what kind of business?" Suzette frowned, her suspicions aroused at once.

"If you must know," said Irena, "I am thinking about joining the show."

For a moment, Suzette was speechless. Then she said, "Joining the show? You mean . . . traveling with them?"

Irena nodded.

"Leaving here?"

"Yes."

"But why, Irena?"

Irena fiddled with a button on her dress. "Because,

the show is due to go back to America as soon as their performance here is done. And there is something I need to find in America."

Suzette gulped, and said, "In *America*?"

"Yes."

"Why is this the first time I am hearing of this? What is it that you need to find?"

Irena shrugged, but was silent.

"Would you not agree," said Suzette, "that this is awfully strange . . . and sudden?"

"Perhaps it does seem that way to you, for I am only now mentioning it. But something is pulling me there, and has been pulling me there for some time."

"And what exactly is this that is pulling you there?"

"Oh, I don't know. Could I not simply be looking for a little adventure?"

"Irena, this is me, your granddaughter. I know you. I am not fooled by your attempts to disconcert me."

Irena frowned, slanted Suzette a glance, then said, "Oh, very well. If you must know, I am looking for a particular person—someone I met when I was in America many years ago. I have never forgotten him."

"Him? Are you trying to tell me that you are in love with . . . this man?"

Silence. Then, "Yes, I think I am."

"Think? Irena, you do realize that if you go with this show, you would be changing your entire life?"

"Yes, I realize that."

"And you are willing to do that?"

"I am. They leave tomorrow."

"Tomorrow? But I am to be married in less than a month's time! Could you not wait until after my marriage?"

"You have your mother and father to help you, darling. They will see you through the difficult time."

"A marriage is not a difficult time, it is an . . . enlightening and happy time. One I had hoped to share with you."

"I know you did, dear. I know. I am sorry to tell it to you like this, but I have to go with the show. There are other reasons why this is so."

"Other reasons?" Suzette rose up to her feet, pacing toward one of the room's corners. "Other reasons? You must realize that I cannot let you go without knowing exactly what these reasons are."

Irena sighed yet again. "Can a person not have a secret?"

"Not with her granddaughter, she can't." Suzette smiled.

"Oh, very well. But you must give me your promise that you will not relate this to a soul, not even to your mother, or your father."

"I cannot very well give you a . . ."

"Suzie . . ."

Reluctantly, Suzette nodded. After all, it wasn't terribly difficult to give her word. She had always been closer to Irena than to her own parents. "Very well. I promise."

"Good," said Irena. "If you must know, the man I seek is an American Indian."

Suzette raised an eyebrow. "An American Indian?"

"I met him in Washington, D.C., at the White House, when I was there to perform for the President. Oh, it was years ago, I admit. I was much younger then. But he was . . . handsome. He was such an honorable man, placing the welfare of his tribe before his own needs, and we . . . I didn't mean to fall in love with him, but it had been so long since there had been a man in my life, your grandfather having died much too early."

"I understand," said Suzette. "I think."

"I did not even know I was in love with him until it was too late. By the time I realized it, he was gone. I did try to find him, but no one seemed to remember him, and his name I could not pronounce, nor did I know the translation for it." She grimaced. "I tried again to find him, that time a few years ago, when I sailed to the United States. These searches, however, proved useless."

"What makes you think you will have better luck now?"

"Suzie," Irena began, her voice breathless, "there is someone here who reminds me of the man I fell in love with. Their likeness is uncanny. As though it could have been my own love as he was as a youth."

"Huh! That seems to me to be very little to go on."

"You are right, it is not much," said Irena. "But it is exciting nonetheless, and at my age, I think I can be forgiven for trying once more to recover my love."

"Oh." A silence fell between the two women. "Still," said Suzette at length, "to travel with this show. Isn't that unnecessary? Why not hire this young man who reminds you so much of the one you seek? Why not ask him to help you?"

"Do you think I have not tried?"

"And what happened?"

"Firstly, he would not be bought, at least not by a woman. Secondly, it appears that he is, himself, on a quest of his own."

"Then hire someone else to find this man. Would it not be better than chasing after someone who . . . Pray, forgive me, Irena, but if this man had wanted to be with you, would he not be trying to find you?"

"Would he? He, too, seemed to be involved in a deed of some importance. And besides, if my instincts are right, I think that this young man, the one I have only met tonight, will lead me to the one that I seek. I feel it, Suzie. I feel it is right."

"But Irena, to give up everything because of a mere 'instinct' . . ."

Irena smiled. "Perhaps," she said, "when you reach my age, you will understand why it is necessary."

A lengthy silence ensued. At last, Suzette said, "All right, Irena. If you are determined to do this, then I cannot stand in your way. But I will ask one thing of you."

"Yes?"

"You must take someone with you. A maid, a bodyguard. You must hire someone to look after you and be as a guard for you."

Irena hesitated. "I could do this. Yes, I could do this. Perhaps this young man . . ." She frowned. Clearly, an idea had suddenly occurred to Irena.

"And you will? You promise?"

"I promise."

"Very well, then," said Suzette, with a long look at her grandmother. "But I will miss you."

"And I will miss you."

"Indeed."

CHAPTER 4

Lady Blair, the Earl of Lankersheim's mother, was a woman of some weight. Both socially and literally. At five foot two, and weighing perhaps two hundred and fifty pounds, her small frame was inclined to teeter beneath the extra poundage. But here any impression of frailness ended, superseded by that lady's voice, which was moderately pitched, but coarse and loud.

Suzette, however, had always gotten on well with the woman; had always found her visits with Lady Blair enjoyable. Therefore, there was no reason to suspect that this particular call would prove to be quite different.

With William at her side, Suzette swept into the parlor and smiled cheerily at the lady. "Lady Blair," she said, with a dainty curtsy. "How happy I am to see you again."

"And I you," Lady Blair responded. "Please, will you not be seated?" She gestured toward a chair, where Suzette obliged her by gracefully descending into it.

"William," said Lady Blair, "please fetch one of the servants. I think tea and crumpets are in order."

"Of course," said William, leaving at once to do her bidding.

Happily, Suzette gave her attention over completely to her future mother-in-law. Clutching her stylish pink and white parasol in hand, Suzette favored Lady Blair with a sweet smile and said, "William tells me that you have some last-minute details for the wedding party that you wish to discuss with me."

"That I do."

Suzette's smile widened, her happiness apparent. And with reason. In only a few days, she, too, would bear the title of Lady Blair.

She said, "Then, pray tell me your concerns and I will be more than happy to allay your fears. Need I tell you that the arrangements are all in order? All is as it should be. My trousseau is ready, and the bridesmaids' dresses are finished, and oh, they are so beautiful. The church is reserved for the occasion, and of course, my parents have made my settlement ready to be available upon the day that we say our vows." She perched forward on her chair. "But I understand that there are a few details that I must attend to with you."

"Yes, dear, so there are." Lady Blair pursed her full lips. "Countess Bishop has related to me a most dreadful particular, I am afraid."

"Oh?"

"Yes, I fear it is regarding your dear grandmother, child."

"Yes," said Suzette, her smile fading but little. "I realize that she will not be in attendance at the wedding, for she is en route to America. But it is not so dreadful after all. My parents and aunts and uncles will be at the wedding to ensure all goes well."

"It is not her traveling to America that I find

objectionable," said Lady Blair. "Rather, it is with whom she is traveling that is the point in question."

"Whom? What do you mean?"

"What I mean is, dear girl, that it has come to my attention that your grandmother is touring with a circus."

"Oh, no. No, no, no. She is not accompanying a circus. No, indeed." Suzette frowned. "From where did you glean such information?"

"From Countess Bishop herself."

"Oh," said Suzette, puzzled, but only momentarily. She brightened. "Well, I am glad that you have brought this to my notice so that I might be able to impart to you the particulars concerning Iren—my grandmother. The facts are that she has been engaged by Mr. William Cody of the Wild West Show. It is her honor to sing at the receptions that Mr. Cody presents after each engagement. Indeed, it is quite a privilege, for she has now entertained such people as the Queen of England, the Duchess of Kent, and many, many others, including members of state and of course, presidents." Suzette's eyes glowed with pride over Irena's accomplishments.

"The Wild West Show, you say?"

"Yes, that is correct," said Suzette, a slight frown pulling at her brow. Was it her imagination or did Lady Blair's voice hold a note of censure?

"Now to the point, dear," said Lady Blair. "It is with a heavy heart, my dear girl, that I must inform you that I can no longer countenance your marriage to my son."

Suzette paused as the air gradually left her lungs. Surely Lady Blair was jesting. At some length, Suzette took a breath, and said, "I beg your pardon?"

"A Wild West Show. Why, my dear, it is no more than a carnival, do you not agree?"

"A carnival?" Was that all that was bothering Lady

Blair? "Oh, no," said Suzette at once, "let me explain, for I think you misunderstand. While carnivals are, indeed, establishments of ill repute, this particular Wild West show is no carnival. It is of the best possible entertainment and has even been attended by the Queen, herself, as well as princesses and other royalty."

"But dear, their majesties often attend carnivals, do they not?"

"I . . . I . . ." Suzette stopped as words deserted her. Perhaps this was more serious than she had first realized.

"Now I am aware," Lady Blair was continuing, "that we will need to compensate you for the breach in contract, but there is nothing else for it, you see. It must be done. You must see this."

"Breach in contract? But—"

"Perhaps I should meet with your parents so that the proper arrangements can be made."

"But," said Suzette again, "the preparations for the wedding have all been made. The church is reserved. The guests are invited, the bridesmaids' dresses are done, the reception is set, the breakfast . . ." Her voice faded away.

"It is to be regretted, it is true. But we shall recompense you."

"Regretted? Recompense?"

"Yes, dear."

Suzette swallowed with some difficulty. For many moments, she was quiet. At length, she said, "Does William know that you intend this?"

When Lady Blair didn't answer at once, Suzette persisted. "Did he have knowledge of this when he brought me here?"

"Yes, my dear. He did."

"But he did not say a word to me about it."

"I asked him not to utter a thing to you, my dear girl, for I believed it would be better that I speak to you about it personally."

"Better for whom?" Suzette asked. "Better for me? I am not certain that I agree with you about that."

"I understand. You are upset. It is to be expected. But, then, we are not asking for your agreement, are we?"

For the first time since Lady Blair had delivered this fait accompli, Suzette raised her gaze to meet that of her elder. What she saw there was startling.

Had Lady Blair's eyes always held a glimmer of spite? Had her demeanor always been so arrogant? The tilt of her chin so haughty that she appeared to be sniffing something distasteful?

Fleetingly, Irena's words of caution drifted through Suzette's mind:

"He is ruled by his mother. Beware."

It is said, thought Suzette, that love is blind. Perhaps the saying is true. But if this is so, then she had been blinded not only by William, but by his mother, as well.

She said, "You are wrong, Lady Blair. My grandmother is an upstanding woman. I am proud that she is touring with the Wild West Show, and I am delighted that she is able to provide entertainment that is moral and honorable."

"I see." Lady Blair's mouth tightened. "Do you seek to contradict me in this, then?"

"Yes. I fear that I must."

Lady Blair raised the angle of her chin until she was practically staring down her nose at Suzette. Only then did she say, "Do you know who I am?"

"Oh, yes," said Suzette, rising to her feet, "indeed, I do. I now know who you *really* are. And for the first time in my acquaintance with you, Lady Blair, I am displeased with what I find."

Lady Blair's hands pounded down on the arms of her chair. "Of all the impertinence!"

"Pray do excuse me," said Suzette, "for I am certain that you can have nothing more to say to me. And I, for my part, have nothing more to say to you."

"Do be seated, child. Though there might be cause for your anger, I am not so savage that I will not send for a servant to escort you back to your home." Lady Blair's voice was at once sweet with sympathy.

"No, thank you," said Suzette. "And do not bother with a servant, for I will seek out William. He will escort me."

"Why, my dear girl, that would be most unbecoming of you. Now that the engagement is broken, the two of you must not be alone together. I would not think of it."

"Still, I would like a word with William in private, thank you very much."

And with nothing more than an urgent need to escape Lady Blair's presence, Suzette swept out of the room, finding William cowering on the opposite side of the door.

"Ah," she said. How much of their conversation had he overheard? she wondered. And why had he not been there to champion her? Pushing these thoughts aside, she continued, "There you are. I believe we have some matters to discuss. If you will accompany me to my home, let us put these things in order."

That William shot an inquiring look toward his mother did not escape Suzette's notice. However, she was not about to give mother and son a chance to conspire.

"Do come along," Suzette said, taking hold of his arm, "for there is a matter of some concern that we must discuss."

And William, realizing at last that he had no choice in the matter, faced up to his duty.

CHAPTER 5

Colorado Territory
Three Months Later

Snow was falling gently as the train slid into the Denver station. The screech of the brakes, the blare of the horn, the sounds of humanity scrambling for their possessions broke into Suzette's thoughts. But even still, such things barely registered.

Cold, weary of the constant traveling, and anxious about the sort of reception that awaited her, Suzette's mind was as far away from the business of the Atchison, Topeka and Santa Fe Railway as if such matters as new trains and their stations were commonplace. To Suzette, it was simply another conveyance, and there had been many in this past month: ships, stagecoaches, trains. However, she did grab hold of her purse and bag, lingering in her semiprivate compartment when the others on the train were scrambling to depart.

What was Irena going to say to her? Suzette wondered. Would she shoot questions at her one after the other, curious to know why Suzette had come to join her here in the American West? Would she want to know the details as to why she had left England?

Of course by now Irena would know of her broken engagement; Suzette's mother was sure to have included that tidbit in her letter to Suzette's grandmother. But did Irena know of her granddaughter's embarrassment? Worse yet, was she aware of the scandal of Suzette's predicament?

Hopefully not. Certainly Suzette would try to hide the particulars of her condition for as long as possible.

A whistle blew, bringing Suzette back to the present. Looking around her, she realized that most everyone who was going to depart had left the car, save her. Squaring back her shoulders and drawing in a deep breath, Suzette at last rose up from her seat, settled her hat on her head, and stepped away from the refuge of the train.

"Suzette! Suzette! Dear, how good it is to see you!"

Irena rushed toward Suzette, accompanied by the colorful figure of Buffalo Bill Cody, a man Suzette remembered quite well.

Suzette smiled reservedly at her grandmother as the two of them approached. "Irena," Suzette said, setting down her bags. "How glad I am to see you! I'm also happy to realize that you must have received my mother's letter."

"Of course we did, my dear. We're not entirely away from all civilization here. But come closer, my dear, and give me a hug."

Suzette did as requested. As soon as Irena's arms wound around her, Suzette knew an uncanny desire to cry. She refrained from doing so, however. Indeed, much too much English blood flowed through her veins to break her reserve in so public a place.

"You do remember Mr. Cody, don't you, dear?"

"Of course." Suzette offered Cody her gloved hand.

"Welcome to Colorado, Miss Joselyn," said Cody, accepting her hand and bending to present a kiss upon it. "Your grandmother tells me you are quite the actress, as well as a singer. Maybe we could—"

"That's all in my past," Suzette said, smiling at him. "Indeed, it's all in my past."

"Yes, well, come along, dear," Irena said. "We'll collect the rest of your luggage—I am assuming that you have a trunk?"

Suzette nodded.

"Very well. This way, then. I imagine you're tired and hungry and ready to do nothing more than sleep for several days in a row. And there's no better place to do so than Buffalo Bill's Wild West Show. I have ample space in my very luxurious tent . . ." Irena smiled at Cody. ". . . and you can even have your own room within my rather large . . . well, I've come to think of it as my apartment, although it is only a tent."

"Yes," agreed Suzette. "That would be good. Very good, indeed. Pray, I think I could use a rest. The journey here has been . . . pleasant, but perhaps it has also been long, and in my . . ." She paused, realizing she had been about to say, "in my condition." Instead, she drew in a deep breath, then said, "I am, indeed, tired."

Irena took hold of Suzette's arm, and though the action was simple, Suzette immediately felt better. "Then come along, dear. You'll soon be back on your feet again, good as new."

Suzette smiled at Irena. Perhaps, she thought, that might be true in five or six more months. But more about that later. For now, she did, indeed, need the rest. And later, she and Irena would talk.

* * *

Black Lion trudged through the snow en route to the Song Bird's tent, the woman whom the white people knew and referred to as Irena. As his feet sank into the sprinkling of the cold, white flakes, Black Lion blessed his good luck. In addition to a business arrangement, he had nurtured an unusual friendship with this woman. It was luck to have done so, because the Song Bird was a being of music and art.

It was also his good fortune that he basked in her friendship. Perhaps in time it would be through her that he might discover *the* song, the one special song that would free his people.

Although in this he was uncertain, since, though his dreams were filled with a feminine voice, it was not the voice of the Song Bird. However, he could be wrong.

Still, when they were together, Black Lion would often ask the Song Bird to sing for him; always he requested her to render him a different song, and there was a purpose behind his entreaties. Someday, when all this was over, he might confess his soul to her, for, even though he must, he felt as though he were using her for his own gain.

However, that time of confession was not now.

At present, time was his enemy. Alas, he had only one year remaining in which to end his people's enchantment, only one more year to solve the riddle of the song.

If he failed . . . But that was unthinkable. He mustn't fail.

"Auntie," he called out, as he reached the Song Bird's tent and scratched on the entry flap. "Auntie?" He alone addressed her in this manner. Since the Wild West Show had come to roost here in Colorado, Black Lion had begun to think of this woman more as family than as a friend. In truth, she looked after his needs, checked on his comfort and spoke to him as a mother might a son. This was why he had started calling her "Auntie."

Still, there was one aspect of their friendship that Black Lion wished were different: She paid him money to stand watch over her and to act as her guard. Because it was not in his nature to take money from a woman, oftentimes, he felt the guilt of doing this. Many times he had tried to tell her that it was his duty to protect his elders, and that he should not receive remuneration. But her only reaction to this had been to laugh.

"Elder?" she had asked him, batting her eyelashes at him.

Black Lion had grinned, but the point had been made. He had never mentioned the matter again, nor had she, although she still continued to pay him wages for his services as a watchdog. As a consequence, since he, himself, had no use for the white man's money, he was sending what little he had back to the reservation. His friend, Two Bears, would need it. With the deep snows of winter upon them, and because he feared that Two Bears might still be ill, he suspected that Two Bears would be only too happy to receive the gift.

"Auntie," Black Lion called out again, "I have come to you as your note asked."

No answer.

Black Lion waited a moment, then called out again. "Auntie?"

Should he linger?

He knew the answer, of course. If she needed him, he would stay here all day, if necessary. Though his feet were cold, he sat on his haunches, ready and willing to wait.

He turned his attention outward, at the snow that was gently falling to the earth. He appreciated this time of year; he prized the lack of sound that a good snowstorm lent to the air, and he basked in the quiet that was cast all around him.

However, were he at home, he might not feel so kindly toward the winter. For this time of year was often brutal for his people; food could be scarce.

But this was not so here at the Wild West Show. There was more food to go around than any of them could possibly eat, a circumstance that left Black Lion full, happy and able to relish the beauty of the season without fear of imminent peril.

With his attention directed outward, he at last heard it. What was it? Tinkling, as white man's glasses sound when they touch? No, this was different. This had a melody to it.

Curious, he rose up, turning his notice to the Song Bird's tent. The sound was coming from in there.

"Auntie?" he cried out again.

Still no answer. But someone was in there. He could hear their movements, like the faint swish of silk over canvas.

Cautiously, as quietly as his namesake, he ducked in beneath the tent's entrance flap, and like a cat, crept into the inner sanctuary of the Song Bird's private quarters. Hers was an unusual tepee. It was quartered off into sections, with drapes and room dividers making four separate spaces. The sound came from the very back room. There, he could see a soft beam flickering, and the scent of a gaslight wafted to him.

Creeping softly across the outer parlor, as the Song Bird liked to call this room, Black Lion paced one careful step after another, until at last, he had reached the Japanese-constructed room dividers.

Squatting down, he peeked around the partition.

A woman swayed to the pulsing sound of a music

box. Her back was turned toward him, and all he could see was the cascade of long dark hair, a slim body and gentle curves beneath a robe that hugged her silhouette.

She danced. And she danced. After a while, she began to hum in time to the music, as well. As though bewitched, Black Lion couldn't move.

Who was she?

She began to sing, softly at first, but then with more conviction. Her voice was spellbinding, like nothing of this world. And he wondered if he had stumbled upon a goddess.

The tinkling music in the box slowed. The woman walked over to the music container, turned the key, and the tune began all over again.

Barely daring to breathe, Black Lion continued to watch.

Should he announce himself? Was it right to stay here and stare without her knowledge? But if he made her aware of his presence, he thought contrarily, would that knowledge end the enchantment?

Because he feared it might be so, he remained hidden.

Still swaying to the slow beat of the music, she turned her profile toward him, and for the first time since arriving here, he saw her in full. He also witnessed the tears falling down her face. She inhaled a ragged breath, breathed out, and more tears slid down a perfect profile. It was a countenance he recognized.

It was she, the beauty from England. The one he had knocked into the mud so unceremoniously.

But what was she doing here? And why was she so sad? She had been anything but melancholy that day when he had met her.

Black Lion rose up to his full height. Within him was an urge to reach out and give the woman comfort.

Fortunately, the memory of her sharp tongue that day countered the feeling.

He would stay where he was for the moment.

And so she danced, and she danced. She cried, her sobs seemed to wrack his soul. How long he stood there, entranced by her, watching her, he could never be certain.

It wasn't until she pulled back her hair, fixing it away from her face, that she walked toward the music box, where she picked it up and shut its lid. And that was it; the music faded from the room.

But not so the magic.

He inhaled deeply. Either he should leave or announce himself. To continue to spy on her was not an action of honor.

He decided on the former, and had turned away from her, when he heard another of her weakened sobs. He couldn't go. It was simply not in him to do so.

Breathing in deeply, he stepped from around the divider. He cleared his throat.

At the sound, she spun around toward him. Wide red eyes clashed with his.

"You!" she said. "What are you doing here?"

"I am honored that you remember me, and I am here because—"

"How long have you been here?" she interrupted.

"Long enough," he said.

She lifted her chin as if to say that she didn't care that he had seen her in a moment of weakness.

She wiped her eyes, and said, "Why are you here?"

"I . . ." What could he say to justify his presence? "I . . . heard the music," he said, "and I feared something might be wrong with the Song Bird. I thought to investigate."

"The Song Bird?"

"The woman the white-eyes call Irena."

"Oh, Irena." She laughed grimly. "You have business with Irena, then?"

"I do sometimes."

"Yes, well, she was here earlier, but has gone seeking a young warrior, I'm afraid."

He lifted his chin. "It may be that she seeks me."

Shadows, cast from the soft, single light in the room, crossed over her face, lending her a fairylike appeal. She studied him momentarily before she said, "It's funny how these things happen, is it not?"

"Funny?"

"I thought to never see you again. And yet, here you are. Here I am."

"*Hau*, here we are." He paused. "And we are alone together. It is enough to ruin your reputation yet again." He cast her a lopsided grin. "I fear that now you truly have no choice but to accept my proposal of marriage, if only for your own sake."

"Marry you?" She frowned, then shook her head and turned away from him, presenting him with only her profile. "I . . . thank you for coming." She stared toward the floor. "I will tell Irena that you were here." There was a tremble in her voice.

He swallowed, hard. It was not in his heart's nature to intrude on another's privacy; yet, he would give comfort if he could. He said, "Jesting aside, is there anything I can do for you? Is there anything that you need?"

"You mean besides a chance at another life? Oh, please . . ."

He watched her profile as a tear escaped and fell down over her cheek. And then, as he surveyed her, it came to him what his first observation of her had missed. Her belly was bigger than it had been the last time he had seen her. The difference was slight, yet . . .

He took a step forward. "You are with child," he said simply. "I will help you if I can."

Her sob was deep, strained. And though she said nothing to affirm his words, the tears now flowed freely over her face.

At last, gaining control over herself, she said, "You wish to help me?"

"If it is within my power."

She breathed in a deep breath, then sent him a look that might have been mocking, if not for the sadness in her countenance. She said, "Perhaps I should take you up on your joke, and . . ." Her face cleared suddenly, then staring up at him, she frowned at him as though she might be seeing him for the first time.

"Joke? You mean, to marry me?"

"Yes, that is what I meant. Do you think your wife would object?" Through her tears, her gaze turned sarcastic, yet sad, all at the same time.

It was his turn to frown at her. "My wife?"

"Yes," she said. "The wife who is supposed to tame me?"

"*Hau*," he responded, smiling slightly. "Now I recall."

"How convenient of you to forget it."

"Convenient, perhaps," he said, "but unnecessary. I am not married. Alas, I fear there would be no one but myself to tame you."

She paused. "But if I recall correctly, you said that a man had to be married to be with the show."

"An Indian man has to be married," he corrected.

"You *are* Indian."

"So I am. I hope you can keep a secret, for this is something I have not told the Long-haired Show Man."

"Who?"

"Buffalo Bill," he supplied.

"Oh, I see," she said, a taunting smile hovering over her lips. "Well, I suppose now you will have to marry me . . . and not simply to save my honor."

"*Ece*? And why is that?"

"Because in the white man's world, a woman is not able to say anything bad about her husband. We call it testifying. She cannot tell his secrets in public . . ."

"*Eya*, I understand." He paused; then, keeping the conversation in the same vein as she, he continued, "There is nothing else we can do, then. I will have to make you my bride, provided you are not already married to the one who did this to you."

"I am not."

He nodded.

"Well, good," she said, her lips quivering. "I'm glad that is settled. When shall the deed be done?" she asked.

"You do not jest with me?"

She regarded him for a moment, her expression unreadable. Then slowly, as if she herself could scarcely credit her own decision, she said, "No. I do not jest. I will marry you."

His brows came together as he took a step forward. He was intrigued by this woman, greatly intrigued. But more than that, he wanted to take her in his arms, this very minute. He wanted to wash away the shadows that hovered over her, if only for a little while.

However, in such situations as this—being alone with a woman—someone has to think clearly, and it appeared that at this time and place, he was that very person. He said, "Let us discuss this in a greater way. We must consider other things."

"Other things?" Her voice quivered.

And the desire to comfort her was almost more than he could suppress. But he had to tell her; she needed to know. He said, "We are no longer across the water in England. You are white. In this country, a marriage between us is not allowed."

She set back her shoulders. "That's not true. And besides, I am not from this country."

"There is also the fact that we know little of each other. We have not grown up with one another. How do you know that you can depend on me to be a good husband? How do I know you will make me a good wife?"

"Yes, yes," she said. "You are right. It is awkward and we should think about this in greater detail." She spun away from him, and walked to a far corner of the room. He followed her with a step or two.

Then he said, "But know this: If you need a husband for your baby, as well as for you, I will be that to you. Tell me, how many months along are you?"

"A few. Perhaps four." Her voice caught on a sob.

"The babe will not look like me," he said, the observation meant to lighten her mood.

"Does it matter?"

"*Hiya.*"

"What does that word mean?"

"It means no, it does not matter to me. If you truly mean to accept . . ."

"I have said so already. I accept."

"*Li'la tanyan,* very well. When shall we commit this act?"

"Tonight." She looked at him defiantly.

He swallowed. "Very well. We will marry tonight." To his surprise, with the utterance, every male instinct within him came suddenly to life. He became aware of her, truly aware of her—of her beauty, her scent, her sensuality.

Moments ago, he had wanted only to comfort one so beautiful, but now he could think of nothing more than taking her in his arms and imprinting himself upon her. Intending to put his thoughts into action, he stepped quickly across the room, closing the distance between them. He said, "Shall we seal the arrangement with a kiss?"

"A kiss?" The contempt in her voice was unmistakable. Was it contempt for him?

He was not left long wondering, however, as she said, "I think that it is a kiss that has served this trouble upon me. Perhaps in the future I shall avoid kisses in any form from any person."

"*Hau*, I can understand that you would think so," he said. "Yet still I would like one, if you are willing."

She raised her chin. "Willing? Mayhap it would be wise if I tell you that I do what I do out of desperation. Therefore, you should be apprised of the fact that I may never voluntarily kiss you."

"*Hau*. That is to be regretted." Then in a most typical American Indian gesture, he jerked his chin swiftly to the left. It was at some length that he finally spoke again, saying, "This will be a strange marriage, I fear."

"Yes," she agreed. "It will indeed be a strange marriage." And before the last word left her lips, he bent down toward her and pressed a kiss upon her mouth.

CHAPTER 6

The moment his lips met hers, she knew she was in trouble. It wasn't in her mind to respond. Yet, she did. One moment, the man was all but a stranger to her, the next, he was an undeniable part of her.

His hands came up to cup her face, his fingers massaging her neck, her cheeks, her ears, the back of her neck, as though only by the sense of touch could he come to know her.

She breathed in and his masculine scent, fresh and musky, filled her senses. Her head spun as she inhaled again, committing his clean fragrance and this moment to memory. Briefly, he ended the kiss to press his cheek against hers, and absentmindedly, she noted his lack of a beard. Was this an American Indian characteristic?

She had no chance, however, to debate the observation. His breathing was taut, deep and ragged, and the knowledge that she was affecting him in this way made her own pulse race.

She pressed herself against him. She couldn't help

herself. It was madness. Pure madness, for they knew nothing of one another, and yet . . .

Once again, his lips captured hers, only this time his tongue nudged her mouth open. It was not in her to refuse, and when she consented, he invaded her mouth, his tongue sliding over her teeth, the inner makings of her mouth, her own tongue. It was as though he would commit the very act of love with no more than a kiss.

But this was no mere kiss. Certainly, she thought, William's affectionate embraces had been nothing like this. This was different from anything in her experience; this was soul stirring, an awakening of spirit to spirit, being to being.

His tongue rampaged the inside of her mouth, and all the while, his hands were caressing every part of her face, her ears, her cheeks, her eyes. Downward his touch ranged, down over the sensitive spot on her neck, downward still, stopping at her shoulders.

Again, he drew back. Again, she surged forward.

"Who are you?" she asked as she fought to catch her breath.

"I am called Black Lion," he said.

"No, I mean *who* are you?"

"Your soon-to-be husband," he whispered against her lips. "Perhaps it is good that we desire each other."

"But I . . ."

"Do not deny it. You are here in my arms."

She should leave those very arms. She should simply step away from him; it would be the right thing to do. But she didn't. It was as though, in this matter, her body and mind operated without her consent, as though they knew exactly what they wanted, even if she did not.

"There is a medicine man here amongst my people. He will marry us tonight."

"No," she said. "A man of the cloth—a person from

one of our churches—he must administer the ceremony."

Black Lion shook his head. "Mark my words," he said. "The white people will not marry us. If we are to do this, it will have to be a secret marriage, I think."

"I dare to disagree. I will find a minister. You will see, for I must find one. Perhaps you do not yet understand, but in the eyes of the world, our marriage must be legal."

He nodded. "*Hau*, you are right. I do not understand, but I will wait, then, and see if you are able to do this. Still, I will tell the medicine man to be in preparation . . ."

She frowned at him.

". . . in the event he is needed. Shall I arrive here for you tonight?"

"Yes," she said, "once the others are well asleep."

Again, he nodded. It was only then that he dropped his arms from around her and stepped away, and despite herself, Suzette felt bereft. With a dangerous light in his eye, he said, "I do not think that we will have a problem with kisses."

Amazingly enough, she grinned up at him. "No," she said, "I don't expect that we will."

She watched him walk away from her. Truthfully, she had little choice in the matter, since her gaze followed the man as though her mind, temporarily separated from her will, would imprint his image on her, whether she wished it or not.

Who was he? she wondered for the second time in so many minutes.

Tall, his was a slender build, she was keen to observe as her eyes caught and held onto his jean-clad figure. His shoulders were wide, his hips slim, and those jeans clung indiscriminately to rock-hard rear muscles. The jeans disappeared, however, into high, over-the-knee, leather boots, while the man's hair, loose and long, and almost reaching to his hips, tumbled down his back. His image was a mixture of stark contrasts, she decided, black mane against a crisp white shirt.

He had worn beaded earrings tonight, she recalled; a look that seemed more than a little exotic for a man. And though one might usually consider such jewelry to be reserved for the female of the species, there was nothing but pure masculinity in the manner of this man. He had also worn a breastplate, which was made of bone and beads, an item he had worn in England, as well, she recollected. Atop that necklace and dangling around his neck had been a navy blue and white neckerchief, neatly tied. Half cowboy, half American Indian, his was a strange way of dressing.

But it was also uniquely his own. Who was this man, she wondered, that he should affect her so? And why was she affected?

Had it been because he had shown himself to have a sympathetic ear? Perhaps this was it, for it was a welcome relief to meet someone willing to take on her cause without so much as a word of judgment. But there was more to it than this, she decided, for she had responded to him as though he were perfect for her . . . and she for him.

She prayed, however, that this was not so. Indeed, if truth be known, she was counting on him being her exact opposite.

Still, whether they were one another's antithesis or rather a match made by the gods, it made little difference to her. They were to be married . . . and tonight.

* * *

Did people in the Wild West Show never sleep? she wondered. Suzette inspected the timepiece that Irena had given her: It was a little after one o'clock in the morning. Where was he?

Pacing the width of the small room that was marked off by a set of three partitions, Suzette listened to the faint sound of the Indian drums, which was coming from the opposite side of the camp. An occasional gunshot broke the monotony, but even that was fast becoming a commonplace sound. Irena was gone, had not returned from the reception that Buffalo Bill was hosting—an event meant to entertain a few visiting dignitaries.

Fortunately for her, Suzette had warned the show's chaplain that she and her "fiancé" would be arriving late. But she hadn't meant to be this negligent.

Suzette was undecided as to what to do. Should she put Black Lion's tardiness down to the fact that show people rarely, if ever, arrived on time? Assume that he wasn't having doubts and leave to go in search of him? And, if she did have the nerve to go out and find him, what would she say to him?

She was saved from answering her own questions, however, when a softly spoken male voice said from behind her, "Put out the light."

She spun around quickly, too quickly. She lost her balance and fell forward. At once he stepped to her side and, reaching out, prevented her from falling.

Of necessity, Black Lion's arms came around her, and feeling much like a rabbit looking up into the eyes of a lion, she gazed up at him. Immediately, his brisk male scent, enhanced with the fragrance of mint, enshrouded her. She swayed slightly.

"Are you hurt?"

She backed away from him—but only minutely. "No," she replied, "I am fine."

"I am happy to hear it." He stepped back from her, then instructed, "Put out the light."

She gaped at him.

And he repeated, "Put out the light."

"But why?"

He didn't answer. Instead, he stepped toward the gaslight himself, reached for the knob that lowered the flame, and with a flick of his wrist, threw the room into darkness.

At once, Suzette was aware that they stood no more than the distance of a hand's breadth apart. She shut her eyes momentarily as she wondered again why this man created such havoc within her.

He leaned in toward her, and she whispered, "Why did you shut off the light?"

"Because shadows are easily seen through the canvas of these tents," he answered, his voice low. "And unless you wish to announce my presence here, it is better that we have our talk in the dark."

"Our talk?"

"*Hau*, we must talk."

"Of what?"

"I have questions I must ask you."

His statement earned a frown from her, but all she said was, "Very well. Won't you be seated, Mr. Lion?"

"*Hau*, I will, but we will sit on the floor close together, I think, for we must speak in whispers."

Taking hold of her waist, he guided her to the floor, her body tingling at his touch. But she ignored the feeling, and complained instead, "It is cold here."

"Sit close to me—our body heat will warm us, each one."

Body heat? The thought of this man's body pressed up close against hers stirred her pulse. She swallowed.

Meanwhile, he continued, "We whisper that we

might save your reputation. We are not yet married, and I am here at an hour of the night used traditionally by lovers. I am also in your bedroom."

"Ah," she said. "Again, you try to save my reputation."

"*Hau*," he said. "Someone must think of it." He paused as though to let the implication wash over her. Then, "And now, my questions. They are not many," he said softly, "but they must be asked. First, however, I would present these beaded moccasins to your family in appreciation of the honor of taking you for my wife." He handed over the prize.

"I . . . I thank you, on behalf of my family." Though she couldn't see the moccasins well, she ran her hands over the tough leather that had been softened to fit around the foot. Tiny beads decorated the entire circumference of the shoe. She said, "Though I cannot see them in this light, I am sure they are most beautiful."

"*Sece*, I think they are. They are made by Blue Feather, a *winkte*, whose craft is known throughout the Lakota Nation."

She nodded. However, realizing he could not very well see the action, she added, "I am certain they are beautiful and I thank you. Now, what are these questions that you have for me, Mr. Lion?"

"*Hau*. My first question is this: Does the man who did this to you know that you are with child?"

Suzette sighed. "Yes. I could not very well leave England without informing him of the matter."

"And he was not ready to do his duty to you?"

"No," she replied. "He was not."

"Then he is a fool."

"Yes, I think you are correct on that account, Mr. Lion," she said, "but that does not change my circumstances."

"If we marry—"

"I thought we *were* marrying."

"Hear me on this. If we marry, our way will not be easy. At least not here. Have you thought to seek a white man to marry you instead of me?"

Suzette paused and it was at some length before she said, "If you do not wish to do this, Mr. Lion, you are entitled to tell me that fact directly. Do not spare me, for I will not crumble."

"You misunderstand," he said. "I do not say that I will not, or do not wish to, marry you. You are new to this country, and therefore, you may not realize that there is much prejudice between my people and the white man."

"Is there? May I disagree? Only today I saw a man here at this show, and with him an Indian wife and an Indian family."

"*Hau*, and this is permitted him because he is a white man," said Black Lion.

"And the opposite is not true? I, being a white woman, cannot take an Indian man as husband?"

"*Hau*, you can. But the way will be hard for you. You should know this."

She nodded. "Thank you for your concern," she said. "And now you may happily consider that I am properly apprised of this information."

He sighed. And though the night was filled with other sounds, the tone of his frustration was loud enough that she could hear it. In due time, he said, "As I understand it, you seek a way in which to save your reputation and that of your child. Yet I would be careless if I did not tell you that by marrying me, your reputation would hardly be saved. The whites will forgive you the child, for your child, being white, will of course look completely white. But by marrying me, you may not save *your* reputation."

She paused. "Did you think I would not be aware of the fact?"

Silence fell between them. He didn't answer her. And it was several moments later when he said, "If is it only a man you need as husband for your child, I should tell you that I know a man who is white, who is a good man. I think he would be easily convinced to marry you."

"You have told him of me?"

"I have not. Nor would I do so. That would be left to you to do."

She frowned at his shadow. "You are telling me the truth about that? You have not said anything to this man?"

"*Hau.* I gave you my word that I would hold your secret close to my heart. I would go to my death with your confidence if need be."

"Good."

Another silence ensued between them, broken only by a gunshot in the far distance. The drumming had, for the moment, ceased.

He said, "Do you still wish to do this thing?"

She inhaled deeply, letting her breath out uneasily. She said, "I do."

She watched his shadow as he nodded, although he asked, "Is there a reason?"

"Of course there is a reason," she remarked, but she said not another word about it.

After a moment, he uttered, "Though I know it is impolite to ask, I would know your reason."

She paused while she considered the request. Then, "Very well," she said. "I suppose you have that right. But I warn you that you will not like what I have to say."

Again she watched through the murky darkness as he nodded. He said, "I feared as much, yet I would still know what it is that drives you to do this."

She hesitated yet again, then said, "And if I tell you, you will not change your mind about our marrying?"

"I will not."

"I must have your word on this."

"I promise."

She inhaled deeply. "I suppose that is all very well," she stated. "And so I will tell you. It is quite simple: I do not want a man in my life. A white man might desire more from me than I am willing to give. Also, he could very well come to think he had a husband's rights with me. Or worse, he might envision that my child is his own and wish to keep it."

She watched as Black Lion waited for her to continue. When she did not, he said, "And you do not fear this fate from me?"

"No, I do not."

He chuckled slightly. "I do not know if I should be flattered or insulted."

"Perhaps you should feel both," she offered. "The truth is that I want only the fact that I am married legally, so that my child is not born out of wedlock. But beyond that, I want nothing. I will require not a thing from you, not even your presence in my life, for, once the child is born, I fully intend to return to England."

"Without your husband." It was no question.

"Yes," she affirmed. "Definitely without my husband."

Again, he paused. "It is a fine plan," he said. "For you. But what if I want more from my wife?"

"You could still be free to marry another, could you not?" She frowned. "Within your society, it is permitted to have more than one wife, is it not?"

"In the past," he answered, "this was true. But we are now a part of the white man's world, and I believe that the missionaries on my reservation would disapprove."

"Oh," she said. "I did not realize. And this is your objection?"

"No," he said. "I have no objections, except that it has never been part of my plan to marry . . . anyone. Yet, I agreed to help you, and I will, but I would ask one thing of you."

"Yes?"

"I would like to kiss you from time to time while you are here. And—"

"What kind of kissing?

"A simple kiss, and perhaps all the acts that go with it."

"Acts?"

"When we kiss, I would like to touch you like this." He held up a hand to run his fingers down her cheek.

In response, and quite against her will, she felt herself go limp.

"Or perhaps like this." He brought his hand down to massage a sensitive place on her neck.

She gulped, and with eyes closed, shivered. She asked, "And that is all you would expect?"

"If you will it."

Her eyes flew open. "Will it? What does that mean?"

"Simply, that if you are ever willing and wanting more, I, too, might be agreeable. But if that time never comes, then I will have to be satisfied with a mere kiss."

What an understatement that was, she thought. *There was nothing "mere" about this man's kisses.*

She said, "This sounds like something that I could do."

But he wasn't finished. "There is one more thing."

"Oh?"

"Though the child will not be my own, I would like to come to know him. If I am to be a father, then I should like to see him, if only so that he might become familiar with a man, and what is expected of a man in the society he finds himself. I will not try to possess him or take him from you."

"And if it's a girl?"

"I would also like to come to know her, as well."

"You realize," she said, "that I intend to return to England after the babe's birth?"

"I do. Do you agree?"

"Are you expecting to come with me back to England?"

"*Hiya.*"

"And that word means 'no'?"

"It means no. Are we in agreement?"

"Yes."

"That is good," he uttered softly. "Do you have a father or brother whom I should seek to gain permission?"

"No, not here. My father and mother are in England."

"They know you are here? You did not run away?"

"They know I am here."

He nodded. "And the Song Bird, the one the whites call Irena, is she a relation to you?"

"She is my grandmother."

"Your grandmother . . ." He arched a brow. "She looks good for a grandmother. I am glad, though, that she is not your mother. For a man must not speak to his mother-in-law, and must avoid her by all possible means. Irena is a friend and we have had many conversations. I would not like to have to avoid her because of marrying you."

"No. I should think that would not be pleasant. So, if Irena were my mother, you would really have to avoid her?"

"*Hau*, that is correct. A man must not look at his mother-in-law, nor should he speak to her. But gifts can be sent to show one's respect."

"How strange," she said.

"It is not strange," he defended. "To talk to the mother of one's wife would be very unusual, I think. It makes for ill-relations in the family."

Suzette tilted her head to the side. "How peculiar. You are an odd one, I must say. But I am bound to marry you anyway . . ." She sent him a surreptitious glance. ". . . on the pure understanding, of course, that it is in name only."

"*Hau.* I have not misunderstood you or your desires on this matter. But I think you forget one thing."

"Oh? What is that?"

"Once you become accustomed to my kisses, you may find it difficult to leave me . . ." And without any further conversation, he leaned toward her and kissed her soundly on the lips.

CHAPTER 7

The wedding ceremony was short, as well as grudgingly done. The chaplain, Reverend Hopkins, was proving to be anything but cooperative. It seemed that in regards to the prejudices between the whites and the Indians, Black Lion had, indeed, been accurate. In truth, were it not for the derringer that Suzette carried in her purse, the ceremony would likely have not taken place at all.

The only witness to the affair was Mrs. Hopkins, who stood off to Suzette's side, where she was tut-tutting and muttering to herself. However, the word "savage" was distinctly heard now and again.

Suzette ignored her. All she required was the woman's signature on a piece of paper. No more. No less.

"Do you take this man to be your lawfully wedded husband?"

"Yes," Suzette said, even while she held the gun pointed directly at the reverend. "I do."

"And do you . . ." The chaplain did not look directly at Black Lion. ". . . take this woman to be your wife?"

"*Hau.*"

"And that means? . . ." The minister peered over his glasses at Black Lion.

"Yes. I do."

Reverend Hopkins sighed and hesitated, as though he prayed for some miracle to save him what he was required next to do. At length, however, he continued, though the words seemed to be dragged from him, "Then I pronounce you husband and wife." Closing the Bible in his hand, the minister said not a word more to them. Instead, he turned away from them and trod straight to his desk.

Minutes ticked by. At last, looking up at her, he said, "If this is to be legal, I will require both of your signatures, that is, providing your husband knows how to sign his name."

Black Lion made no reply to the insult, but instead stood behind Suzette as she signed her name. Suzette held her breath as she passed the pen to her new husband, but it seemed that Black Lion had no problem with letters or the signing of his name. Unfortunately, that fact appeared to dishearten the reverend, and it was with great reluctance that he handed the pen to his own wife, Mrs. Hopkins, who was the last to sign.

Shaking his head doubtfully, Reverend Hopkins peered over his glasses at Suzette. He said, "I only hope I do not come to regret this."

Suzette smiled. "You will not. Besides, I fear you had no choice. You can always, in all honesty, tell people that the deed was done at the point of a gun." Uncocking her pistol, she returned the weapon to her purse.

However, when both Suzette and Black Lion lingered, Reverend Hopkins appeared even less sympathetic to them, and he stated, "Well, that will be all now. Mrs. Hopkins will show you out." Rising, he turned his back on them, as though the simple action might put the entire affair from his mind. Slowly, he paced toward the other side of the room.

Mrs. Hopkins was no more cordial than her husband. Reaching out to throw the entrance flap of their tent open, she said simply, "Through here," slapping the flap down as hard as she could as soon as Suzette and Black Lion had crossed over the threshold.

Once outside, a feeling of uneasiness swept over Suzette, and she let out a breath, watching its evidence in the frigid air. She noticed that Black Lion did the same.

"I did warn you about that," he said with a quick glance at her.

"So you did. But the chaplain's antagonism matters very little to me. The deed is done."

"*Hau.* The deed is done."

Silence. She wondered if he felt as awkward as she did. If so, he didn't mention it.

Finally he said, "I will escort you to Irena's tepee for your wedding night."

"Yes. I would like that."

They began their trek toward Irena's tent. Suddenly, Black Lion placed his hands on her shoulders, and turned her to face him. "I promise to defend you against your enemies," he said, "and to hold you in honor within my heart."

Wide-eyed, Suzette stared up at him. *What?*

"The Black Robe did not mention these things," he explained, "and since we are taking vows this night, I thought I should say those details that the Black Robe should have said."

"Yes," she muttered, "and I thank you for that, but so that you know, I can promise you nothing of a similar nature in return. You do remember that, do you not? That I need only your name? Nothing more?"

"I remember it very well. But though you require little from me, you are still my wife. I would give you what protection it is within my ability to give you."

"Yes. And again, I thank you."

"That is all." He grinned at her. "For now."

"For now?"

Black Lion did not elaborate. Instead, he said, "We must conclude this in the right way. Follow me."

"Why?"

"If we are to marry—"

"We *are* married."

But he ignored her. "We must do this in an honorable manner."

"We *have* done this in an honorable way."

He smiled at her. "Come," he said, holding out his hand to her.

She hesitated. After all, what did she really know of this person? That he was handsome? Yes. That she felt alive, enjoyed his company, felt secure in his presence? Yes. But was that enough?

She stared at that hand, as though within it were the secrets to this man's character.

"Come," he repeated.

She looked up into his dark eyes, which were calmly observing her. She exhaled, again watching her breath mirror the temperature in the air. She brought her gloved hand up to meet his, where he grasped it against his own.

There were some things, she decided, that one had to take on trust. Call it instinct, call it feminine intuition. Whatever it was, she sensed that she could believe in this man's integrity. For now, that was enough.

He didn't escort her into the Indian encampment, which was what she had thought he might do. Instead, he guided her into the woods that adjoined the entire Wild West encampment.

Even in the frosty air, the distinct scent of the ever-present pine trees greeted her. Aside from several large cottonwood trees, and a few birch dotting the landscape, it was a wonderland of pine.

He led her to one of the larger trees, there being much room beneath its balmy branches to shelter them. Here, he positioned her against the toughened bark of the tree. Moonlight shone into their little grove; it was a gentle shaft of light that highlighted his features with the silvery moonbeam. At this moment, she was more than aware of her heightened emotions and everything about the moment seemed exaggerated, the sight of him more handsome than anything her imagination could have presented, the scent of his flesh more enticing than those aromas from a grandmother's kitchen.

It was a strangely intimate environment, protected somewhat from the cold air, and it hid them and any-thing they might do or say from the world at large. Truly, this was their own private haven.

She felt close to him.

"I am glad now that I brought this," he said.

"What?" she whispered. "What did you bring?"

"This," he said, and he pulled out a piece of buckskin from a bag that was tied around his waist.

Buckskin? She stared at it, then at him.

"I am going to tie your hand to mine."

She nodded, though her expression was a puzzled one.

"But first," he continued, "I am going to cleanse you and myself, that we might make our ceremony pure, and that the smoke from the sage we use will drift up to the heavens where the Above One will know what it is that we do on this very cold morning."

Again she nodded, and this time, with a little more understanding. This was to be their own private wedding ceremony. No priest. No witnesses to approve. Just her, him. And of course, God.

He lit a small bundle of sage, reciting something in his own language as he directed the smoke over her head, on down to her shoulders, her chest, downward still, toward her legs. It didn't require knowledge of his language to understand that he prayed.

"Take the smoke into your hands," he said to her, "and use it as though you were washing yourself. And spread it over your face and your body."

She did as he directed, inhaling at the same time the scent of burning sage.

"And say a prayer to yourself as you do this."

Once again, she did as he instructed.

"*Waste*," he said. "Good. It is good. And now I will cleanse myself in the same way." He proceeded to do so, whisking the smoke from the sage over his head, his shoulders, his body.

When it was done, he took hold of the piece of buckskin and tied it first around her wrist, then his. When their two arms were tied securely, he said, "A wedding requires a song, I think. I own such a song, and I will sing it to you, though I will change the words. In my song, I am going to thank the Creator for giving you to me. And I am going to ask Him to watch over you, over me and over our marriage. To make it strong." He placed one arm over his chest as he spoke.

Suzette, listening to him, felt as though she had fallen into the moment. As the moon danced over his features, she couldn't help but feel as though she were caught up in a fairy tale. He was superb, in body and in spirit. And her throat choked up on the enchantment that the two of them were creating. He truly meant to marry her; he honestly wanted to help her, and all without asking for a single thing in return.

It was the kind of gesture one might expect from a family member, but not necessarily from someone who was practically a stranger. And if he became a little dearer to her at this time, and in this place, she might be forgiven. She stared up at him without saying a word, but on another level entirely, she was trying to memorize every little thing about him, if only to try to understand this man a little better.

And then he began to sing:

> "Taku oci'ciyakin kte, *I will tell you something.*
> Cica'nnigapi, *I choose you.*
> Cajeciyata, *I call thee by name,*
> Cica'nnigapi Suzette, *Suzette, I choose you.*
> Heci'ciye, *I say that to thee,*
> Cica'nnigapi Suzette, *Suzette, I choose you.*
> Le anpe'tu kin cica'nnigapi, *This day I choose you.*
> Cajeciyata, *I call thee by name.*
> Toke' Wak'antanka niya'waste ni, *May God bless
>   thee.*
> Cica'nnigapi Suzette, *Suzette, I choose you.*
> Toke' Wak'antanka niya'waste ni, *May God bless
>   thee.*"

The song was in a minor key, although it ended in one that was major, and as his words and the melody enveloped her in a feeling of warmth, a few snowflakes fell down from the tree branches above them, reminding her that it was, after all, winter. It was a moment out of time.

She was afraid to move, lest she break the spell, the moment was that magical. She was moved. She, who was accustomed to having men sing to her—for she made it her career—was yet touched.

True, there was no orchestra to accompany him, no chorus, no audience, save herself. No, indeed. The song was sung simply from one heart to another.

"And now it is your turn," he said. "You sing to me whatever is in your heart, on this day when we have become one."

Suzette opened her mouth to speak, but at first no sound would come forth. Clearing her throat, however, she was at last able to whisper, "Yes, I will sing, but . . ." Should she make the point? She hated to bring up a particular that might cause the mystique of the moment to vanish. Yet, she felt compelled to say what she must, and she added, "You do still understand that this is in name only?"

"*Hau.* This I understand." He leaned toward her. "But," he whispered against her ear, his breath warm against her, "if we are to say our vows before the Great Spirit, we should recite them with whatever is in our hearts. And if all that you feel is the necessity to have my name, then you should sing of that, for you now have it."

She nodded, again feeling touched by this man. "I feel rather inadequate. You have been most eloquent and—"

"Nothing is inadequate," he responded. "Sing from your heart, for only in that way will it be pure."

"Yes," she said. "All right." Clearing her throat once again, she began to sing, using the same melody of his song—at least as much of it as she could remember. She sang in the same key with the same style as he had done, and these were her words:

> *"I thank this man who is showing me kindness.*
> *I thank this man who has love in his heart and*
> *I thank this man who gives without asking favor.*

*Great Spirit, bless him. Great Spirit, bless our
     marriage.*
*Though I seek only his name for the favor of my
     child,*
*In my heart I will never forget him, nor his
     kindness.*
Black Lion, I, too, choose thee."

When she had finished, she looked up at Black Lion
and found him staring at her as though she might have
said a thing quite alien.

"Is something wrong?" she asked. "You look . . .
startled."

"*Hiya*," he said. "*Hiya*, nothing is wrong. Truly, I
think something is very right."

She grinned at him. "I am glad."

"As I am, also," he responded in kind. "Your voice is
very beautiful."

"Thank you."

"And I have heard it before."

"You have? Did you attend the opera in England,
then?"

"Opera? *Hiya*, no. No opera. I have heard your voice
in my dreams."

"Your dreams?" A smile pulled at the corners of her
mouth. "How poetic."

"Poetic?" he said. "Perhaps. All I know is that in
some way, in some unknown course in my life, I have
had the good sense to do something very right this day.
I have married you."

Her stomach flip-flopped in her abdomen. She was
flattered, and she smiled at him as though his words
were as precious as a discovery of a precious metal.

He returned the gesture, and they stood close, looking into one another's eyes, searching, as though each

would understand the other better. Then, glancing down at their hands, he said, "The time has come for me to break the physical tie that binds us, for there is no longer a need of it, because we are now of one heart." Thus saying, he let go of the buckskin. "At last it is done. We are truly married."

"Yes, we are," she agreed. However, again constrained by conscience, she added, "But, please, in name only."

He smiled at her. He simply smiled at her. "Come," he said, "I think it time to take you back to Irena's tent. For I do not believe that you are ready to spend the night in mine?"

"I think not."

"But before we go, there is one more detail that we should discuss."

"Oh?"

"*Hau*, there is." And without another word, he kissed her, a sweet, lingering kiss. But it didn't last. Pulling slightly away, he said, against her lips, "It is done."

"Yes." And the good Lord help her, she responded to this man and his kiss, once again.

CHAPTER 8

"Ladies and gentlemen, what you are about to witness is not a mere show. What you are about to see here today are the real people who made America into the great country she is today. The characters you will witness before you are not actors. These are the people who have lived their lives on America's Great Plains. Ladies and gentlemen, permit me to introduce to you a Congress of Riders of the West!"

"I don't know, Frank." It was Buffalo Bill speaking. "I think the introduction is too long-winded. Let's hear it again."

The announcer, Frank Richmond, repeated word for word the opening introduction. Meanwhile, the participants of the show filtered into the arena for this, a dress rehearsal. All those first entering were cowboys who each one sat atop a multicolored steed. Behind them, a tall and elaborate painting of the Great Plains provided a backdrop over about one half of the arena.

How interesting, thought Suzette, staring at the painting. Like the theater, the show used props.

"I think," said Buffalo Bill to Richmond, "that you could leave out one of those sentences somewhere there in the middle. Brief, to the point. That's the best sort of introduction."

"Bill . . . Bill!" A short, dark-haired man ran across the arena toward Buffalo Bill. "Red Hand is not gonna be able to do the fight with you," he said, out of breath. "Just got injured. Horse kicked him—we'll be needing someone to replace him in the 'fight to the death' scene."

"Damn! Is he being cared for?"

"Yep, near as I can tell."

"Good, then who else have we got who could do it?" As he spoke, both Buffalo Bill and the other gentleman left the podium to drift away from the arena.

"All right, is everybody ready?" It was Richmond, the announcer, speaking. "We're about to start again. Resume your original positions." He paused as the cowboys filtered out of the arena. "Here we go from the top. Ladies and gentlemen, what you are about to witness is not a mere show. The characters you see before you are not actors. These are the people who have lived out their lives on America's Great Plains. Ladies and gentlemen, permit me to introduce to you a Congress of Riders of the West!"

The noisy band started to play, a band that Suzette now realized consisted of a woodwind section—clarinets and flutes—as well as a brass section. It was a marching song they were rendering—a rather loud marching song—but as soon as it began, into the arena pranced a procession of some of the finest specimens of horseflesh that Suzette had ever seen.

Of course their cowboy riders were even wilder and

more dangerous looking than the animals, Suzette thought. All the young men wore cowboy hats, which they removed as they rode farther into the arena, for as they came in, they waved them in the air. Many in the small rehearsal audience waved back.

Some of those cowboys, Suzette noted as she stared out at them, had grown their hair long, but most kept their hair cropped short. All were groomed with a mustache, some with beards grown full out. Most had donned jeans or plain trousers, as well as chaps, multicolored shirts and leather gloves.

Several of the cowboys in the front guard held flags, but there were a few who had hopped off their horses and, while continuing to walk, whisked out their ropes and began a series of rope tricks. It was amazing!

Next into the arena galloped the Mexicans, their guns held high as they sent off one shot after another. A few of their fellows followed on foot, strumming their guitars and singing a song that was in competition with the one being belted out by the band.

It was a noisy concatenation at best, but spectacular all the same. At last, pulling up the rear, came the Indians. No women were in the procession; it was all warriors who were adorned with full headdress, buckskin shirts, leggings, breechclothes and moccasins. Each man, in his right hand, held a staff decorated with feathers. Each lifted that staff high into the air, much as the cowboys had waved their hats. Those few in the audience responded with a round of applause.

"All right," said the announcer, "that's fine. That's good. Now at this point, we'll play the Star-Spangled Banner—the song that Buffalo Bill thinks should be America's national anthem—and then we clear the arena. Are you ready? All right, let's do that now."

Suzette strained to see if Black Lion was among the

impressive-looking warriors, but either her vision was
at fault or he was missing from this particular performance. Placing her hand over her forehead, she strained
forward in her seat.

"Are you looking for anyone in particular?" asked
Irena, who was seated beside her.

"Uh, yes. I was . . . uh . . . looking at the Indians."
Suzette glanced away from her grandmother. She had yet
to confide to Irena that she was pregnant, let alone that
she was married to a man who was not her babe's father.
Indeed, because she was British to the very end, Suzette
hardly knew where to start. But one thing was certain:
This was not the time and place to make a confession.
Still looking in the opposite direction, Suzette said, "The
Indians, the cowboys are quite a sight, are they not?"

"Yes. It's why I thought we should come here to see
the dress rehearsal. Of course, you'll be invited to watch
the show, itself, when it plays this weekend, but the re-
hearsals are more intimate . . . less people. I thought
you would enjoy it."

"And so I do," replied Suzette.

"Careful. Careful," came Richmond's voice over the
megaphone. "We'll do the buffalo hunt first. Now I want
every rider to form a protective line around the audience.
Do this as soon as the Star-Spangled Banner is done playing. And I'll say something like this: 'Ladies and gentlemen, for your protection, our riders are forming a
protective line around the arena so that you may witness
a buffalo chase in safety.' That's right. That's right. Take
your positions now. Jed, a little to your left. That's right.
All right now, are you ready? Because as soon as you're
in position, we'll let the buffalo into the ring. Remember,
your job is to keep the buffalo toward the center of the
arena. That's right. Okay, let 'em loose."

Suzette could hear the buffalo before she saw them.

It would have been hard to miss the sound, since the ground literally shook. They burst through the open gates, and entered the ring—there must have been as many as fifty of them.

Were they being controlled? Suzette hoped so, because they seemed to be on a path aimed directly at her. Suzette jumped out of her seat, ready to run, and would have done so, too, except for Irena, who was still seated beside her.

"It's all right, Suzie," said Irena. "Sit back down. It is dangerous, but only to the cowboys and the hunters. You'll see."

Reluctantly, Suzette sat as instructed, though she wasn't sure she could trust her grandmother's logic. She peered out toward the arena. She had never seen a live buffalo before; they were massive, wild and hairy beasts, and she shuddered to think of meeting one of them without the safety of the arena.

It was while she was staring at the beasts that she saw him. Riding a spotted pony that was no taller than were the buffalo, Black Lion rode hard into the fast-moving herd. He was yelping and urging his mount to run up to the side of a buffalo. Without saddle, without even a hold on the reins, he performed the stunt hands free.

In awe, she watched as his pony nudged itself in close to one of those buffalo. Closer and closer it pushed until its master, Black Lion, at last shot off round after round of the arrows, aimed directly at the buffalo. No buffalo bull fell, however, since, as Suzette learned later, the arrows the Indians used were rubber tipped. But the pony acted as though its master had killed the beast, and dropped back to find another target. Once again, it was the pony who brought his master in close to the buffalo, so close that Suzette was certain that Black Lion could have reached out and touched the beast.

Again, hands free, Black Lion shot off round after round of arrows. What happened next was surely not in the script. One buffalo slowed, it turned. It pawed the ground. Then it rushed toward Black Lion.

Those who were seated in the audience leaped to their feet. A few of the women screamed. Several of the cowboys, those who had lined up around the arena, prodded their mounts slowly forward.

"Stay where you are!" came the announcement over the megaphone. "Protect the audience!"

The cowboys retreated.

The bull charged. Was Black Lion prepared for the attack? He looked relaxed in the saddle. Was he too relaxed?

The bull stormed forward. Suzette screamed.

The pony stood still. However, in the nick of time, the pony darted to the side, then swung around to meet the bull's next challenge. Again, the bull lunged forward, but this time Black Lion sent off one arrow after another, directly toward the bull's head. Quickly, he fired over and over, and though each arrow hit its target harmlessly, their force still stunned the bull.

The bull stopped, but he didn't turn. And that gave Black Lion's companions, the two other Indians, the opportunity they had been awaiting. Yelling and hollering, each holding out a blanket, the two other Indians provided a diversion, and the bull, confused, caught sight of one of its own herd, one who was exiting the arena. Luckily, the bull followed its companion out of the arena.

It was over.

A feeling of relief quickly swept through Suzette, which was followed at once by a round of applause from the audience. For her own part, Suzette let go of a long-held breath.

All it would have taken was one foul step, thought Suzette, and her newly acquired husband's life would have been over. The feeling of loss that accompanied the thought seemed out of place for a man she barely knew.

Or did she know him better than she thought? . . .

At present the three main players in the little drama were taking their bows, then with a wave to the audience, the three Indians exited the arena. But the roar from the relatively small audience would not let them go.

"Yes, yes," said Richmond, the announcer, "come back in here, boys. Take another bow."

As the three young men rode once more into the arena, the clamor from the people rose up in a crescendo. In their hands, the Indians held bows and arrows and on cue, they threw their hands high into the air. The small crowd went riotous, Suzette included. Even the cowboys who had placed a protective guard around the arena applauded.

"That's right. Give them a hand, folks. They certainly deserve it," said the announcer.

At last Black Lion looked directly at her in the audience. But what was this? What was he doing?

Without dropping his gaze from hers, Black Lion set his mount in a direction that would take him to stand directly in front of her. Then, reining in the Appaloosa that he rode, Black Lion wasted not a single effort, and in a salute to her, he placed his right arm over his breast.

It was an honor. Suzette grinned back at him, and caught up in the moment, she whipped her hat off her head, and threw the thing into the arena.

It was a bad toss, a girl's toss, and it fell to the ground well short of its mark. But it didn't matter, because, turning his pony around, and reining the animal into a run, Black Lion rushed toward the hat at a full gallop. Leaning over the side of the animal as it approached the hat, Black Lion plucked the bonnet up from the ground with ease. Straightening in his seat, he waved the headgear in the air as one final salute to her. And no sooner had the act been committed than he rushed from the arena.

Suzette, however, stood still, staring at the place where Black Lion had exited long after his image had faded from view. He had been magnificent, she thought; he had been thrilling. And this from a person who had been raised in the drama of the opera.

He had also been in danger. But it wasn't merely this that worried her. There, in the midst of the buffalo hunt, she had feared for him, truly feared for him.

Suzette wondered what this meant. She had married this man for his name alone. Did she already have stronger feelings for the man than she ought? Certainly she respected him, and particularly what he had done, was doing, for her. Certainly she responded to him physically, but . . .

On the tail end of that idea images materialized in her mind's eye, those of Black Lion. There he was, confronting the buffalo; there he was, listening to her, reasoning with her, arguing with her, tying their hands together, marrying her . . . kissing her.

She touched her lips. She had returned each of those kisses, she reminded herself. But it seemed to her that she could have done little to help herself. Especially because his kisses were as untamed as the man was, himself. If she were to be honest, and she really should be, she would have to admit to yearning for more contact with the man.

In the form of what? she asked herself. More kisses, more embracing, more fondling? What was it that he had said to her, there in the beginning of their relationship?

"If you are ever willing and wanting more, I, too, might be agreeable . . ."

Like a fine vein of gold marbling through a rock, his words laced through her thoughts, and without conscious effort, desire, pure and carnal, leaped through her. And it was with a certain degree of self-abhorrence that Suzette knew she was not only married to this man, she *wanted* this man, and on a very physical level.

But in so short a space of time? Surely, he was kind. Surely, she liked him. Surely, he created feelings of lust in her. But . . . ?

Could such a thing be a result of being pregnant? she reasoned. After all, was it not said that pregnancy could cause unusual cravings?

Still, on a subconscious level she knew that this thing that stirred within her was not a matter of bodily hormones. *She* wanted *him* as a woman wants her mate.

It was an alarming realization. She sat back down, feeling as though the wind had been knocked from her. In truth, she felt both frightened and excited.

It also unsettled her. Had she not hoped to escape this very scenario? Was that not one of the reasons she had sought out a man with whom she ought not to associate?

Truth was, she didn't want to experience love or lovemaking. As far as she was concerned, men did hurtful deeds; said hurtful things. Hadn't she learned her lesson with William?

Quite unconsciously, she stiffened her back, and at the same time she tried to tighten her resolve against her feelings for Black Lion. She was here to do no more than give birth to her child, return to the opera and hopefully regain not only her self-respect, but the veneration of a society that had shunned her. That was all.

Still, she was more than aware that she was not

immune to this man's charm. That this could pose a problem was also without doubt.

However, perhaps she worried needlessly. Indeed, Black Lion had his life to lead, she had hers. There really should be no trouble at keeping the man at a distance.

She sighed . . .

As Black Lion rubbed down his pony, he wondered again how he should proceed. His luck, it would appear, had changed, for at last he had found the owner of the voice from his dreams. Of course he couldn't be certain, but he believed that she could be the one who owned the sacred song.

Why had he not recognized before now that her voice was the one from his dreams? Surely, he had heard her sing that first day he had found her in Irena's tent. Perhaps he had been too bewildered by her requests at the time. Or mayhap he had found her beauty too distracting.

But, regardless of the reason, he wondered what he should do now. How should he approach her? Undoubtedly, she was his wife, and although a man might solicit his wife's help with ease, this was not the situation between the two of them.

Could he sing the song to his wife? Perhaps. But if she were not the one, and he did sing it, would he lose forever his only chance to help his people?

It was a good question, an important question, and one he could not answer.

It was hard to know what to do, and he wished fervently for guidance. If only someone else were here to help him, or better yet, if only White Claw, the wise man from the Lost Clan, were here. White Claw would know what to do.

Black Lion instinctively wanted to seek out his wife, to sing to her and to free his people. How happy he and the Clan would be. Yet, he must control himself, for if he acted in a way that he should not, all could be lost.

He frowned.

He could seek out a medicine man here amongst the Lakota with the show. But, though he had grown to manhood amongst the Lakota, they were not truly *his* people. And except for Two Bears, Black Lion had never confided to anyone the truth of who he was. Fear of the consequences of doing so had made him hesitate. Instead, he had sought out advice from the Great Spirit, He who spoke to him through his spirit protector.

Black Lion paused in his train of thought. That was it. His spirit protector. His spirit protector would know what to do, for the mountain lioness spoke words that came from the Creator.

Yes. He would go into the mountains.

Speaking gently to his pony, and leading her back to her stall, Black Lion closed the door on the animal, petted her, and left the stables to seek out the wisdom from his spirit protector.

CHAPTER 9

"Do you want to tell me about it?"

The rehearsal for the show had ended hours ago. At present, Suzette and Irena were at their leisure, seated within what amounted to Irena's best attempt at a parlor. The murky white tent's flaps were closed, the music box sounded in the background, giving the two women a feeling of privacy. Indeed, it was as perfect an atmosphere as any, were a person of the mind to admit the secrets of her heart. However, Suzette was not so inclined.

She said, "Tell you about what?"

"Come now, Suzie. This is *me* you are talking to."

Suzette scowled at her grandmother. "I have no idea what it is that you are asking of me."

"Today. You. Black Lion. You threw your hat to him."

"Only because he greeted me."

"Yes, but why did he greet you?"

Suzette paused.

"Yes?" Irena encouraged.

"Well, we do know each other. We met in England, actually."

"In England?"

"Yes, he ran over me."

"He did what?"

"He had not meant to," said Suzette. "But he was in a hurry that day, and was not watching where he was going, and he ran into me, pushed me into a mud hole, as it were."

"Oh, so that's why . . . Although I never asked, I always wondered how your clothes had become so muddy that day."

"Yes, well . . ." said Suzette. "Now, about another matter entirely different. Have you told Mr. Cody your true age?"

"Of course I have, dear. I signed a contract," said Irena matter-of-factly. "But let's return the subject to Black Lion . . ."

Suzette twisted in her chair, and though the chair was more than comfortable, she was not. But she said nothing.

"Well?" prompted Irena. "Are you going to tell me about it?"

"About what? There's nothing to say, really. On that day in England, I was trying to find *you*, if you might remember. But I ran into the man, he pushed me in the mud, I got angry at him, and he proposed."

Irena's head came up. "He what?"

"Oh, didn't I tell you about that?"

"No, you most certainly did not tell me." Irena had come to sit forward in her seat. "He proposed?"

"Well, he meant it as a jest, I would venture to say, because I was taking up his time and I refused to let him go when he was late for a performance. He said that because we had spent so much time in one another's company that to save my reputation, he would have to marry me."

Irena was perched at the end of her seat. "That does sound like something he would say. And what did you say back to him?"

"I laughed at him."

Irena bobbed her head up and down. "Yes, I can see that you might have done that. And then?"

"That's all there was to it really. We had a moment's conversation, and then I went my way and he went his."

"Hmmmm . . ." said Irena. "And yet, there must have been something unusual about it for you both, for him to have bestowed the honor of his attention on you . . . and, might I add, for you to throw your hat to him."

"Yes, well . . ."

"Indeed, it must have been quite a memorable experience."

Suzette remained silent.

"Unless you have seen him in between that time and now."

Suzette frowned. "What do you mean?"

"What I mean is this: A man does not shower attention on a person when he is performing, unless that person . . . means something to him."

"Oh, Irena that's silly. You and I were both raised in the theater, and you know that . . ."

Irena gave her a knowing look.

"Besides," Suzette continued, "how could I possibly *mean* something to the man?"

"That is exactly my question to you. Come, Suzie, dear, tell me everything."

Suzette shut her eyes, opened them, looked Irena directly in the eye and said, "I suppose I will have to tell you the truth."

"That sounds like an excellent idea."

"After all, you will probably hound me about it until you learn every little detail."

"I should think so."

"Then, I guess I am forced to tell you."

"Indeed."

"Very well. Here it is: We are married."

An uncomfortable, deep and protracted silence followed the announcement. "Did you say married?" Irena said finally.

"I did."

Irena, who had been practically ready to pop out of her chair, did the opposite and flopped back into it. "Married?"

"Don't tell me that you, too, are prejudiced against him or our marriage because he is Indian. To do so would be the height of hypocrisy, since I know very well that you are here for no other reason than to find an Indian man whom you profess to love."

"It's not that I am prejudiced. Rather, I am . . . shocked."

"Well, as long as you are shocked, I might as well tell you something else. Are you prepared for this next?"

Irena sat up stiffly. "No, but tell me anyway."

"Very well. If you must know, I am pregnant."

"By Black——"

"Oh, no! No, no, no. By William, of course."

"Oh," said Irena. "Of course. And William knows of this?"

"Yes."

"And . . ."

Suzette sucked in her breath. "I imagine I should tell you the entire thing, shouldn't I?"

"That would be best, dear, yes. I did hear of your broken engagement . . . Your dear mother wrote to me about it. And I learned also that Lady Blair tried in every way she could to damage your reputation . . . because of me joining the Wild West Show, your mother tells me."

"Yes. Lady Blair did try to blacken my character," said Suzette, "but she was not as successful as she might have thought. Indeed, on my last evening in England, I sang to a full house, and were it not for this small problem, I would be there now, attending to my reputation without any needed help, I might add."

"The problem that you speak of, of course, being your pregnancy?"

"Yes, of course. I made William swear to tell no one about it, not even his mother."

"And I suppose he agreed readily?"

"Yes. I do believe he was frightened that he might be forced to marry me and stand up to his mother. I must say, she is rather formidable."

"But she is his mother, not his jailer, and he should have done right by you."

"I do think so, as well, particularly since I was under the impression that we were to be married within a matter of days when the deed happened. I know it was wrong of me to relax my guard with him, but it seemed a harmless thing at the time. I never suspected . . ."

Irena pulled her mouth into a grimace. "I should go home," she said. "I don't have to be here. As a matter of fact, I shall go home. For when I do so, you can be married in an honorable way."

"I am already married in an honorable way."

"Yes, but . . ."

"Surely you do not think that Black Lion is anything but honorable?"

"Of course he is. But it is, after all, because of me that you are in this predicament. Therefore, I will settle it."

"No," said Suzette. "I forbid you to do so. The situation has changed. I no longer love William, and I no longer wish him to be my husband. Not only did he fail to defend me against his mother, he also proved himself to be a cad. If anything, Irena, what you did saved me from a terrible mistake, for I am afraid that I was quite blinded by his charm and his position. Remember? I thought I was the luckiest girl in all of England because he loved me, and because he was not using me as some men would a diva."

"Yes, we all know this is true. Now, Suzie, listen to me. It is kind of you to say these things to exonerate me. But never did I envision that my actions would ruin your engagement. And now that I know the details of it, I would make it right. If you are with his child, then you should be married to him."

"No, I should not be," said Suzette. "And I am not going back to England at this time. I am married to Black Lion, and I intend to remain married to him."

Silence greeted this statement. "I see," said Irena at last. "Tell me, have you had your wedding night with him yet?"

Suzette raised her chin. "If you mean has the marriage been consummated, I will have to say that this is between myself and . . . my husband."

"Of course. You are right." She paused. She smiled. "But have you?"

"Irena! I refuse to answer that question. Clearly, I can see that if I say no, then you might try to urge me to annul the marriage. If I say yes, the marriage is consummated, what will you do then? Confront him?"

"I will confront him with this sooner or later regardless of your answer."

"No, you will not," said Suzette.

"But I—"

"The man does me a favor. If you must know, I have married Black Lion because I will *not* marry William, and I will not have my child born out of wedlock. Black

Lion understands that all I require from him is his
name, nothing more. And pray, do not bring this matter
to his attention."

Irena remained silent.

"You must *not*," said Suzette. "I will have your word
on it."

"And why should I give it?"

"Because if you do not, I will not detail to you the
rest of the adventure."

"There is more?"

"Oh, yes, indeed. There are my plans for the future to
tell, and also I have not yet disclosed to you what happened between myself, William and Lady Blair."

Irena drew her brows together, frowning at her
granddaughter. She said, "That's blackmail."

Suzette pressed her lips together and crossed her
arms in front of her.

"Had I known that Lady Blair would take such a
stand with you," said Irena, "I would never have agreed
to this engagement with the Wild West Show."

"I know that," said Suzette. "Do you give me your
word?"

"Not to speak my mind to Black Lion?"

Suzette nodded.

"I cannot. I, myself, have become close to that young
man, and a thing such as this can fester between people
if they do not have it out. However, I will promise you
that I will speak to him intelligently, gently, and I will
not accuse him."

Suzette paused, weighing the possibilities, for she
knew she would receive no better promise than this. At
length, she said, "I guess that will have to do."

"Yes," said Irena. "And now, tell me about William
and Lady Blair. Besides being a mother's boy and break-
ing your engagement, what has set you so against him?"

Suzette hesitated for a moment. Then, "No more than a trifling, perhaps."

"A trifling?"

"Well, maybe more. He did, only a few days after our engagement was broken, set his attentions upon my understudy, Miss Abernathy. It was whispered about the opera that he had promised to accelerate Miss Abernathy's career in the opera."

"And, of course, there is no worse crime than that . . ."

"Do not jest—as you well know, it is a point of contention with me that he could so easily dally with another woman, and one whom I not only knew, but one who aspires, herself, to become a prima donna."

"But sponsoring a diva is not the same as—"

"I first saw the two of them together after a performance," Suzette interrupted to say. "He came backstage. I was there, and yet, although he did acknowledge me slightly, he went directly to her. I saw them leave together. I saw him kiss her."

"Ah," said Irena. "I begin to understand. This being the case, naturally, you cannot marry him."

"Indeed not."

"And so you decided to follow me? That you might marry Black Lion?"

"No," said Suzette. "I followed you because I was angry with you, and because I needed to leave England, William, his mother and those memories behind me."

"Of course. Yes, of course. And are you still angry with me?"

"No." Suzette grinned. "Performance is in our blood. It would be stranger to me if, presented with what you were, you remained behind to see me safely married."

"Thank you for that." Irena fixed Suzette with a look,

then said, "But did it not occur to you on the trip here that you might find Black Lion and use him as a means of handling your situation?"

"No, it did not. Of course his unusual proposal did enter my mind on occasion, but I understood that he had meant it as a jest. Yet, when I saw him here, in your tent—"

"You met him here?"

"That first day, he had come here to see you. I was . . . melancholy, for despite what has happened between myself and William, I was happy for a time with him, and I had fancied myself in love with him. But, getting back to the story, there was Black Lion, and there was I and he seemed to understand me somehow and I . . . it just came out."

Irena nodded.

"It wasn't until after I said it that I realized it would be perfect, if he would do it. Marry him, have my child and return to England a married woman. And yet, it is not as perfect as it could have been. For it was never my intention to use Black Lion completely. If he were already married, it could have been done with little inconvenience to him."

"Ah," said Irena, "yes. But he is not married, I know that. Or perhaps I should say he *was* not married. Now tell me, did he object to the rather harsh living arrangements that will be necessary between the two of you? . . . If you are to live apart?"

"He did not seem to. Although, again, it would have eased my conscience considerably if he could take a wife besides me . . . But alas, it does no good to think of such things. It appears that the old ways of the American Indian are not well tolerated on the new reservations."

"Indeed, not. I do, however, think it strange that Black Lion should so willingly agree to the arrangement. He is a robust man. One would think that he would aspire to the marital state, in all its bliss."

Suzette, despite herself, could feel herself blush. She said, "He did tell me that he has never intended to marry, and so it mattered little to him if he were able to take another wife or not."

"Did he?" Irena arched a brow. "I wonder why?"

Suzette shrugged.

"Well, be that as it may," said Irena, "your mother did write to me that Lady Blair gave you problems."

"That is true." Suzette pulled a face. "I must say that Lady Blair can be quite cruel in her whisperings."

"Her kind is often cruel."

"Perhaps, but I had liked her very much at one time."

"Your mother did tell me that you had done something that had her quite put out. What exactly did you do?"

"Well," said Suzette, "it happened after a performance. I saw William and Miss Abernathy together, and I . . . If you must know, I took off my glove, I slapped William's face and I called him a cad."

"He is a cad."

"Very true. Yet, it was put about that I did much more than this, that I begged him to come back to me . . . offering myself to him . . ."

"Considering your position, it would not have been a great crime, my dear, even if you had done so."

"But I did not do it." Her head came up and she squinted her eyes. "If I am to be punished," she said, "let it be for something that I did, not a thing that I did not and never would do."

"Yes, of course, this would be most unfair," said Irena.

"It was also said," continued Suzette, "that I misrepresented myself to him as being a woman of honor, and when he had discovered that I was not, due to . . . circumstances . . . he had no choice but to break the engagement." Even now, Suzette could feel herself blush with the remembrance. Never had she been so humiliated, nor so angry.

"What terrible gossip." Irena's face was red as she spoke. "Terrible, ugly, and so much a lie. Who was it, do you think, who fueled the gossip? William, himself, or his mother?"

"I am not clear on that fact," said Suzette. "It could have been William, himself, although, as I further considered that, I do think that he is too inept to have invented such a lie. Then there was my understudy, Miss Abernathy, as well, for you and I know well the jealousy that abounds in our profession. Or mayhap it truly was Lady Blair, herself, who set the gossip into motion. But regardless of my feelings in the matter, whoever first started the rumor is not important now. Not anymore. I am over it. The only thing critical to me now is my child, and making a good home for him or her." Absentmindedly, she rubbed her stomach.

"And so that should be your first thought, Suzie. Yes, indeed, so it should be." She paused. "Tell me, does Black Lion know of your condition?"

"Yes," said Suzette. "It was one of the first things that he asked me."

"And he is willing to be your husband in all the ways, except perhaps one, yet let you raise the child alone?"

Suzette made a face. "No. He was quite adamant about his rights concerning the child. While he will not take him or her away from me, he would like to come to know the child."

"Yes," said Irena, "I would imagine he would. The American Indians take seriously their duty as a mother or father. Though he will not do anything with the child that would upset you, he will want to figure largely in the child's life."

"And he may . . . while I am here. But perhaps you should be alert to the fact that I intend to leave here after the babe is born. It has never been my plan to stay here. I plan to return to England and when I do, I will devote my life to my child and to my career."

Irena nodded. "It is a worthy endeavor. Quite. And now, I have one further question. Are you hungry?"

"Indeed, I am. Especially after a talk such as this." Suzette smiled.

"Then pray, let us ring for the servant and attend to our dinner."

"Yes," said Suzette, "that would be most fine, indeed."

CHAPTER 10

It was too cold for the clouds to be making thunder. Yet, thunder loomed above him, its grumbling so vigorous that, were it not the dead of winter, one might have been fooled into thinking it was the prelude to a summer shower. Above him, black and gray clouds raced across the midday sky, as though they were chased by some unforeseen element of nature. However, there was little, if any, wind this day to cause their speed.

Small hailstones spit around Black Lion from those clouds, some hitting him full face. They stung, and ofttimes they hurt, for Black Lion had come before the Great Spirit as naked as a young babe.

He was cold. He was discouraged, but Black Lion would not be swayed from his task. He had come to this place, high in the mountains, to pray and to seek counsel with his spirit protector; he would have that counsel.

With smoldering sage in hand, he sang out:

> *"Mountain lioness, spirit protector*
> *Hear my plea.*

I have been gone from here, my country, it is true,
But I am home now, and I need seek your advice.
I did as you asked, and I sought the song
Across the seas.
I did not find it.
I did as you asked, again,
I searched for it while traveling here and there.
I did not find it. I still have not found it.
But spirit protector, something new has happened.
I have married, and the voice that sings the sacred
Song to me each night is she who is my wife.
Is she the one who has it?
May I sing it to her? Or if I sing it,
And she does not know it,
Will I forever have failed the Clan?
Mountain lioness, spirit protector, hear me.
I have not forgotten my people;
I have not laid their plight to rest.
Mountain lioness, protector, I would ask your help."

Ha! Ha!

Had the sound came from above him? What was it?
Ha!

There it was again. *Hau!* It was above him, in the
clouds.

"Ha! Ha, ha!"

"Who is there?" Black Lion asked, addressing his
words to the low-ranging, and ever-moving, black puffs
of vapor.

"Ha! You dare to come this close to me? You, who are
no more than a human being?"

It was the Thunderer, his enemy. There could be no
mistaking the identity of that voice.

"Human being I may be," called out Black Lion.
"But I would best you if you would dare to come to

earth to fight me. Because of you, my people are enslaved. Because of you, my people weep. Because of
you, my heart is filled with the desire for revenge, so do
not taunt me, Thunder Being. Either meet me in a hand-
to-hand fight, or leave this place."

"*Ha! Ha, ha, ha!*"

The dark clouds rolled, gathering force, and Black
Lion thought that at any moment a lightning bolt might
strike him down. Still, he did not retreat. Instead, he
bared his breast to the god of thunder, physically issu-
ing a challenge.

But there was to be no fight this day. Still laughing, the
Thunderer moved along in the sky, forcing the clouds to
speed elsewhere, perhaps to torment some other unfortu-
nate soul. Gradually, the Thunderer's laughter faded into
the distance. But not so Black Lion's resentment.

In protest, Black Lion raised his arms to the sky and
shouted, "Come back again and challenge me, if you
dare, Thunderer. I will best you!" Lowering his arms, he
repeated, this time more softly, "I will best you."

But the Thunderer was gone, taking the blackened
clouds with him.

Black Lion paused, if only to clear his heart, for it
would do no good to address the Great Spirit and his
protector with anger. At last he was ready to continue
his prayer, and he sang:

> "*Mountain lioness, spirit protector,*
> *Can you tell me if my wife is the one who owns the*
>   *song?*
> *May I sing to her?*
> *Help me discover the truth of this,*
> *For I am lost in this land of the whites.*
> *Protector, I would give my life in service to my*
> *People,*

For I am not afraid.
But to wait when she, who may know the song, is
     close,
Is torture.
Help me, Spirit Protector. For if you do, I promise
That I and my people will sing songs of your praise so
Long as we exist."

Again, Black Lion raised his arms to the heavens. This time, his exposed face was lifted toward the sky. Hope burned deep within him, and he waited for a reply.

But it seemed that his spirit protector was not here this day. Lowering his arms, Black Lion squatted next to the fire, warming himself but a moment. Though the fire's heat called to him, he could not linger here. Need drove him to find the mountain lioness for time was growing short.

Standing, Black Lion made a decision. He would leave the safety of his camp to go in search of his name-sake, his protector. Though Black Lion was naked, he would endure the cold, the sleet and the snow. Some-how, in some way, he would find the guidance he desperately sought.

Damping down the fire, he set out upon his journey, and since this was a vision quest, he began his trek naked. He traipsed in a circle around the mountain, and all the while, he called out, "Mountain lioness, protector, come. I have need of counsel."

But there was nothing.

Almost delirious from hunger, cold and disappointment, Black Lion trod back toward his camp. Reaching it, he noticed that the fire was still alive, but almost out. Quickly he rekindled it. He would remain here one more night, but he feared he could devote no more time than that. Already he had been on this mountain two days and nights, and the white man's show would not allow him more than this.

One more night.

"Human!"

Black Lion came fully awake.

"Human, you have called my name the day through. I have watched you. I have seen how you suffer. I have taken pity on you, and I will help you if I can. What is it that you seek from me?"

Black Lion sat up, his buffalo robe falling from around his shoulders and onto his lap. At last, he had come face-to-face with his protector, the mountain lioness, for that animal sat close to him, the lion's hind legs folded beneath her, her front legs and paws stretched out in front of her.

Black Lion tried to speak, but his voice took leave of him. He coughed, he sputtered in his attempt, and at last he was able to say, "I seek counsel."

"I am here."

"Thank you. Mountain lioness, I would seek to know if I am on the right path. I have found the voice of the woman who sings the sacred song to me each night in my dreams. I long to sing the song to her, to see if I can break the spell for my people, but I fear to do it, in case she is not the one. Will you not tell me, mountain lioness, is she the one who will proclaim the song?"

"Human, you must discover this yourself."

"Hau, hau. But protector, are you saying that I may sing it to her?"

"Human, do not misunderstand. Listen well to me. You have one chance and only one chance to chant this song without missing a word. If you sing it to your wife, and she does not know it, then you will have failed, for

you will not have found the song. Know that if this happens, you will have lost the opportunity to save your people . . . forever . . ."

At these words, Black Lion sank inward on himself, bringing up his hands to cover his face. He must have appeared utterly dejected, for his spirit protector continued to speak, saying, *"But come, it is not hopeless. I will cleanse you in the right way and afterward, I will give you my own song, the song of the lion. While it is not the sacred song, it is one that you may sing freely to anyone you choose. Perhaps the one who knows the sacred melody may recognize this, a lion's song, and then perhaps that person might help you."*

As she spoke, the mountain lioness had come up onto all fours, so that the two of them, human being and lion, stared at one another, face-to-face.

At length, Black Lion said, "I thank you for your wisdom, protector. It is, indeed, a great gift that you offer me. For this I will honor you, and I will sing your song with a glad heart."

The mountain lioness seemed well satisfied with this and turned to walk a few steps away. Black Lion commenced to follow, but the mountain lioness hadn't gone far before she leaped onto a ledge, spun around toward Black Lion, and said, *"It is good, human being. I am honored by your words. Know this in warning. Nothing in this life is certain; nothing, no man, no animal, is perfect. But there are those who help others more than they harm. Seek to be he who helps, not he who harms, and if you do this, your pure heart will guide you straight.*

"But beware. The white man's ways are tempting. I will do what I can to help you, but you must keep to your purpose. Do not become distracted by ways of the flesh. Though you are married, you, your people, must be willing to sacrifice pleasures of the flesh.

"Now come, and I will lead you to a stream where you may cleanse yourself. Then I will sing my song to you."

"*Hau*, you speak wisely, my friend, and I will honor your words. If you will guide me, I will follow." And Black Lion, gaining his feet, adhered well to his promise, chasing after that mountain lioness as they sped over the rocky terrain of the high mountains.

The Deadwood stagecoach was a piece of history, and was in fact the same coach that years earlier had been held up by Indians. Pulled by six mules, the coach sped into and around the large open-air arena as if pursued by Indians.

And it was.

The stunt was meant to be a reenactment, not simply a show. As a matter of fact, Suzette had come to learn that Bill Cody did not consider the Wild West a "show" at all. Rather, the Wild West was a depiction of the history of the West, as Cody had known and lived it.

In the reenactment, the coach was driven by Tom Duffey, a man who had been one of the original drivers of the Deadwood coach years earlier. Seated atop the rear of the coach was John Nelson, another colorful frontiersman who was rumored to have wed several Indian maids during his career—and at the same time. At present, Nelson and family were among several authentic characters in the show.

Suzette was seated within the coach. Her role in this drama was to be the maiden in distress, the one who would be rescued by Buffalo Bill, himself. It was Saturday, late in the afternoon, and this would be the last of three shows for the day.

The coach jerked back and forth as dirt from the mules kicked up enough dust to create a cloud. Suzette was reclining next to an open-air window, and with the coach running at full speed, she was joggled this way and that, often sliding into the gentleman seated next to her, necessitating several apologies from them both.

Behind the coach could be heard the war cries and the high-pitched whooping of the Indians, as they gained speed over the coach. In anxiety, Suzette's stomach lurched over once, causing Suzette to lay a protective hand across her abdomen. Funny, she thought, the Indians hadn't sounded so frightening in rehearsal. What was it about the actual performance that made the event seem so real?

Perhaps in rehearsal the Indians were not so loud or so intent on their prey, or maybe the crack of the whip was not quite so ominous or desperate. Whatever it was, it took no stretch of the imagination to envision how it would have felt to be involved in the real thing . . . even knowing that Buffalo Bill and his riders were to come to their "rescue."

Jittery now, she glanced toward her fellow passengers seated across from her, a man and his "wife." They all three shared a smile, and then, on cue, the man drew out his pistol, leaned out the window and commenced firing the blanks from his gun.

Gazing once again out her own window, Suzette marveled at the skill of the Indian brave who rode up to the front of the coach on her side; the warrior sent a round of arrows toward the driver, who immediately fell over, "dead." But the stagecoach kept going.

The Indian jumped from his seat on his pony to the coach, grappling to hold on while he wormed his way onto the topmost seat. Truly, it was a most athletic move. Meanwhile another one of the Indians, a man she knew was called Red Shirt, rode up to her window, and drawing his bow taut, sent an arrow, aimed directly at her.

She screamed, even as the arrow whizzed harmlessly past her. Of course she'd known this was to happen; they had rehearsed it many times. Be that as it may, whether the stunt was "real" or not, it was still shocking.

At last the stagecoach came to a halt. The Indians dismounted and surrounded them; one Indian, whom she believed to be the man she knew as Red Shirt, ripped her door open.

Suzette screamed, again according to script. But even without the inducement of the script, she might have done the same thing regardless. Indians were everywhere—and they were painted for war.

And then the oddest thing happened: The Indian who had ripped open her door winked at her.

Winked at her? Red Shirt?

Eyes wide, she studied her "attacker" more carefully. Ah, here was the reason. This was not Red Shirt at all; this man was . . . It was Black Lion, and beneath all that war paint on his face, he was grinning at her.

Stepping into character for a moment, he frowned at her, sized her up and down, from the top of her bonnet to the tips of her boots. Then he said, "I think you will decorate my tepee well. Although my wife may be jealous of one so beautiful."

Suzette shook her head at him, then shivered, remembering that she was supposed to be frightened. She said, "Why sir, do you mean to tell me you are already married?"

"Alas, I am," he replied in an accent that sounded more British than Native American. "My wife is a white woman, too, and very beautiful, also. It is strange, for she looks much like you."

Suzette almost laughed. "Oh, do stop," she admonished, damping down the smile. "If you keep this up, Black Lion, you are going to cause me to laugh instead

of doing what I am supposed to do—which is screaming and begging for mercy."

"Scream away," he said as he pulled her from the
coach. But his touch was hardly rough. Indeed, he brought
her into his arms, and for a moment only, he pressed his
face up close against hers.

"Sir," she said, adding a scream to the word for good
artistic measure. "This is sudden, is it not?"

"So it is," he replied. "But I must work fast, I fear, for
even now, the cavalry is sounding their horns in the distance, and I suspect that soon, I will be lying here dead
at your feet. Ah, what a man must do to hold his own
wife in his arms."

She burst out laughing.

He frowned at her and shook his head. "And now you
laugh at me when you should be screaming."

"Oh, of course. I forgot." And she added a shriek.

His hand came up to cover her mouth, but instead of
jerking her toward his horse, as he was supposed to do,
he leaned down, took his hand away for the barest of
moments, and pressed a kiss against her open lips.

She wasn't supposed to respond. Dear Lord, she was
performing in front of thousands of people. How could
this happen?

Yet, she answered him back in the only way she
could. She fell in against him, and for a moment, his
arms encircled her. A cavalry trumpet sounded close at
hand, which must have prompted him to remember the
script, for he said, "Lean on me," and then he dragged
her as gently as possible toward his pony.

"You should not have done that. You should not have
kissed me," she said, even while she pretended to struggle to get away from him. "Someone is sure to have
seen. Do you wish to bring trouble to yourself?"

"A man might dare much," he responded while fielding

her attempts to hit him, "when he discovers his wife has not a single moment to spend with him."

"But I thought you understood that—"

He winked at her, and then, as he had "predicted," soldiers and the Wild West riders sped onto the scene, coming to the "rescue" of the coach. Within a matter of minutes, Cody galloped toward her and Black Lion, and jumping down from his mount, Cody had no sooner pulled Black Lion away from her than the two men commenced upon a completely scripted yet desperate fight.

Suzette found herself silently cheering for the Indian, and she wondered if any of her counterparts of old might have done much the same . . .

Cody won, of course, and when it was over, Black Lion lay at her feet. Alas, it was done. Her honor had been "saved" a terrible fate.

"My lady," said Cody, bowing. Then he smiled at her and gallantly extended a hand to help her up to her feet.

"Sir," she repeated loudly so that the audience could hear. "You have saved me. You have saved my father. How can I ever repay you?"

"No need to do that, ma'am," answered Cody in his best theatrical voice. "I am only doing my duty."

"Ah! You are so brave. You are my hero!" With this said, as she was supposed to do in this little drama, she collapsed into a faint, directly into Cody's waiting arms.

CHAPTER 11

"Good show," said a smiling John Burke, the Wild West Show's manager and press agent. "Good show." With a drink teetering precariously in each hand, he mingled in between and amongst the assembled guests in the after-the-show party, passing by Suzette and her grandmother.

He acknowledged Irena, extended a glass of champagne to her, and offered the other to Suzette. Suzette declined, but Irena accepted gracefully.

"Thank you," said Irena, smiling at Burke.

Burke nodded, then turned and retraced his steps, presumably to find more champagne.

Irena looked at Suzette over her glass. She said, "That is a beautiful gown, Suzie. White is a good color on you. The material is very soft. Is it silk?"

"Yes."

"And the cut is quite flattering, as well, the neckline not too low, not too high."

"Thank you."

And then, still eyeing her granddaughter over the

glass of champagne, Irena commented, "Oh, and by the way, I saw him kiss you."

"Did you?" said Suzette, not bothering to ask who *he* was. "Let us hope that no one else did."

"Suzie, I fear that it could not have been missed."

It was true. She said, "Do you know if he is in trouble?"

"I must admit that I have no idea."

"But why did he do it?"

Irena smiled at her as though she knew something that Suzette didn't. She said, "Perhaps you could spend some time with him. You must be aware that it is well over a few weeks since you first wed. Perhaps, if you were more attentive to him, he might not look upon a public demonstration as a way to become closer to you." Irena paused.

"We are *not* supposed to become closer."

"Need I remind you that you are wed."

"Irena, do stop this. You know the particulars on that."

Irena shrugged. "He is a man, and you went into this arrangement willingly."

"Has he said something to you, then?"

"No, he has not. But I think he would like to get to know you better."

Suzette didn't respond.

Completely unnecessarily, Irena repeated, "He is your husband, after all."

"No, he is not," Suzette denied. "Well, maybe," she said more honestly. "But not really. I bear his name. That is all."

"And so it is your plan to take his name and ignore the man?"

Annoyed, yet keeping a smile affixed to her countenance, Suzette turned on her grandmother. "What do you expect from me, Irena? The man knew what he was doing, as well as I. I did not lie to him about what I needed or what our relationship would be after the deed was done. He agreed."

Irena shrugged.

Suzette abruptly changed the subject. "When do you perform?"

"As soon as dinner is finished."

"What are you singing?"

"The Barcarolle, 'Belle Nuit,' 'Oh Lovely Night,' from *The Tales of Hoffmann*, by Jacques Offenbach."

Suzette nodded. "Good choice."

"Yes. I think the Denver officials might enjoy the performance."

"I am sure that they will."

Irena eyed her granddaughter with a raised eyebrow. She said, "Would you like to sing after I do? It would be easy to arrange."

"Oh, no," said Suzette at once. "I am unprepared for it, and I think I am attached to the idea that no one here knows that I am a prima donna in my real life."

"In your real life . . ." Irena's expression took on a dreamlike appeal. "How strange those words sound. We have not been here in Colorado that long, and yet England seems so far away."

"But it is far away."

"I was not speaking about the distance in miles."

"I knew you weren't, Irena. It is different here, I will admit. Do you miss England, then?"

"No. Do you?"

Suzette thought for a moment. "No," she said carefully. "When I first set out to join you, I believed that I would miss my home, but oddly, I do not. There is something about this place. One is allowed to . . . breathe . . . and not be expected to rush through one's life, with little attention to anything but the need for wealth, power and position. One is simply let to . . . well, to live. I think the people here call it freedom. And I, too, seem to favor it. Very much, I should say."

"Yes," said Irena. She nodded. "Quite. Ah, look there, dear. Mr. Cody approaches, and I do have a need to speak to him alone. Would you mind?"

"Of course not."

"Hello, Mr. Cody," cooed Irena, as soon as the man came within hearing distance. She smiled and offered him her gloved hand.

"Lady Irena," he responded in his deep voice, as he took hold of her hand. Bowing low over it, he pressed a kiss to it. He turned to Suzette. "And here's the pretty little miss who decorated the Deadwood stagecoach so beautifully today."

Suzette smiled. "Mr. Cody," she acknowledged, offering him her white-gloved hand, as well, which he accepted at once. "How much I enjoyed being rescued."

"My pleasure, ma'am. My pleasure. I hear that you might have had trouble today when—"

"Mr. Cody," interrupted Irena. "Do you have a moment?"

Cody grinned at her. "I have many of them that I should like to spend with you, if that is what you are suggesting."

Irena's smile deepened. "That would be very agreeable, indeed. Suzette, will you excuse us?"

"By all means." Suzette beamed at them both. "By all means. And Mr. Cody? There was no trouble. None at all."

"Glad to hear it, ma'am. Glad to hear it." And with a parting smile at her, Cody guided Irena away.

Sighing, Suzette glanced around the room, taking in the assembled company. There were few here that she recognized, fewer yet that she wished to speak to, though she supposed it would be to her advantage to mingle with the cowboys and cowgirls. However, the brisk cold of the evening outside Cody's welcome tent seemed inviting to her.

In England, one would not dare to venture into the night alone for fear of ruining one's reputation. But here in the American West, considerations were not so inflexible. Besides, it wasn't as though she would be alone, in truth. It seemed to her that the people who populated the Wild West Show seemed to never sleep, that someone was always nearby regardless of the hour of the day.

She drifted toward the entryway as inconspicuously as possible. She might have stepped outside, as well, but directly across the short midway between the two areas was the Indian encampment, and now that the orchestra music was distant from her, the Indian drums from that camp rang out their distinctive beat.

Something drew her irresistibly toward those tepees. She could not explain the attraction to that camp, however, for she had never been there. Unless the allure was because of *him*.

Was it? She supposed that it could be.

Whatever the reason, Suzette determined to ignore the enticement, and take a walk instead. The air was fresh, though cold in this place, and it invited a person to partake of it. Placing her cloak around her shoulders, she stepped out into the darkened black of the night.

As she strolled over the lush, wet grass that cushioned her feet, the familiar sound of gunshots rang out in the distance; perhaps Annie Oakley or some other sharpshooter was practicing. A sprinkling of frosty moisture touched the night air, its humidity enveloping her like a mantle. It felt good and with pleasure, she inhaled.

The scent of smoke from the Indian encampment wafted to her on a gentle breeze, carrying with it the smell of roasting meat. Suzette's stomach churned in response.

"Are you hungry?" she asked the little one that she carried, and she patted her stomach.

"Are you?" came a baritone voice, one that she recognized all too well.

She started, then turned to confront Black Lion. "I wish you would take more care when you approach me. You seem to creep up on me without my awareness and then . . . Well, have you been here all this time? Following me?"

"No. When I saw you step away from the tent, I decided to take a moment to talk to you. I do not mean to 'creep' up on you. Perhaps you would benefit by being more aware of your environment."

"I *am* aware of my environment," she defended. "But you . . . you move with the stealth of a cat."

"Perhaps I am named aptly, then."

They both fell silent, and Suzette took a few steps forward on a path that would lead them into a treed grove, the same one they had visited on the night of their marriage. She took a few more steps, for she had to move. To stand still, with him watching her so closely, was somehow dangerous. Black Lion followed her.

She said, "Was there trouble for you because of today?"

"*Hiya.*"

"And again, that word means? . . ."

"No."

"Then no one saw you kiss me?"

"People saw. They believed it was part of the performance."

"Oh." Suzette nodded. "I am glad." Again, she fell into an uncomfortable silence with him. After a time, she said, "Where was Red Shirt?"

"He is enjoying his new pony, I believe."

"New pony?"

"It is what I traded with him to take his place to-day."

Suzette stopped and turned to face Black Lion. "You traded a pony with Red Shirt so that you might take his place?"

"I did. My best pony, too."

"But why?"

Black Lion shrugged. "I would be with my wife."

She shook her head. "You do recall that we are not really married . . ."

He raised an eyebrow. "Did we not say our vows in front of your Black Robe?" he asked. "Did we not also say them in front of the Great Spirit?"

"Yes, but . . . But I thought you understood that our marriage is . . . even still . . . in name only."

"And so I do. It does not follow, however, that I do not desire to be close to the woman who bears my name, and my child."

"He or she is not your child."

"Not by blood," he said. "Yet he is mine, nonetheless, for I have given you my name, that he will be protected. This makes him mine."

"I repeat," she said, "he is not yours. Besides, you promised me that you would not try to take him from me."

"Did I say that I wish to take him from you? You should know that I am aware of my promises to you, and that I would sooner die than break any one of them."

She nodded.

"Are you?" He reached out a hand to smooth a lock of her hair back from her face.

"Am I what?" Suzette turned her face in toward his touch, and resisted the temptation to lean farther toward him. Why was she so affected by this man?

His hand slipped down to her neck, and Suzette caught her breath. His fingers upon her, however, were light, barely more than a simple caress.

"Are you aware of your promises to me?"

"I made none."

He smiled slightly as his hand came to rest on her shoulder. "And yet I remember the white man's minister asking you to obey me and to give yourself to no one but me. What of those promises?"

"I thought you understood that we said those things only so that we might marry. They weren't said to be 'meant.'"

"Were they not? And what of the vows that we took together, here in this glen? Do you think the Creator is so easily fooled?"

"But we agreed . . . Besides, I made no vows here. I thanked you for your help. That is all."

"'I choose thee, Black Lion,'" he repeated, reminding her. "Do you think the Great Spirit agrees with us that it is not real?"

"Choosing you, and saying thank you for your kindness, does not denote that . . ." She jerked up her head. "Are you insinuating that you want this marriage to be real?" It was strange that, with that thought, a rush of sensation exploded within her.

"No, not completely. At the time, I agreed that you would have only my name, so long as that is all you wish. I only make the point that we did seek His will, and that we did make vows between us . . . before Him. With my body, I thee worship," he uttered. "And how easy it would be, I think, to worship . . . thee."

Suzette frowned up at him. He barely touched her, for his fingers lay gently atop her shoulder. But she might as well have been branded, for his touch invoked excitement all through her. She said, "Please understand. I . . . I am not ready to be romantically involved with anyone."

"Are you not?" He leaned forward, and she stared up at him as though mesmerized.

At last, she said, "No. I already told you that nothing like that would happen unless . . ."

". . . you agree to it," he added. "I remember."

"And I . . . I . . ." She jerked away from his touch, which seemed to be the cause of her problem, and took a few steps back, putting more distance between them.

With a slight grimace, as well as a smile, he said, "A man can always hope."

She ignored his words, and turned her back on him, pacing a few steps away, farther into the forest. She stopped beneath the same large pine where they had said their vows to the Great Spirit.

He did not follow her, but remained a few yards away.

"You have been gone for a few days, have you not?" she said.

"I have."

"Where did you go?"

"I went to the mountains," he replied, "there to seek guidance from my spirit protector."

"Spirit protector? What is that?"

"It is an animal, or a plant, or a spirit that has heard your plea for assistance, and has expressed its desire to help you. Taking pity on you, a spirit protector gives you its power."

"Oh," she said as though she understood him perfectly. "Help you to do what?"

"To ease a situation that plagues me."

"You are plagued?"

"I am troubled," he admitted.

"I am sorry to hear that. And this spirit protector . . . does what?"

He frowned at her. "It is not an easy matter to explain, and a man should not talk about such things. But I see that you do not truly understand. Therefore, I will try to help. In the past, before the white man came to this country, a man would seek out a spiritual helper to aid him in war, or because of some other matter of importance."

"Ah," she said, "does this mean that you worship this animal or spirit?"

"*Hiya*, no. It is well known that in a war, the Creator will not choose sides, for He is neutral, and loves all His creatures. Besides, one's enemies could very well speak to the Creator, as well as you. And so, to compensate for this, a man will endeavor to find a helper from the animal or spirit world. Someone or something that will give him the secret of its power, thus giving that man medicine."

"Medicine?"

"Medicine to the Indian heart means the great mystery of all things. It is a mystical strength."

"Oh, I think I understand," she said. "Mystical. Is your need to seek out this 'medicine' because of me? Have I upset you so greatly?"

"*Hiya*, it is not because of you, and you have not upset me."

"Are you going to war, then?"

He moved forward an inch. "I am already at war," he said.

"But you are with the show and so you surely are not still fighting the white man, are you?"

"I do not fight the white man." He sighed. "It is a long story."

"Well . . ." She shrugged. "I seem to have . . . time at present . . . to listen . . ."

"And yet," he responded, hesitating, "even if I bare my soul to you, you will not believe me, I think."

"And it is necessary for you to believe that *I* will believe before you tell me?"

"*Hiya*, no."

"Then come," she sank down gracefully onto the ground, which was made soft by pine needles and only a little snow, and patted the earth beside her. "Sit beside me. Tell me what it is that you fight."

CHAPTER 12

He didn't move to join her. However, he did say, "I do not know if I can speak to you of it, for I have never told another living soul about the full burden that I carry."

"But you will tell me?"

"*Hau*, yes. And this is odd, for men and women are often antagonistic to each other, even in marriage. It is often so that a man amongst the Lakota might try to count coup on a woman and steal her virtue, and a woman might often feel put-upon by men. But with you, I feel . . . it is different."

"Yes, I, too . . . feel this. But, let us go back to something you said only a moment ago, for I do not understand it. What do you mean by counting coup?"

"It is what we call a deed that is either hard to do or involves danger," he explained. "It is a deed of honor against an enemy."

"So by counting coup on a woman, you mean that the men look upon a woman—any woman—as an enemy?"

"It is often so."

She shook her head. "This is a very strange viewpoint to me."

He didn't say a word to defend the practice; he merely shrugged.

"So tell me what it is that plagues you."

"I hesitate, for you will think that the sun has gotten into my mind. I have never confided the full extent of this to anyone."

"Then let it be to me that you trust to tell. After all, I am your wife."

He smiled. "So you are," he said, "when it suits you."

She overlooked this last statement. "Very well. I do not mean to pry, and if you are not at your ease, do not feel obligated to tell me. But I promise that if you do, I will listen."

"And will you promise me, as well, that you will not think that I am mad?"

"I promise. Besides, in my society, husbands and wives share their hopes and desires, and their plights. Because we are husband and wife, it is only fitting that I should be the one you tell."

Even in the dark, she could see that he eyed her suspiciously, as though he would like to read her mind. She could feel the intensity of his scrutiny, and she lifted her chin a little because of it.

At length, he said, "Very well. The truth is that I am at war with he who has ruined my life and the lives of my people. It is he that I fight, he who is the Thunderer."

For a moment, Suzette felt as though she had left this world for another more mystical place, so strange were the images his words invoked . . . But she had promised not to think ill of him, so she merely said, "You do battle with the Thunderer? Who is the Thunderer?"

Black Lion was silent for so long that Suzette began to wonder if he would ever answer. In due time, however, he paced toward her and came to stand above her. It seemed again as though he debated with himself and it was a long moment, indeed, before Black Lion, at last, sank onto the ground beside her. He said, "It is hard for me to tell you these things, even though you are my wife, for they are dear to my heart. But if I do share them with you, which you say is often the way of married people, I would ask that you not tell another soul what it is that I relate to you."

She didn't answer; her throat had become suddenly tight, for it did appear that she might have earned his trust.

"Do you think you can do this? That, with this secret I am about to tell you, you will keep it forever in your heart?"

She swallowed. "Yes," she said. "I promise."

"And do you, like the real wife you speak of, seek to relieve my spirit and share my troubles?"

Suzette nodded. "I do," she said. "Though I may never lie with you in the marriage bed, I will try to be a wife to you in other ways. In truth, it seems the least I can do. You are, after all, sharing my troubles, and you have relieved my burden. If I could do the same for you, I would try."

He paused. "*Waste*, good. Give me your hand, then, for it is dark here and if I am to tell you the secrets of my soul, I would know the touch of she with whom I have entrusted my heart."

Suzette hesitated barely a second, then dutifully held out her gloved hand to him, which he took within his own. His hand was bare, and the knowledge that it was so, as well as his warmth against her, sent her pulse into an erratic beat.

He said, "May I slip off your glove so that my skin may touch yours?"

It was no more than one hand against another, nothing to excite her. Except that it did. She nodded, and whispered, "Yes."

One finger at a time, he pulled the glove completely from her hand. The action was seductive, whether he meant it to be or not. He offered the thing back to her, which she accepted immediately. As soon as her bare palm touched his, she knew she was in trouble, for a cascade of lightning-fast charges surged up and down her nervous system.

And that place most private to her, there between her legs, answered in the age-old feminine way. She ached there.

Holding her hand with both of his, he said, "Very well, I will tell you of my people and of the Thunderer. I warn you again that you will not believe me. You will say that I lie. Yet, every word from my mouth will be the truth."

She nodded. For the moment, her voice failed her.

He continued, "It happened long ago, many thousands of years ago."

"Thousands?"

"Shhh," he said. "I have already said that you will not believe me. Let me tell you the story without interruption, for there will be many times that you will wish to do so."

Again, she nodded. And staring up at the handsome image of him, as the moon and shadows washed over the hills and valleys of his complexion, she found herself not only seduced by his nearness, but enchanted with the vitality that was his alone.

"It happened long ago," he started again, his voice low and soothing. He went on at length, telling her of the being he referred to as the Thunderer, speaking of his own people who were imprisoned in a mist, telling her of the Creator's promise to give his people a chance to end the curse, and of the boys chosen to go out into the world to do so.

When at last he finished, she was silent as she tried to digest what he had said. She realized that he was right. She didn't really believe him.

But, it didn't matter what she thought. The point was that *he* believed it . . . and that she had come to trust him. She said, "Are you one of those boys who was chosen to end the curse?"

"I am."

"And so the task that imperils you is to free your people?"

"*Hau*, yes."

"And how do you seek to do it? You must have some idea?"

"A little, perhaps," he said. "But this is why I ask for guidance and power from my spiritual helper. Without that I would be lost, for as you can well see, the traditional enemies of the Lakota no longer make war."

"Yes, I can certainly understand that. And how has this spiritual helper aided you?"

"I cannot speak of it. To do so would be as to make it powerless."

"Oh, I see. Well, then," she said, "is there anything that you can tell me about it?"

"I can only say this one thing: My spirit protector has given me a song."

"A song?"

"It is a good gift, for it is a sacred song."

"A sacred song to help you on your task. Well, I think I should like to hear it. That is, if I may?"

"*Hau*, though the song belongs to the mountain lioness, she has given me permission to sing it freely."

"Mountain lioness?"

"She is my spirit protector, and this is her song."

With his free hand, Black Lion began to beat out a rhythm against the denim that covered his legs. Nodding his head to that rhythm, he sang:

> "Haye-haye, hey, hey.
> Haye-haye, hey, hey.
> *Come run with me.*
> *Come feel the air rush quickly over your back.*
> Haye-haye, hey, hey.
> *Come sit with me on this rock*
> *In the sunshine.*
> *Come feel the warmth of he who rises in the sky*
> *Each day.*
> Haye-haye, hey, hey.
> *Come share the fresh meat I have brought you this*
> *   day.*
> *Come sink your teeth into it and fill your stomach.*
> Haye-haye, hey, hey.
> *Come nestle close to me. Feel my warmth.*
> *Come, my children. For you, I do all this. For you, I*
> *   love.*
> Haye-haye, hey, hey.
> Haye-haye, hey, hey."

His voice had been low, barely audible, the song a mixture of minor and major keys. When he said, "Come, sing it with me," Suzette was unprepared.

"Sing it once again," she said.

He indulged her, then, "Are you ready to lift your voice with mine?"

"I think so," she answered. "At least I will try."

And so they sang together.

He helped her with the words when she stumbled. When it was finished, they sat still, each taking the measure of the other.

After a moment, she asked, softly, "Does 'haye-haye' mean anything?"

"It means to be glad," he answered, "usually because of a gift. The mountain lioness is happy because she has her children. They are a gift to her from the Creator, and so she made this song to sing to them and to the one who made them, that they all might appreciate her love."

"That's very beautiful," said Suzette.

"And so is your voice," he commented, his fingers squeezing hers.

His touch was unlike anything she had ever experienced as far as its effect on her. Her breasts swelled, a portion of her body most private ached, and her nerve endings were on fire. Indeed, she found herself saying, "Please, do that again."

"What?" he asked. "Sing the song with you?"

In truth, that was not what she had in mind. But she wasn't certain she could admit that to him. Did a woman talk of her need to a man, even if that man was her husband? And if she did mention these things, what would he think of her?

Confused, she uttered the only thing that she felt she could, "Yes, let us sing it again."

They did so, and when the song was over, they stared at each other.

At last, he said, "At this moment, I feel as though I know you very well."

"I, too."

"I would very much like to kiss you."

"I would like that, also."

Pressing her hand, which he still held firmly within his own, he brought it up to and around his neck. Then, bending toward her, he placed a gentle kiss on her lips.

"You taste of honey and nectar," he said against her mouth as he pushed himself a little closer to her.

"And you taste of mint," she whispered, then she frowned at him. "Why do you taste of mint?"

"I chew the leaves, which are to be found all over this prairie," he said. "I have done so most of my life, as is common with my people. Mint is a good medicine, for it aids one in social surroundings, and it helps with a stomachache, too."

"Do you have a stomachache?"

"No," he replied, "but when you sit near me, as you do now, I often feel as though I have leaped from a high cliff."

"Do you?" At his words, an involuntary quiver raced over her skin. "Sometimes I feel that way, too . . . about you . . ."

"Truly?"

Suzette, however, didn't answer. Alas, she was afraid to do so, if only because she craved something from this man that she could not quite admit . . . something quite sensual. And a proper young lady didn't speak of such matters, did she?

In the end, she chose a safe topic, and said, "But you have no need for the mint, I think, for your breath is quite . . . invigorating."

"Invigorating?" He seemed to mull over the meaning of this word. "It is good that you feel this way. In the days of old, before the white man's liquor stole away our vigor, a warrior took pride in all things concerning his appearance, and that included the way he was perceived by others."

She nodded. "Yes." And then because she grew tired of trying to second-guess herself and him, she threw away all caution, and whispered, "Kiss me again."

He was not slow on the uptake, and within moments he had enfolded her fully in his arms, bringing her body in close to his. He said, "Let us make ourselves comfortable."

To this end, he eased her onto the ground, which was made soft by the pine needles, leaves and snow.

He did not raise himself over her fully, but rather lay by her side, with only his upper body pressed in against hers. "Is your position comfortable?" he asked, even while he smoothed his lips against her cheek, then moved steadily toward her ear.

"Somewhat," she said softly, barely able to think when his lips were making magic over her. "I do believe, however, that a pillow would be quite to my liking."

He at once obliged her by removing his jacket, folding it carefully and placing it under her head. Immediately, the scent of horseflesh, fresh air and the unmistakable fragrance of his distinct masculinity assailed her. Again, excitement burst within her. But all she said was, "That's perfect."

They shared a sweet smile, until at last she said, "I feel I should like to inform you that I have been searching within myself for . . . courage."

"Courage?"

"Yes. I fear that if I tell you what is happening with me, you will not like me very much."

"Not like you? That will never happen, for I already like you; nothing can change that. *Nacece*, I have liked you from the very first moment I ever saw you."

"Have you? Still, I am uncertain."

"I understand, but tell me anyway. I promise that regardless of what you say, I will always like you."

"Truly?" She raised an eyebrow at him. "I have your word?"

He nodded, "You have my word."

With as much dignity as she could muster, she said, "Very well. It is this: I do believe that if you were to agree, I should not object to having an affair with you."

"An affair? Ah, I see." He grinned at her. "But we

already have an affair," he countered, and even as he said it, he leaned down to kiss her, an overture she returned eagerly.

Coming up for breath, however, she thought she should be very clear on the subject, and she said, "I think I mean more than an affair. I was considering . . . something more."

"More?"

"Like . . . the marriage bed . . . perhaps . . ."

He was quiet for a long, long time. She became nervous.

At length, however, slipping down to lay by her side, he murmured, "I, too, would like that, very much. But you must know that I am bound by honor. An honest man does not take his pleasure with a woman who is with child. After you have the babe—"

"Yes, yes, of course," she said. "I am certain you are right about this. I should never have mentioned it."

"*Hiya*, no, my heart is happy to hear you feel free to speak to me about this," he replied. "We should always be honest with each other. And perhaps it is not wise that I tell you this: I, too, crave that. But there are some things more important than physical need."

"Yes, again you know best, I am sure."

"But it does not mean," he continued as though she hadn't spoken, "that I cannot kiss you like this." And no sooner had he said it than he opened his mouth over hers, his tongue dipping into hers, tasting every inch of her, while his hand eased over her cheeks, her eyes, her ears, tracing over her nose, on down to her lips, which were plump and wet from his kisses. His hand continued its journey down to her neck, to her chest, which was more exposed than usual due to the cut of her evening gown.

She moaned. "That feels good."

"*Hau*, it does."

She smiled, and as he returned the gesture, he made a foray over her, moving his hand downward, avoiding her chest—as though in respect to her—but coming to rest on her stomach. He whispered, "How is the little one? Does he stir?"

"I have felt very little," she said, "but it is still somewhat early in my pregnancy, and I am told that I may not be aware of his or her movements until I am a few more weeks along."

He nodded slightly. "If he moves, I would ask that you come and seek me out, no matter where I am, for I would like to feel this, also."

"I will do that," she said, and any tendency that she might have had in the past to remind him that the child was not his evaporated within her.

"Are you eating the right things?" he asked.

"I eat well."

"But you must dine on very specific foods when you are with child. Foods that will ensure that he will be healthy; meat from the buffalo and certain plants should be part of your diet, that these will aid his growth, and nourish his spirit."

"Truly? I have not been aware of this. Alas, until now, I have not been enlightened about such things."

"All of our women know and seek to learn this knowledge when they are carrying a child. If you would like, I will ask someone from my tribe, for they will remember what these special foods are. And then if it pleases you, I will seek out these foods for you. Tell me, do you keep your thoughts on deeds that are happy?"

"I try to do so," she said, "but it is not always so easy."

"But it is good that you try," he said. "For you would want your child healthy of mind, as well, I think."

"Yes," she agreed, patting her stomach.

He took her hand in his. "I will seek out the wisdom from the old women of my tribe. And now I think I should take you back."

"Back? So soon?" Wasn't the night only beginning? Why did he want to take her back?

"It may be soon to return you to the party, but I feel it is the right thing to do."

"Why? Why do you say this? Mr. Cody's festivity means nothing to me and I have been enjoying myself . . . with you."

"I, too," he said, although he was frowning. "Perhaps though a little too much. It would be a simple deed for me to take advantage of you, especially after your confession to me this night."

"But—"

"I must not take advantage of you. Understand this: Many times the old men of my tribe have told us boys that to take a woman who is carrying a child is bad; it could harm the child, and it might cause the mother to miscarry. It could incite both of their deaths. I would not take that risk with you."

"But my doctor said I could . . . without risk to the child."

Black Lion was silent for a moment, until at last he nodded. "The white man's ways are strange to us, for a Lakota man would never seek his pleasure from a pregnant wife, for fear of damaging both . . . if not physically, then perhaps spiritually. But know this, if my honor did not keep me from it, you would not have to offer yourself to me, for we would have already made love . . . now . . . always . . ."

She swallowed. "Black Lion . . . Thank you . . . I think . . ."

"You do not need to thank me. It is the way I have been taught."

She scoffed a little, blowing out her breath. "And I was raised knowing that I should 'save' myself for my wedding night—and look at what I have done. As you say, you may have been raised in a particular way, but you honor it. And there's the difference." She bobbed her head up and down. "There's the difference."

"Do not blame yourself for what has happened to you," he said. "The roles of men and women are often opposed, and because of the way a man is, he will try to seek his pleasure regardless of his regard for the woman or her reputation. But if a man loves a woman, it is his duty to draw a line in regards to passion, for it is well known that a maid pushed too far is easily convinced; it is why she must be so carefully guarded by her family. An honorable man marries the girl of his choice." He grinned at her. "Recall again that I married you."

"Yes, so you did."

His smile turned solemn. "And now we should go back, while I still possess the will to stop."

"I suppose you are right, and I am certain you have more experience than I do in this regard," she agreed. "But come, it is dark here, the moon is shining in a very romantic way, and I am wanting one more kiss. Surely you could afford to give me that without . . ."

He inhaled deeply, but he nodded all the same. "Perhaps I could do that," he said judiciously. And she caught her breath as he bent over her, and as he positioned his open lips over her own . . .

CHAPTER 13

Like a blossom, her mouth opened to him, and his tongue delved into the inner recesses of that moist haven. In and out, over and over, he tasted the clean fragrance that was her. Her tongue met his, danced with his, and then she groaned.

At the sound, he died a little. He wanted her; he was ready for her. And she wanted him, no mistake. Yet, if he were to remain honorable, and he must, he knew he had to ignore the urgings of his body.

He ended the kiss, let out a sigh, and sat up. She followed him into a sitting position. Leaning forward, she reached up to spread her arms around his neck.

He grasped hold of her arms, as though to remove them from around him, yet he couldn't quite manage it. Instead, he turned his face in toward her, rubbing his head along the skin of her upper arms. After a moment, he said, "You surely test me. But you know that we cannot carry on in this manner much longer. Already I fear I will obtain little sleep this night."

"Indeed?"

At that moment, something in her abdomen moved. He felt it.

"Was that the child?" he asked.

She looked surprised, as well as he. "I think it was. It is the first movement I have felt." She grinned up at him. "How delightful it happened now. I believe he might approve of what we are doing."

Black Lion returned her smile, and at the same time, placed his hand over her stomach. "Maybe he will move again."

As she eased her hand over his, Black Lion let his gaze wash over her, and he would have had to be a blind fool not to recognize the raw hunger that was illuminated there, within her eyes.

But he shut himself off from the sight; it did nothing to help his resolve. Delicately, she rubbed her hand over his, then reaching out she smoothed the backs of her fingers over his cheek. He groaned, even while his stomach took a steep dive.

"Your cheekbones are high," she commented, "and your skin is soft."

"I am not soft."

"Well, perhaps soft is the wrong word. What I mean is smooth-shaven. Have you a beard?"

"Not as the white man has," he responded quietly. "There are a few whiskers that grow on my face, perhaps, but I, like my fathers before me, pluck these, and they are few. I fear it would be a wasted effort for me to shave as does the white man. And if I let the hair grow on my face, I would still never have a full beard."

"It is interesting, I think. You are so different from everything that I am accustomed to. I wonder," she said, "about your chest."

He swallowed, holding himself rigidly back from her. "My chest?"

"Yes. Do you have hair on your chest or do you shave it?"

"Shave it? I have no hair on my chest," he said, "nor do I have any on my arms or legs, as the white man does."

Again, she traced her hand over the contours of his face. He grabbed hold of that hand, placing his lips against her fingers, as he urged himself to keep control, not only over himself, but of their situation.

She said, quietly, "I would like to see your chest."

And he almost lost it. "Do you try to seduce me, even after all I have said?"

"No, well . . . maybe. It is only that I am curious."

"Curious? Perhaps I should also remind you that I am doing all that I can to keep your honor and mine close to my heart."

"And you do that very well," she said. Then, "I would still like to see it."

"My chest? Now?"

"Now would, indeed, be a most fitting time."

He smiled at her slightly. He could not very well help doing so, and he said, as though in challenge, "If I take off my shirt, will you lower your dress for me that I may also see your bosom?"

Her eyelids lifted, to reveal the blue depths of her eyes, which stared up at him so innocently. She whispered, "Do you dare me to do it, then?"

"If you are to see me without my shirt, then I think it only fair."

He was playing with fire and he knew it, for he had no intention of undressing her . . . or did he? As though struck by a tomahawk, a realization came to him.

What was wrong with him? There was more than one way to give and receive satisfaction. Yes, the old ones had spent many hours lecturing the young boys on the duties of a husband, but that didn't mean he had to be stupid about it.

She was his wife. She deserved pleasure, as did he. There were other ways of making love . . . and the thought of those ways almost sent him spiraling out of control. But again, he held himself in check.

"My wife," he muttered, "I will show you my chest, if you like, but realize if I do this, there will be no going back for us. Once we begin going down this path—"

But he had no more than started speaking when she threw herself into his arms. "Would you stop talking?"

"*Hau*," he said. "I can stop talking." And he gently lowered her back to the ground, whereupon he followed her down. "It is cold."

"I am not cold," she uttered.

"Still, we will place your cloak over you, for I intend to see you naked."

"Oh."

"But I may need your help, for the white man's clothes confuse me . . . and white women wear so many of them."

She smiled at him, and he smiled back. She said, "I do not think that will be a problem."

"That is good," he said. "That is good."

Kneeling beside her, he removed his shirt, and Suzette stared at him as though he might have been a Greek statue, rather than flesh and blood. One thing was certain: He rivaled those Greek specimens as to the image of the ideal man. Firm muscles met her vision, a view completely unhampered by the unsightliness of hair. Light and shadows danced over his silhouette, causing her to wonder, was it simply her perspective of him?

Was it the way the moonlight shone on him? Or was he simply beautiful?

Here in the deep shadows of the place where they had said their vows, the moment seemed somehow sacred. And perhaps it was only right that they should consummate their marriage here.

Exactly how this deed would affect their future life, she could only speculate. In truth, however, such reflections didn't seem important. Right now, all that mattered to her was him, and the way he gazed at her as though he adored her.

She whispered, "I think you are beautiful."

He shook his head. "No," he murmured. "You . . . you are the one who is beautiful. I have always thought so, from that first instant I saw you. Though our first words to one another might have been said in anger, this does not make a man blind. And I have much admired your physical beauty. Perhaps it was not in jest that I proposed to you on that day. Maybe I was wise in ways I do not understand. I can only now thank the Above Ones for giving me the sense to suggest what I did to you.

"But come," he continued, "I am much ready for this, as you are, too, I think. And I have yet to undress you."

"Yes," she agreed, sitting up, and turning slightly, she presented her backside to him. "I will help you. There are buttons at the back of this dress. I think you could undo those easier than I."

"*Hau.*"

She felt his fingers against her, and she shivered as tingles raced over her skin.

"Are you cold?"

"No," she replied. "I am . . . wanting this . . . very much, I think."

At last it was done, and he lowered the front of her

gown, but far from being naked, there were yet other layers of clothing to be considered.

"It is a chemise and a corset," she whispered, "but these I can easily remove."

"I am glad of that," he said. "This one piece of your clothing looks unmovable to me."

She said, "There are hooks and ties that hold this garment together, and you may have to help me again, for the ties are at the back of the corset."

"*Hau*, I see them. They are quite tight. Ah, now I understand why the white woman has an uncanny tiny waist. She is helped."

"Indeed." Suzette grinned, and glanced at him over her shoulder. While yet working over the lacing, he glanced at her, returned her smile and reached up to place a kiss along her cheek.

At last, it was done and Suzette felt the relief that she always experienced upon the relaxing of her corset. But the garment looked as though it were glued to her, for it continued to hug her curves. At least it did until he released her from it, pulling the clothing away from her body.

Then, still kneeling at her back, he reached around to caress her breasts, showering her neck with kisses at the same time. And she sighed, leaning back against him and opening herself up to him. "Oh, what you do to me."

He mumbled, "And what you do to me."

"Hmmmm . . ." she purred. "But I wonder, what would it be like to experience the solid contours of your chest against mine? Its rigidness against me?"

"*Hau*, let us discover this," he whispered, and he turned her around to face him, pulling her in so close to him that their bodies might have been one.

The sensation was achingly exquisite, and she twisted

against him, back and forth, up and down, as though she would imprint his image on her. And he was not motionless, moving with her, rubbing against her, as though they both were involved in the sensuousness of dance.

He growled, the sound low in his throat, and she moaned, then murmured, "Your skin is a superb shade of brown—do you see how it looks against the paleness of mine? I wish I were as brown as you. The color is delicious."

"*Hiya*. You are perfect as you are," he whispered. "I would not have you change for me or for anyone or anything."

"How you flatter me."

"No flattery. Truth. But I think we talk too much." Leaning down, he pressed his lips against the bud of her breast.

He growled, the sound reminding her of his namesake. Moreover, hearing it aroused her, sent her insides into a frenzy, and casting back her shoulders and head, she offered herself to him, as though she were a feast.

Indeed, he did partake, first suckling on one breast, then the other, his hand kneading the one mound while his lips and tongue relished the other. His free hand slipped down to her pantalettes, pushing them down, until they pooled at her knees.

Still kneeling against her, his fingers found that throbbing place—down there, at that so very private junction between her legs. She moaned. In reaction, she felt the rigid form of his sex jerk against her stomach. Ah! She moaned again.

"You are ready for me, I think," he murmured, and as he lowered her to the ground, he threw her cloak over them both, and added, "Open your legs for me."

It was not within her to argue with him, and she

obeyed him at once. But instead of joining himself with her, as she had expected, he lowered himself down over her belly, rubbing it and spreading kisses over each part of her as his range of activity kept centering lower and lower over her.

"What is this that you are doing?" she asked, not really caring, for it felt delectable. Merely, she was curious.

He said, quietly, "We must not seek our pleasure in the regular way men and women love one another, for harm might come to you or the babe. Rather, we will indulge in a different form of lovemaking that will give us both much pleasure, I think. You will see. Lie back."

And as she did so, his kisses crept ever so slowly downward. At last, his tongue found her throbbing need, and she jerked upward with the pleasure of it.

"Oh, my goodness!" she groaned, sighing in complete pleasure. And she really didn't need his saying "Spread your legs farther" to do so. It seemed the most natural deed in the world.

He kissed her there between her legs, his tongue taking over the duty of what might be considered the more natural pattern of lovemaking; so intense was the sensation, she thought she would surely spiral out of her head. She twisted against him, seeking release.

But what release that was, she was uncertain. Surely, she had enjoyed lovemaking with William, but it had been nothing like this. Yes, it had been pleasant, but not so acutely exhilarating. As Black Lion continued his ministrations over her, she wiggled and twisted, her body seeming to know what to do, until something began to build up inside her.

What was this? This had never happened with William. And then it built, and it built, and she was reaching a place, a plateau, then tripping over the edge of it . . . She groaned with the experience, she moaned and tiny whimperings sounded from her lips.

The pleasure went on and on until suddenly it was too much, too sensual. And she jerked away from him, coming to lie still beneath him. Her breathing was erratic and her body shivered in pure ecstasy.

He had come up onto his forearms over her, resting his weight against his elbows, and grabbing hold of some snow that littered the ground. Gently, he washed his lips. Then he grinned at her.

"What was that?" she murmured between gasps. "I never experienced anything like that with William," she said in all honesty.

"Did you not?"

"No. That time with him was pleasant, yes, but this was . . . this was . . ."

Black Lion jerked his head to the left. "He was more than a fool, then, to seek his pleasure without giving you yours. I am glad I am the first to show you the real enjoyment between a man and woman. Very much."

"Yes," she said. Then a thought occurred to her. "But you? You haven't met your pleasure, have you? Let me return the gesture."

"That would, indeed, be fitting," he said, "but I fear it is unnecessary." Coming up onto his knees, she was treated to the view of a very aroused male. However, taking hold of her hand, he pressed it against him privately, and she was startled at the firmness of him. He said, "It has been too long since I have been with a woman, and as you can see, I have already met my pleasure."

"Oh," she muttered, intrigued, but somewhat disappointed. The thought of doing to him the same that he had done to her was, indeed, quite arousing. Then she added, "Maybe yet this night? . . . Later?"

"*Hau*," he said, with a moan. "I will anticipate that with much pleasure, very much, Little Blue Eyes."

"Little Blue Eyes?"

"It is the name I gave to you that first day we met. You were wearing blue, and the blue of your eyes was startling to me. I have never forgotten."

"Little Blue Eyes," she repeated with a smile. "I like it. I like it very much, I think."

"Then it is what I will call you from this day forward. Little Blue Eyes, wife of mine."

Coming down over her, they shared several rare, sweet and elegant kisses, and scooting his weight to the side of her, it was not long before they had both drifted off to a well-earned nap, her cloak gently imparting them both with a warmth they hardly needed.

Black Lion was jerked awake. What was that? Something had roused him. Had it been the crack of a twig against a footstep?

Alert now, Black Lion remained absolutely still, although his mind raced. If the whites discovered him and his wife here, wrapped as they were in each other's arms, there would be little point in announcing the fact that they were married and that they were committing no crime. Actions could be taken that could harm, while questions might be asked later, perhaps much too late . . . for him.

Gently, he roused his wife awake with a kiss, then placed a finger over her lips to keep her from speaking out. Quietly, he whispered against her ear, "I have heard something in the forest, and I fear we may no longer be alone. You stay here, dress yourself as quietly as you can, then hide in the bushes. I will leave here to go and investigate whether someone is here, or whether we have been joined this night by an elk or a deer."

She nodded.

Grabbing hold of his jeans, he pulled them on, then slipped his feet into his moccasins. He didn't bother with his shirt or his jacket, for when scouting, whether it was warm or cold, clothes were an encumbrance. As soon as he was dressed, he became instantly the scout. Lowering himself to his hands and knees, he slithered noiselessly away.

First he searched for clues over the ground close by to them. However, when he found nothing, he scoured the ground farther afield, his investigation taking him through the bushes and the brambles in the forest, over its rises and falls. Expanding his awareness outward, he let his mind extend into the environment around him, seeking anything unusual in the natural order of things. But he could discern nothing.

Finally, he saw what he had missed before, there by a stream. A broken twig, and the imprints of a doe. He let out a sigh of relief.

It would seem that for now, their secret was safe.

However, he had no more than relaxed his guard when another detail came all too vividly to mind: *You must keep to your purpose. Do not become distracted by ways of the flesh. Though you are married, you, your people, must be willing to sacrifice pleasures of the flesh.*

The voice was loud in his ears, as though his spirit protector were here with him now. He frowned. Why was he recalling this now? It was not as though he had forgotten the warning; a man did not ignore his vision.

It did, however, cause him to question: *Was he distracted? By his wife?*

No, that didn't feel right, plus he didn't think that his wife was a mere "distraction." Rather, what had happened tonight was completely natural. Although, in truth, he would have to admit that he had forgotten about his vision, at least for the time when she had held him in her arms. But what man wouldn't have done the same?

"Remember, a man who ignores his dreams merely exists, and much trouble will come to him."

So had spoken his elders.

"Eya!" he uttered the word aloud.

Was he not permitted a brief diversion? She was his wife, and as such, she deserved a husband who would initiate her into the ways of married life. What he had done was not a vice.

Yet he couldn't shake the idea that he might have erred.

Quietly, he played his own devil's advocate.

As his tribe's champion, he was not as free as other men. Indeed, until he had accomplished his task, he was bound by the needs of others. But did those needs include abstaining from relations with his wife?

No. No man need do that.

Yet, should he even *be* married, when he had yet to accomplish the task before him? In truth, until he had met his wife, nothing else had ruled his life. Previously, his romantic encounters had been pleasant, yes, but certainly not as important as his responsibility to his people.

Perhaps this was what was causing his doubt. Somehow, in some way, *she* had become as important to him as his own people.

How could he have let that happen?

How could she have become the center of his thoughts, when his duty to his people was, as yet, unfulfilled?

Perhaps she had medicine, strong medicine. Indeed, it could be true. For, when he was with her, thoughts of his tribe, his duty, his obligation disappeared, as though they were mere obstacles to something greater. Nothing, except her, mattered.

This was not good. Not that she, herself, had done anything wrong; she had merely been female, acting in the role of his wife.

Rather he recognized that the fault was his. Was a man not supposed to face the rigors of living with a firm resolve? Indeed, as the old ones would say, a man should not be swayed by the physical pleasures of life, nor be cowardly in the face of danger. Instead, he should show fortitude, and perhaps in this instance, abstinence.

Abstinence?

The thought was not a pleasant one. Was it even possible to be married to his wife and abstain from the pleasure of her beauty? Even when she so sweetly teased him with it?

You must keep to your purpose. Do not become distracted by ways of the flesh. Though you are married, you, your people, must be willing to sacrifice pleasures of the flesh.

Damn! He cursed softly to himself, then sighed. Whether it was possible to forego the intimacy of marriage or not, he knew he had to try. But how?

Should he refuse to see her? Impossible. Not only was she his wife, he could very little deny that she was also a part of the remedy for his people. After all, was it not her voice from his dreams?

Here, indeed, was a dilemma. One that could create bigger problems. What to do?

Should he tell her? Would she leave him if he did?

"The truth is that I want only the fact that I am married legally, so that my child is not born out of wedlock. But beyond that, I want nothing. I will require not a thing from you, not even your presence in my life, for, once the child is born, I fully intend to return to England."

There it was, then. He already had the answer to his question. But might she not have changed her mind about him, especially after tonight?

The truth was, from the very beginning, when she had declared her intentions, a very male part of him had taken up the challenge. Essentially, he had scooped up the dare so easily, that he had inadvertently made it his plan to cause her to change her mind.

It was an intention that he still possessed.

It would appear that she distracted him too greatly from his duty. Yet, if he were to keep her with him, he should be ready and willing to satisfy her physical need.

Unless . . .

If he could induce her to love him, perhaps the erotic nature of their life together might become unimportant . . .

However, could he make her love him?

Perhaps. He already possessed her passion . . . Was love not the next stage?

Did he love her?

For all that the question was natural, it still startled him. But he was quick to recover; it was a pointless debate.

Whether he loved her or not, he did desire her, and therein was the root of the problem. He could not have her. At least not until such a time when he had released himself from this nearly impossible duty.

"*Eya!* Damn!" he cursed. It was a maddening predicament.

CHAPTER 14

It was with a heavy heart that at last his path brought him back to her. As he silently crept up on her, he found that she had hidden herself beneath her cloak, there, under their tree.

Coming up next to her, he startled her when he spoke: "Do not worry. It was only the footprint of a doe that I found. We are safe here, I think, but—"

She sighed. "Will I ever become used to your sneaking up on me?"

"Next time I will make more noise so that I will not surprise you."

"I would be grateful." Then, with a teasing smile aimed directly at him, she opened up her cloak, whereupon he saw disturbingly that she was not fully dressed; that she sat before him in a see-through white slip.

While he groaned, she said, "Come, you look cold, and I am warm inside my coat. Come here, share the warmth with me." Her smile was so alluring, he almost lost all his good intentions, right there.

He swallowed. He stared at her.

And when she continued to speak, saying, "I would love to return the favor that you have done me. Indeed, I would seek to indulge you with those very secret seductions that you have shown to me this evening . . ." only the very real destiny of his people held him back from her. And even then . . .

"Come," she urged again, and she patted the ground next to her, "let us have more fun."

He swallowed several times before he was able to find his voice. "That would, indeed, be very good. But— We have managed to avoid detection thus far, and I fear that if we stay here longer, we might risk others finding us."

"Oh? There is reason for you to believe we are in danger of discovery?"

He paused, while he debated if he could resort to the white man's way, and tell her a lie. He opened his mouth to do so, but found that he couldn't. He was not a white man, and lying to his wife was not a deed that he could honor. Alas, all he found he could say was, "No, we are not in imminent danger of discovery, but—"

"Then come here," she said with a sweet smile.

He paused a beat while he collected his wits about him. Could he distract her? "Ah . . . do you hear that music?"

"Music?" She set her head to the side.

"*Hau.* Is not the Song Bird singing tonight? Perhaps it is her voice that I hear."

"Your ear must be quite acute, then," she said, "for I detect nothing more than the drums from your encampment."

"And yet," he said, "I think your grandmother is singing tonight. We should go back there now."

She frowned at him. "You would rather go back to the party and listen to Irena than to join me and . . ."

He knelt down next to her and picked up her hand, holding it within his own. "Listen to me, my wife, for I must speak to you solemnly."

"Very well. I am listening," she purred softly, and brought up her hand to run her fingers down his cheek.

He inhaled sharply, then continued, "There are reasons that I cannot tell you, that we must not repeat what we have done this night, not until I have finished the quest that I am bound to do."

Her brow furrowed, but she didn't say a word.

"Perhaps it has been a fault of mine to not open my heart to you until now. From the start, it has been my intention to cause you to change your mind, and take me for a real husband. That this requires intimacy is something that I have desired. But this has been unwise, I fear, and I can no longer give you the familiarity that a wife deserves . . . until . . ."

Her frown deepened. "Until . . ."

"You recall my informing you about my people's misfortune?"

"Yes."

"I have come to realize that I must complete my mission. I fear that only after I free my people will I be at liberty to make love to you again."

"Oh?" She sat unmoving for a time, then said, "Indeed? And when will your mission be complete?"

"Very soon, I hope. But in truth, it could last my lifetime."

"Your lifetime?"

"*Hau.* I fear that is so. Do not fret overly much, however, for I believe I am close to solving the mystery that keeps my people enslaved."

"Oh," was all she said.

"Will you wait for me?"

"I have little choice. As you might remember, I have

my own problems, and keeping you as my husband is a good solution to them."

He nodded. "So it is," he said. "Then perhaps I have much luck this night, for it is not my desire to lose you as my wife."

She withdrew her hand from his, and very carefully sat up. "Then, this one time tonight is all we are to have?" Her frown deepened. "What was that all about, then, when you said that if I should change my mind, you would be more than willing? Do you remember saying that to me when we were first married?"

"*Hau*. It is true. But other things have happened since then."

"Other things?"

"My mission."

"Indeed? Your mission . . . your people . . . but, they have always been there, haven't they?"

Another silence stretched out between them. She turned her face away from him and he was at once presented with her beautiful profile. Again, he sighed, and she went on to say, "I do believe this is very similar to what happened between myself and William. One night of love, and then . . . Are you spurning me, as well?"

She came up onto her knees, sitting back against her calf muscles. Her cloak, upon which she sat, was as soft as the feathered down of a goose, was spilled out over the ground around her, making her appear as if she sat in the middle of a cloud. And he thought he had never seen anything or anyone more exquisite.

"Spurned?" he asked. "I am uncertain I know this word."

"It means to slight an . . . invitation . . ."

"Slight? I do not understand. Does not 'slight' mean very little of something?"

"Yes, sometimes it does, but not in this case." She tightened her lips, and her voice took on an edge as she said, "What would you have me do, spell it out for you? I think, Mr. Lion, that you know well what it means. Your English is very good, I must say."

He frowned. "I try to be very good. But I do not understand. Why are you becoming angry with me over a word?"

"I am *not* becoming angry with you. I am . . . all right . . . I'll define it for you. Slight . . . it means to snub, to . . . rebuff . . . to insult one."

"Insult? What have *I* said that is insulting?"

She sighed. "I no longer wish to have this conversation with you. I think you are right. You should take me back."

"Take you back? *Hiya*, no, not like this. If it helps, I should tell you that it is not you. Perhaps I should have made that plainer from the start. I cannot take any woman to my bed, no matter who she is, until my duty to my people is complete."

But Suzette had already come up onto her feet. He followed her up. Her gaze, however, looked anywhere but at him. Instead she was slipping into her clothes as fast as she could. If she had heard his explanation, he would not know it, for all she said was, "Thank you for the walk, Mr. Lion, but I—"

He reached out for her hand, touched her, but she jerked away from him. She stepped back, putting some distance between them.

As though to fill the gap, he said, "I do what I do because I must. I do not *slight* you, and believe me, if I could make love to you without possible harm coming to my people, I would do so."

"So now *I* am the cause of you possibly harming your people."

"*Hiya*, no, it is only that—"

"You expect me to believe this?"

"About my people?"

"No," she said, "your excuses." She shoved her arms into her dress. "Perhaps the problem is not your people, but rather your will. Perhaps gaining that thing which most men seek from a woman has caused you to think that you can insult my intelligence with your excuses."

"Do you think that I lie?"

"Yes, I do."

He drew back, stunned. "Though I realize the white man can have a forked tongue when the occasion suits him, you should know that there is no greater insult than to call an Indian a liar. For my people, there is no dog so low. I will tell you the truth one last time, and I dare you to believe me. It is not that I do not wish to have more relations with you. It is that, for a time, I must not."

In response, she sent her chin into the air, and said, "Forgive me, but I still cling to the notion that you are lying, and I think you try to play me for a fool. What is it? What is the real reason? Is it despite the laws on the reservations, you already have another wife, as you once told me so long ago? That you dare not tell me about it, for fear of . . . ? Or another girlfriend, perhaps, who will be upset that you have had this pleasant interlude with me?"

"If that were so, I would tell you about it."

"*You?* You would? When most men would not?"

"I would not have taken you for a wife, had I another. What I say to you is the truth."

"Is it? Very well, then. I will consider it. When I go home tonight, I will think much over what you have said, and I will decide then if I trust what you say or not. But at this moment, it stretches credulity."

Bending down, she picked up her cloak and swung it over her shoulders. "And now I must leave."

She turned and started to go, whereupon he reached out to detain her. "I will see you back."

"No," she said, "I will see myself back to the party, Mr. Lion, thank you very much." She turned away from him and paced several more steps forward.

He followed her and as he did so, his frown deepened. He placed a hand on her shoulder and said, "Do not leave yet, let us talk about this more . . . and tonight."

"No," she said. "I need to think clearly, without the influence of you being beside me." And with this said, she shook off his hold, picked up the front of her dress and ran from their sheltered glen as though pursued by the white man's devil.

He watched the place where she had been for a long, long time, and eventually he followed her, if only to ensure that she returned to the party safely. He understood her upset; he could only hope that upon further thought, she would come to believe him.

In the meanwhile, he would wait. But not for long. Whether he made love to this woman or not, she was still his wife, and the voice of the sacred song. Before too much time had elapsed, he needed to discover if she, indeed, could help him or not.

Unfortunately, now more than his people's freedom seemed to depend upon that discovery.

In the end, he took a bath before going to his bed, for the icy water often helped to chase away the shadows in his mind. Though the bath had been freezingly cold, it had been invigorating, and had accomplished what he had hoped. Treading back toward his lodge, Black Lion was curious to see the image of a fire blazing merrily within his lodge. So, too, did he observe the shadows of two people who were sitting around it.

All the better, he thought, for he would welcome visitors. As Black Lion pushed back the tepee flap and stepped into his lodge, he was greeted by the sight of two friendly and familiar faces.

It was Two Bears and his wife, Rabbit Leggings, who welcomed him. Immediately, the two men greeted each other as was the Lakota way, with solemn appreciation. However, toward Two Bears's wife, Black Lion was permitted a more appreciative nature, and he said, "*Hau, kola*, hello, friends, my heart is filled with gladness to see you." Coming around to the left of the lodge circle, Black Lion squatted next to his friend, placing his hand over Two Bears's shoulder. Two Bears returned the gesture.

It is probably safe to say that to an American onlooker, little joy would have been observed in the reunion, and such could have been confusing, for the two men were close friends. But such was the Lakota way of expressing the warmth of a deep friendship, since, to the Lakota, an overly excited manner was considered bad manners.

"*Lel unkunpi kin he waste*. It is good for us to be here," said Two Bears.

"*Hau*, and my heart is happy to see you," Black Lion responded. "However, let us speak in English so you may practice it. The Long-haired Show Man demands that we speak it and only it, while we are here with his show. It is a burden, I admit, but I fear we must."

"*Hau, hau*," said Two Bears. "I wish to thank you for the money that you have been sending me and my wife with the coming of each new moon," continued Two Bears. "It has helped us through a hard winter."

"My heart is glad to hear this," said Black Lion. "And I am filled with happiness, for you are both a much welcome sight. I hope you will make my lodge your home."

"*Waste,*" said Two Bears, with a hand motion out away from his chest—it was the sign language for "good." He continued, saying, "It is good to come visiting."

Black Lion nodded. Meanwhile, Rabbit Leggings served the two men a supper of prairie soup. Metal bowls were used, bowls that both she and her husband must have obtained from trade, for they were white-man made. Accompanying the soup was pemmican and bone marrow.

Ah, here at last was a meal that Black Lion could fully appreciate, and he accepted the food gladly.

After appeasing his appetite, Black Lion nodded toward Rabbit Leggings, and said, "It is good to know that you still make the best soup in all the Lakota Nation."

Rabbit Leggings smiled and cast her head down. But etiquette allowed her to tease her husband's friend, and she said, "I see . . . you . . . more handsome than does you . . . good. But, friend of my husband, you are . . . hmmm . . . thin. It . . . good that I am here. I feed you well."

"*Hau, hau.* I will appreciate it, too. They give us plenty of food here, but I find the white man's offerings disagreeable, in the main. There is little meat in it and much grain and milk from a cow, and a thing they call bacon. It is not suited well, I think, to an Indian's disposition."

"Then it is good we made journey here."

He smiled at Rabbit Leggings. "Tell me," he said between mouthfuls, addressing Two Bears. "How do you come to be off the reservation? Are they not watching the Indians closely, to ensure that we are all kept there?"

Two Bears didn't answer at once. Instead, he looked at his wife, who then cast her gaze down.

After a time, Two Bears said, "As you know, I am supposed to be here, not on the reservation. But our agent did not notice that I had remained there, so for many moons there was no difficulty."

"The agent is a fool."

"No doubt, he is. But I think a trader must have alerted him that I was not with the show, for the agent came poking his nose at our house, asking my wife questions she could not answer. I hid from him, of course, and I hope he did not discover that I was, indeed, there. It was enough of a scare for both of us, however, that we decided to leave our home there and journey here, since this is where I am supposed to be. We sneaked away in the middle of the night. Do you think the Long-haired Show Man will notice the difference between you and me if I take your place, as I am supposed to do?"

"I do not believe he will," answered Black Lion, "for I have little contact with him, and there are so many people here—Indians and whites alike—that he will probably assume that all is as it should be. But you should alert the others in our tribe to your situation, so that they do not give you away."

Two Bears nodded. "I will do so tomorrow. I will visit each family here in turn."

"*Waste*, good," said Black Lion, and they both became silent as they gave over their attention to finishing their dinner.

After their meal was complete, and a pipe had been produced, the two men sat smoking, and began to talk of other important things. Several moments passed, and when the time seemed right, Black Lion thought he should voice the question uppermost in his mind, even though he dreaded the answer. He said, "Are you here, then, to take your rightful place with the show?"

"*Hau*. Though fear of the agent has sent me here, if I am to be here, I should relieve you of your duty. I know that you have other, more pressing needs."

Black Lion nodded, noticing that Two Bears had set his lips together so firmly that his mouth appeared as though a straight line were etched across his face; he also became suddenly quiet. Even Rabbit Leggings hesitated at her work. Alas, the only sound to be heard within the lodge at present was that of the spitting fire.

Black Lion frowned. What was this odd behavior in these two? Was something wrong?

Black Lion said, "I welcome your honor in doing your duty, but I sense that you are not telling me all that you might."

Again husband and wife exchanged a look, before Two Bears went on to say, "I am . . . I am . . ."

"My husband is weak," Rabbit Leggings supplied. "Him . . . well enough . . . make this journey. But . . ."

"I am well. I am fine. It is only that—" Two Bears coughed.

With that cough came sudden realization, and Black Lion's heart lightened. Two Bears didn't *want* his job back . . . at least not yet.

But as was the way of the American Indian gentleman, Black Lion's only outward response was a nod. He said, "It is no trouble for me to continue in your place. The truth is that being with the show has helped me in my own quest, and I am not yet ready to leave. So if you would stay here with me and hide from the white man's eyes, the current arrangement could still stand. You were right, my friend, I needed to seek out the white man where he is. Many things have happened that I believe have set me on the right path . . ."

Two Bears let out a breath, and even Rabbit Leggings seemed happier. At least she went back to her duties around the fire.

Two Bears said, "I am glad that the show has provided you with an opportunity. And if you would continue in my place, it would afford me the chance to gain back my strength, I think. A few more complete cycles of the moon is all I ask."

"*Hau, hau.* You shall have them. And while you are here, my home is your home. In truth, when I leave the show, this lodge will be yours. But when the white man comes around, I would ask that you hide from him, since to the white man, I am you."

"*Hau, hau. Waste*, this I can do. And now, I hope you will excuse us, but we have had a long trip, yet we desired to await your arrival home. If we might, we would see our bed now."

"*Hau, hau,*" responded Black Lion. "Let us away to our beds. But first, there is one matter that I feel we should discuss."

Two Bears nodded.

"The Long-haired Show Man often comes into our camp to visit," continued Black Lion. "And he believes that not only am I you, he thinks that I am married. I have done nothing to make him suspect that this is not true, since it would be a disfavor to you. There could be a problem, though, since it will be easier to hide you than your wife, if only because she has many duties outside the lodge. What I ask is this: If the Long-haired Show Man or any of the other white men should call on my lodge while I am not here, Rabbit Leggings should pretend to be my wife. In truth, there would be much trouble for me and eventually for you, too, if it is discovered that a woman who is living with me is not my wife."

Two Bears nodded, listening.

"There have been some difficulties with this in the past," continued Black Lion, "especially when the show was performing over the great water, in England, and young women would come brazenly to our lodges. I fear that some of our men, who were not strong of heart, took advantage of the girls. Therefore, if the Long-haired Show Man should come here, I think it best that your wife pretend to be my wife." Black Lion glanced toward Rabbit Leggings. "I know it is a demanding thing that I ask of her, for a woman, even more than a man, must always be truthful. But if your wife could manage it, I think it would avoid much trouble."

"I see no difficulty with this, but then I am not the one who would have to do it. What say you, my wife?"

Rabbit Leggings smiled, but kept her gaze averted downward. She said, "I will do it. We already pretend-ing . . . you"—she gestured toward Black Lion—". . . my husband. You honor us with help. If this avoid trouble, I do it. For you . . ."

"*Waste*," said Black Lion, and he smiled at Rabbit Leggings. "I thank you."

Rabbit Leggings smiled.

"*Waste*. Now that this is settled, let us do as you sug-gested, and retire at once."

And without further conversation, they did exactly that.

CHAPTER 15

After several tears and a full night's rest, Suzette awoke with the realization that she owed Black Lion an apology. Somehow, as these things often do, "sleeping on it" had set her mind to correcting itself.

She had awakened with the understanding that Black Lion was not rejecting her, he was simply being true to what he believed. Whether she thought his adherence to the particulars of his vision was trivial or not, the fact that he deemed it to be important showed that she should at least respect his conviction.

For whatever reason that she could not quite understand, his rejection last night had brought back to mind William's betrayal. However, putting some distance between herself and it had allowed her to look at the situation more realistically. William had been a dishonorable coward. Black Lion was nothing of the sort.

Bearing this in mind, it appeared now that she had behaved badly last night. Therefore, Suzette had decided to go visiting. And of course she would look her best.

Dressing carefully, she donned one of her outing

gowns of white hopsack and, since it was trimmed on the bias with folds of pink, she was the picture of the nineties' modern woman. Her white jacket had the familiar large sleeves so popular in this day and age, and her hat was fashioned of a light, rough straw. She felt well-dressed and ready for the meeting ahead of her. Grabbing her claok, she slipped quietly out of Irena's tent, and was greeted by a cold, sun-drenched morning.

Few people were about at this time of the morning . . . Most likely because of the lateness of the party last night. Suzette was alone. However, lack of an escort, though perhaps scandalous, was not about to detour Suzette.

It was only a short walk across the small medium that separated the Indian encampment from her own quarters.

"Excuse me," she said to the first woman she found in the Indian camp. "Do you speak English?"

The woman nodded.

"Could you direct me, please, toward Black Lion's tepee?"

The woman nodded. "I can. I take you there."

"I would so greatly appreciate that . . . what are you called?"

"My name . . . Little Star, wife of Running Fox, a Hunkpapa Lakota."

"Ah, Little Star. That's a beautiful name." Suzette smiled at the woman, who could not have been more than twenty-odd years in age. "Do you mind if I follow along behind you?"

"*Waste*. Good. You come," said the Little Star. "Follow. Him may not be awake. But maybe he awake since many people . . . have sought him last few days."

"Truly? There are others who have been looking for him?"

"I . . . not lie. This way." She led Suzette into a wooded area, where the Indians had pitched their canvas-tepee camp.

As Suzette lifted her skirts to keep up with the other woman, the smell of smoke, cooked meat and brewed coffee had Suzette's stomach growling, and she felt slightly nauseated. She really should have had something to settle her stomach before coming here. Hopefully, however, this meeting wouldn't take long. She would simply apologize to Black Lion, explain a little of what had made her respond as she had, and be on her way.

"This . . . his lodge," said Little Star.

"Thank you," replied Suzette. "Hmmm . . . how do I knock?"

"Knock?"

"How do I let him know that I am here?"

"Scratch at tepee . . . flap," said Little Star, "like this." And she scraped at the canvas of the entrance flap.

"*Han u ye*, yes, please come?" came a feminine voice from within the lodge.

"*Leciyotan u wo!*"

Suzette laid her hand over the young woman's arm. "That was a woman's voice. We must have the wrong lodge."

"This . . . right lodge," said Little Star, then, "*Leciyotan u wo!*"

"*Han, han!*"

A young woman stuck her face outside the tepee, and frowned at the sight of Suzette.

"No," said Suzette, "this cannot be right."

Timidly, the young woman crawled out of the lodge, her eyes squinting under the glare of the sun. She looked briefly at Little Star and then at Suzette, before lowering her gaze. After a moment, she said, "You want . . . Black Lion?"

Suzette nodded.

"Then . . . this right tepee."

"But, it cannot be . . . unless . . ." Suzette frowned. "Who are you?"

"This one?" The woman pointed to herself.

"Yes, who are you?"

The young woman swallowed, glanced around, as though searching for another to help her with what she was about to confess, and she said, "I . . . Rabbit Leggings."

"Yes, Rabbit Leggings," said Suzette. "How-do-you-do. But what are you doing here?"

Again, the woman swallowed hard. "I here because . . . I . . . his . . ." She gulped, twice. "I his wife."

"Wife?" said Suzette. "Black Lion's wife?"

"I say wrong word? *Wikte?*"

"It right word," said Little Star. "This wife of . . . Two Bears, him the . . . white man knows . . . as Black Lion."

Suzette didn't respond. In truth, at this moment in time, she was uncertain if she could have spoken a word. Her stomach twisted within her abdomen, her nausea became even more pronounced, and she felt as though something she had eaten last night was disagreeing with her horribly. Alas, she could barely think, let alone speak.

"Little Blue Eyes?" Black Lion at last peeked out from the lodge's entrance flap. His eyes were sleepy, his hair was tangled, and his chest was bare.

But Suzette barely took notice. She heard his voice as though she were far away from herself.

"Little Blue Eyes, what are you doing here?"

What, she wondered, in the name of the good Lord did she say to this man?

She stared at him as though she had never seen him

until this moment, and perhaps she never really had. This time, however, her look took in his mussed, though thoroughly masculine, appearance. But she steeled herself against the sexy look of him. She *had* to.

"I . . ." She tried to speak, but nothing, absolutely nothing came to mind to say.

"Little Blue Eyes? What is this? What has happened? Wait, let me pull on my jeans."

He was gone but a second, and, as though her feet had grown roots, she was still there, still in the same position when he appeared out of the lodge, as though she awaited him. Could it have been any more obvious that he had just awakened from sleep? Not only was his hair in disarray, but he was shirtless, and she was certain there was nothing but pure man between himself and those jeans.

The thought was erotic. He was erotic, and silently, she cursed his good looks, as well as herself, for her lack of resistance to him.

Still, she could think of nothing to say—not with an audience. And so she took the only action that came readily to her. With as much dignity as possible, she turned to leave.

But he moved with the speed of a panther, and blocked her way. "My wife?" He leaned in toward her, and whispered for her ear alone. "What has happened?"

"*Wife*? Yes. Pray ask your wife what has happened." And turning at an angle away from him, she took another step away.

He caught hold of her arm and said, still in a whisper, "Am I not looking at her?"

But Suzette wasn't about to argue with him. Perhaps she might do so later. At this moment, she felt too vulnerable. She needed to get away. Twisting her arm out of his grasp, she turned from him, and said, "Pray, do not insult me further." She picked up the edge of her skirt and began running away from him.

The ground, however, was still frozen from the evening hours, and her feet slipped over its icy patches, making her departure far from graceful.

"Little Blue Eyes, wait!" He caught up with her as she stumbled. He grasped hold of her. "Now I know what is wrong. There has been a misunderstanding," he said.

"There certainly has been," she agreed. Since she couldn't outrun him, however, she turned on him, and she said, "How could you do this to me? How could you lie? You, who speak of honor and integrity. And look at you! You! You have lied to me, and I . . . I trusted you! I was coming here to apologize to you."

"But you have the wrong idea about this. She is not my—"

"No wonder you were able to walk away from me last night. Was she waiting for you when you returned?"

"It's not like that. You are putting things here that are not there."

"And you are a liar . . . worse . . . you are worse than a liar, and I want no more to do with you."

"Listen to me. She is not my wife."

"And you expect me to believe you? When two women, not one, but two, say that she is?"

"I can explain."

"Pray, I do not wish to hear it. No more lies. You must think me an extraordinary fool to believe you can talk your way out of this. And I would, indeed, be witless if I were to listen to you." Again, shaking herself out of his hold, she scooted around him.

"I am not a liar," he said, taking step right beside her. "And you are not stupid, although seeking to leave when we have not talked this through is not wise."

"I? Not wise?"

But he ignored her words and went on to say, "I will tell you once again. She is not my wife. There is a misunderstanding. What I am saying to you now is the truth."

Briefly, Suzette glanced toward him, since he was at her side. She said, "I am uncertain you understand the definition of that word. But let me explain it to you. Truth means something that is the way it is—no lies—no pretense. If you had been honest with me from the start—"

"I have been honest with you and I understand what the word means." He practically shouted the words at her, and his face, beneath his tanned skin, had turned red, though his voice was once again calm when he said, "I have not lied to you. She is the wife of—"

"Two Bears. You! I know. She told me. Now, please let me go before we attract more attention than what we already have."

Black Lion glanced around him, looking almost sheepish to see that they had attracted much attention, both Indian and white. His pause, however, was all she needed, and picking up her skirts, she turned and fled across the medium that separated his camp from hers.

"Little Blue Eyes!"

But she was beyond listening to him. She ran through her own encampment, heading straight for Irena's tent. Several interested heads turned to watch her, but she ignored them all.

At this moment, all she could think of was a clean getaway. Thank goodness he would not be able to follow her here. Not easily anyway.

Though their encampments were situated side by side, rarely did the people from one camp enter that of the other. But then again, she had first met him in Irena's tent . . .

Perhaps she would simply walk through Mr. Cody's campground instead of returning home at once. She would keep moving, perhaps talking to several of the cowboys in the show. But she would not settle in one spot, not when Black Lion might find her. It wasn't much to savor, but at this moment, all she wanted was a little peace.

Luckily, Black Lion didn't appear to desire following her this day, either. Or was it lucky? . . .

CHAPTER 16

Suzette would have liked nothing better than to never see Black Lion again. Most certainly it would have been preferable if this could have been accomplished. Alas, such was all but impossible with a show like this. Though the Wild West employed over three hundred people, and there were more than enough women to act out the various parts required, Suzette had somehow found herself being pulled into the show. Perhaps it was because she was accustomed to the stage, and Buffalo Bill, recognizing her ease in it, had put it to work for him.

Or maybe it was simply fate.

Whatever it was, only two days after her argument with Black Lion, Suzette found herself acting out the role of the "wife" in the "Attack upon the Settler's Cabin" scene. It was a Saturday afternoon, the sun was shining, the air was cool and this was the first show of the day.

Standing before the log cabin, which was fashioned exactly as the settler's homes used to be, Suzette was dressed in an old-fashioned blue and white plaid gingham wrapper, complete with a white bonnet on her head.

According to script, her character was to exit the cabin, as though she were to attend to her washing; she was to hear something, glance up at the roof and see the Indian, who was crawling into a shooting position. This was her cue to scream a warning to her "husband" who was working in the fields, run back into the cabin and emerge from it again, this time holding a shotgun.

All this she did according to script, but upon reappearing at the door of the cabin with her rifle, she discovered that something was wrong; the Indian on her roof, who was supposed to be a man by the name of Flies Over, wasn't there. Instead, the Indian atop her cabin was the spitting image of Black Lion.

Drat! She glanced upward again. It *was* Black Lion.

Unfortunately for her heart, he looked uncannily handsome, dressed as he was in only breechcloth, leggings and moccasins. Setting her lips into a frown, she braced herself against the sight, wondering sarcastically how many horses he'd had to trade with Flies Over in order to take his place. Oh, to have some real ammunition.

At this point in the script she was supposed to run to the cornfield to try to help her settler "husband," who was battling there with another Indian. Except that before she took her cue, she aimed her gun carefully at Black Lion, and pulled the trigger.

Of course there were no bullets in the shotgun, but there was a wad of paper that hit him square in the cheek nonetheless. Obviously, it startled him, as he probably hadn't expected Suzette to vary from the script. Glancing down at her, he retaliated and trained a rubber-tipped arrow on her.

"You're dead!" she shouted at him. "I got you fair and square. Fall over." She waved her arm at him.

Luckily, there was so much commotion and so many other dramas going on around them, no one seemed to pay the two of them the least attention. That this made it very likely that no one else saw him wink at her was not the point. She'd gotten him.

"You realize, of course," she said, "that if this were real life, you would never be able to tie me up later because I got you. You're supposed to be dead now."

Remaining silent, Black Lion shook his head at her. Then, instead of keeping to the script himself, he climbed down to the cabin's edge, where, with a carefully aimed jump down, he landed behind her.

Grabbing hold of her from her back side, he dragged her to the ground, and began to gently tie her hands above her head. She struggled with him, fighting like a she-cat defending her territory. In truth, she almost won the fight, for he seemed leery about overly handling her.

Still he held her. "Why are you not following the script?" she shouted at him.

"Because you are not, and because I have come to take my wife home."

"I am *not* your wife," she yelled.

"You are. If I have to tie you up, and steal you in front of these thousands of people, and take you with me out of this arena, I will, for I would have Rabbit Leggings tell you why she said what she did that day."

"After you have paid her and told her what to say?"

"*Eya*, do you think so little of me?"

"Oh, much less. Much less."

"Then you give me no choice. I will tie you up, set you on my horse, and ride with you out of the arena."

"And you'll find yourself in a lot of trouble, Mr. Lion."

"Perhaps I will, but I think it is worth the chance."

"Very well, do it," she challenged, even as she fought with him. But he had already finished the task of tying her hands. "I warn you," she screamed above the commotion, "there will be consequences."

"I am prepared to take them."

"Oh!" And she kicked out at him. Immediately, he seized her legs. "Thank you for reminding me to tie your feet, as well." And he accomplished the deed as if she were a steer and he a rodeo performer.

Then, picking her up, he raced to a pony that another Indian held for him. Running the knife through the rope that held her feet in place, he positioned her on the animal first, not giving her a chance to kick out at him, while he jumped up behind her. Nodding to his friend, Black Lion set her comfortably before him, picked up the reins, and then, spurring the pony into action, raced out of the arena.

No one followed him. In truth, most of the performers were so embroiled in their own actions, only a few noticed that the script was no longer being followed. However, little did the two of them realize that the audience had followed their antics, and had gone wild over what they thought was a performance. As Black Lion raced out of the arena with his captive, the audience went into a frenzy, jumping to their feet with applause.

It was then that Buffalo Bill, at last, noticed the two of them, and what they were doing. But was it for good, or for bad? . . .

"Him . . . husband"—Rabbit Leggings pointed to Black Lion—"him . . . told me . . . say that . . . to you."

Shaking off the ropes that had tied her hands, and dismounting from the pony while shooing away Black Lion's attempts to help, Suzette turned on him. "Why have you gone to this much trouble to get me here? If I am to understand this correctly, Rabbit Leggings is saying that you *are* her husband. This hardly seems to prove your point."

They were standing within the shadows of the arena. In truth, Black Lion hadn't needed to take Suzette as far as his camp; Rabbit Leggings awaited them here. Said Black Lion, "Rabbit Leggings means that I had asked her to tell any white person who might come to the camp that she was married to me. You do recall that in order to be with the show, I am supposed to be married."

"I hardly think I have need of an interpreter between myself and Rabbit Leggings. I do understand English, and pray, I didn't hear her say all that you did. And you have yet to answer me what she was doing in your lodge first thing in the morning."

"I come . . . visiting . . . It . . . truth . . ." said Rabbit Leggings. "Him . . . tell me . . . be wife."

Suzette closed her eyes and sighed. "First thing in the morning?"

"But . . . it . . . true."

Suzette moaned, then turned to Black Lion. "So what you both are saying," she began sarcastically, "is that Rabbit Leggings decided to come visiting in the wee hours of the morning—before you were even awake? And—"

"You! The both of you! Come here!"

Riding a snowy white horse out of the arena, Buffalo Bill galloped to within a few yards of them.

Suzette exchanged a glance with Black Lion, whispering under her breath, "See? I told you there would be trouble."

Buffalo Bill repeated, loudly, "What was that all about, and whose idea was it to change the script?"

Exchanging a glance between them, Suzette and Black Lion both spoke at the same time, saying, "The idea was mine."

Black Lion sent Suzette a private look of amazement, as though he couldn't believe, in the face of everything else, that she was coming to his defense. In turn, she frowned at him. True, she thought, she would protect him from trouble, but that didn't mean she was feeling amiable toward him. Indeed, much the opposite.

Buffalo Bill, however, appeared puzzled. Leaning forward on his horse, he said, "You both came up with the idea, then?"

"Well," began Suzette, "after the stagecoach scene the other day, I thought that—"

"It was my idea, sir. The responsibility is mine, and mine alone," said Black Lion. "And I will understand if you feel it necessary to discharge me."

"Discharge you? Discharge you? Why, I'm going to give you a raise. It was brilliant!" said Cody. "Completely brilliant! And the crowd loved it! Did you see them standing in their seats? Even now they're calling for you both to come back into the arena. You're not going to disappoint them, are you?"

"But, Mr. Cody," said Suzette, "I think that—"

"Come here now, Miss Joselyn. You ride that pony"—he waved toward the Appaloosa—"while the Indian—what's your name?"

"Two Bears, but most people call me 'Lion.'"

"Good enough . . . you ride, Miss Joselyn, while Lion, here, guides the pony back into the arena. When you've reached the center point, stop and take a bow. We'll talk about this more later, and what sort of raise you'll be looking for. Come to think of it"—he scratched his beard—"we could expand on the theme and rescue the lady here from the Indian village later in the presentation . . . maybe even this one . . . Are you both up to it?"

Suzette smiled at Cody, while Black Lion frowned. But neither of them said a word.

"Come on now," said Buffalo Bill, directing the two of them as he kept his seat on the elegant white horse. "You, Lion, help the lady back up onto her seat."

When Black Lion hesitated, Cody said, "Come now, I know it goes against your warrior reasoning, but help her up there anyway, and then come back in for a bow . . . both of you."

Black Lion nodded, coming around Suzette to usher her toward the pony, then to grab her around the waist. With a simple motion, he lifted her up, onto the animal.

"Don't touch me!" she whispered, even while she smiled at him for Cody's benefit.

He returned the gesture, only his was a genuine smile. Beneath his breath, he said, "You tried to shield me against harm. What was that about? Do you begin to believe me?"

"No, I do not," she responded with relish. "Nor do I feel favorable toward you in the least. After all, it is not as though Rabbit Leggings has denied that you are her husband. Nor have either of you enlightened me as to why she was in your lodge in the first place. But I will not continue our argument here. Let us do as Mr. Cody asks, since he awaits us."

Black Lion might have answered her, but at that moment, Cody rode up to them, and said, "I'll ride back into the arena first, and announce you—then you follow. Think you can do that?"

Black Lion nodded.

"Here we go!" And then once more, for good measure, "Brilliant!"

This said, Cody turned his horse around and rode back into the center of the arena. From their position outside the open-air tent, Suzette could hear him announce the two of them as his newest actor and actress.

"Friend of . . . husband, Black Lion, you should know . . . man . . . here . . . see you. He wait . . . in lodge."

Black Lion nodded to Rabbit Leggings, who had come up to the two of them as they awaited their cue.

"*Waste*," said Black Lion. "Did the man announce who he was?"

"*Hiya*, no."

"Very well. Go, tell him I will come to see him as soon as this performance is done."

"*Han, han.* I go. I tell . . . him."

No sooner had Rabbit Leggings turned to leave than Black Lion was leading the pony—with Suzette on it—back before the crowd.

"What was that all about?" she asked.

"I hardly know," Black Lion replied. "But I will discover it forthwith, I suspect."

Suzette might have responded, but it seemed inappropriate at the moment, for no sooner had they both stepped foot into the arena than the people in the stands went riotous with their praise. Most were standing, some were waving and smiling at them.

Suzette waved back, blowing kisses aimed at the crowd, while, having stopped at the midpoint in the arena, Black Lion stood immobile by her side.

She said, "You could raise a hand and wave, too."

"You are doing very well for both of us."

"Someone has to give them a show and accept their accolades."

"Then I am glad it is you. Will you come to my lodge tonight, after the Long-haired Show Man's party? We need to speak on this matter between us at length, and I think it should be soon."

"No, I will not."

"Say yes, you will."

"I will not."

"Then I will kiss you, here, before them all." He grinned slightly. "Let the Long-haired Show Man explain that."

Even as he said it, he had begun to turn the pony around so that they might take a bow for the people on the opposite side of the stands.

"I will not be blackmailed," she said. "How dare you try to do so!"

"And I will enjoy kissing you." As he swung the pony around, he stepped toward her, he even reached up as though to take hold of her, and . . .

"Very well," she said. "You make your point. But I will not come to speak to you until after the party is well finished. So do not wait up for me."

He smiled. "I will wait for you all the same," he said, and at last, grinning madly, he, too, waved at the crowd.

Black Lion treaded back into the Indian encampment and, stepping toward his canvas-covered lodge, saw a stranger awaiting him. Whoever it was, Black Lion had a good feeling about this. Thus, it did not completely startle him to discover that it was White Claw, the medicine man of the Lost Clan, who awaited him.

Though it was true that Black Lion was surprised by the visit—for he did not realize that White Claw had the ability to move between the realms of both realities—as was the way of his people, Black Lion kept the emotion carefully concealed. Instead of an enthusiastic welcome, after climbing into his tepee, Black Lion stepped to the left of the lodge fire, and took his place next to White Claw, acting as though this might be a most commonplace meeting. Two Bears and Rabbit Leggings, as though by a previous agreement, arose and left the lodge.

After several moments of solemn appreciation elapsed, Black Lion said in the Sioux tongue, "*Hepela—hepela!* I am joyful to see you."

White Claw nodded. Then at length, the old medicine man took hold of his pipe and lit it with the dung of the buffalo, offering up the pipe's smoke as a prayer first to the Sky, then to the Earth and lastly to the Four Winds. Only then did White Claw inhale a puff from the pipe, extending it afterward to Black Lion.

Black Lion accepted the gift, drew in a breath from the pipe and gave it back to White Claw. It was only then, after placing the pipe in a position of honor, that White Claw spoke in the language of the Blackfoot, "*Issohka*, Grandson, it is good to see you. And I am pleased to witness that you have grown into a fine man."

"I am happy to see you, also, *Aaahs*, Grandfather. It has been very many years since we last spoke. I have missed my people."

"That is to be expected."

"Do you bring news? Are my father and mother well?"

"They are as well as might be expected," answered White Claw, "living the half-life existence that we do."

"*Aa*, yes. I understand. Know that I am using all my strength and wisdom to break the spell for our people."

White Claw nodded. "I am certain that you are."

Silence followed this statement, and except for the occasional spark that broke away from the fire, all was quiet. Though there were many questions Black Lion would have liked to ask the medicine man, good manners forbid him to speak of such things until asked.

At last, White Claw said, "You are the first of all our

champions that the Great Spirit has allowed me to visit while the spell still remains intact. What the reason is for this, I suspect is not about the spell or helping you to break it. For I fear, this you must do yourself."

"*Aa*, yes," Black Lion said in the Blackfoot tongue. "This I do understand. Therefore, my heart is very glad that you are here."

"As mine is to see you. *Issohka*, let me begin by telling you that I have dreamed of you. Take heed now of what I say, for I have seen your spirit protector and I bring you news from the lioness."

Though surprised anew, Black Lion did no more than nod pleasantly.

"This is what I have to say to you," said White Claw. "There is a new danger, one that we in the Clan have not before experienced. My heart grieves to tell you that Red Belly has died, and as you know, he was the last boy of the right age that we could send forth into the world in our quest to break the curse. Worse, I fear the Thunderer knows this."

Black Lion accepted these tidings calmly yet his soul was filled with dread, for he suspected what other news might be forthcoming.

"If you fail in this quest," White Claw continued, "I fear our Clan will be doomed to remain in the mist forever."

Again, Black Lion simply nodded, though his heart skipped a beat.

"*Haiya*," said White Claw, "the responsibility upon you is grave, and could I take the burden from your shoulders, I would do so. But I cannot. Hear me, Grandson, your spirit protector has this to say to you: Take your wife into your confidence, and tell her what it is that you seek. Do not sing the sacred song to her, for if she does not know it, and you have sung it, you will lose your chance to free your people. But your wife may have knowledge of this song. Remember, it is a white man's song. *Haiya*, take her into your confidence."

Though his pulse was beating heavily in his chest, Black Lion said, simply, "I will do as you say."

"*Soka'piiwa*, that is good. *Soka'piiwa*. *Issohka*, Grandson?"

"*Aa?*"

"There is one other particular your spirit protector wishes you to know."

"*Hannia?*"

"The lioness sees that you are unhappy in your personal life. Do not be." A gleam, not unlike a spark of laughter, lighted the old man's eye, as he continued, "Your spirit protector fears you have misunderstood a detail that she told you."

"*Hannia*, really?"

"*Aa*, it is so. A man is allowed the pleasure of his wife, as long as he is respectful of her condition." White Claw grinned. "Especially when he is only recently wed."

Black Lion raised a single eyebrow; it was his only reaction.

"Think again on the message from your spirit protector, *Issohka*," said White Claw. "Sacrificing the pleasures of the flesh may have many different meanings . . . not only the one. Ponder it again. Remember that the lioness said exactly that though you are married, you, your people, must be willing to sacrifice pleasures of the flesh."

Black Lion nodded. That White Claw should know the particulars of his dream, and of his marital situation, did not astonish him. Far from it. Such were the ways and wonders of the old medicine men.

"Think on it."

"I will," said Black Lion.

"In truth," said White Claw, "one is never too old to love, to show love . . . or to find love. It is all around us, and one only needs to reach out to bring it into our lives. *Mat'-ah-kwi tam-ap-i-ni-po-ke-mi-o-sin*, not found is happiness without woman. And so I am here," he nodded. "*Aa*, I am here."

"*Aaahs*, Grandfather, do you, too, look for love?"

"I have already found love," said White Claw. "*Haiya*, I only require discovering it once again."

Though Black Lion did not understand these words, he did not query further. Instead, he said, "I am truly glad that you have visited me. And my heart is happy to learn that I have misunderstood the spirit protector's words, for these last few days have been difficult . . . Perhaps I can now be a good husband, though I fear that I would be happier yet were the task before me not so serious."

"This is to be expected, *Issohka*. Perhaps the Great Spirit in His wisdom, though he gives you an additional burden, counters it with a freedom. So do ponder your spirit protectors words, by all means, but also take pleasure in being a husband."

No sooner had the words left White Claw's lips than the two men shared a glance, and at last, they both smiled. Though the council was formally ended, the two of them continued to talk at length of Black Lion's vision, and of more general tidings. But interestingly, White Claw was very intent on one detail: They would attend the white man's party this night. And though Black Lion tried to convince the medicine man that the Indian was rarely, if ever, invited to such things, his words had no effect.

And so, donning their very best clothes for the occasion, the two men set out to crash the Long-haired Show Man's celebration.

CHAPTER 17

"You and your husband were spectacular," said Irena as she sipped a glass full of champagne. "And so real to life."

"Yes, well, it *was* real to life. I was truly fighting him. You know that I am upset with him . . . and with good reason."

Above the champagne glass, Irena blinked at her granddaughter, then said, "So you say. However, it was an extraordinary idea of Bill's to rescue you later from the Indian village, setting you free. Pray, I have rarely seen so enthusiastic a crowd. I began to think they might jump over the barrier and into the arena with you. Indeed, I would have to agree with Mr. Cody in this regard. It was an absolutely brilliant maneuver on Black Lion's part to steal you, and you were stunning as a captive, my dear."

Suzette didn't answer. She couldn't, not at this particular moment. In sweeping her glance around the room, her gaze caught onto a very familiar face.

"What is *he* doing here?" she asked no one in particular. "Indians are not usually invited to these parties given for the dignitaries, are they?"

"Is someone here, dear?"

"Yes. It is Black Lion, as well as . . . well, I have not had the acquaintance of the older gentleman who is with him. However, I would say at a glance that they are probably dressed in their finest."

"Oh? Where are they?"

"Over there, in a corner, near the entrance." Suzette nodded toward them. "Do you see them?"

Irena turned to stare at the place Suzette indicated. Oddly, she went suddenly silent, though Irena did grab hold of and squeeze Suzette's hand.

"He's quite handsome, isn't he?" said Suzette, and, though she was at odds with Black Lion, she could not deny that he cut an exotic and incredible figure. He was dressed in a white buckskin shirt that hung well below his knees and strips of the shirt fell to the ground. Fringe as well as blue and silver beads decorated both sleeves, while a beaded circle of blue and silver hung over his chest and the lower part of his shirt. White fringed leggings hugged his legs and on his feet were white, beaded moccasins. His hair was left long, flowing over his face, like a lion's mane. It fell over his shoulders and down his back, while two strands of his front locks had been pulled together and tied there with beads. He carried a lance in his hands, that was decorated with feathers and ermine fur.

He was magnificent, and though she still harbored a less than kindly attitude toward him, she stared at him, agape.

He looked to be exactly what he was: a proud warrior.

"It is he," said Irena at her side, her voice a little breathless.

"Yes, I know. He cuts a good figure, does he not?"

"He does, indeed. Suzette." Irena turned toward her, though her glance remained on the two Indians who still hugged the entryway. "I must go speak to him. Do not be upset with me."

"Why would I be upset with you?"

"Just remember to not be. You will do that, will you not?"

"Of course."

Irena kissed Suzette on the cheek and then hugged her. "I love you, Suzie. I always have, I always will."

"And I love you, too, but Irena—"

"I have to go to him."

"Yes," said Suzette, "I understand. I know the two of you are friends. Do tell him not to wait up for me tonight, though. I plan to be here until the party ends."

Irena nodded, she smiled, and then she was gone, making her way gradually through the crowd, toward the two gentlemen of the Plains.

Smiling, Suzette drew her glance away from the entrance and the men, and decided to mingle with the rest of the show people and cowboys. In another far corner of the room was Annie Oakley. Who would believe, she thought, that such a small, delicate woman could be a professional sharpshooter. That she was also a woman of sympathy toward the Indians was well-known, for Sitting Bull was her fast friend.

Suzette made a move toward Annie, when a deep baritone voice sounded from behind her. "I have heard many people say tonight that you made a good captive."

She grimaced. Even if he hadn't spoken, the scent of rawhide and mint was enough to announce that Black Lion had found her.

She said, without turning to greet him, "I am no man's captive, and I never will be. I am afraid that slavery, Mr. Lion, is dead in our world today."

"*Hau*, that is a good thing, and yet too bad, for I would enjoy seeing you decorate my lodge."

"I am also not *decoration*, and I would like to remind you that I have by no means changed my mind about you." She was afraid to spin around and look at him, apprehensive that he was simply too good-looking for her own peace of mind. "By the way," she said over her shoulder, "who is your friend? I have not seen him before tonight."

"He is an old medicine man from my tribe. He has come here to give me advice."

"Advice?"

"*Hau*," Black Lion said, stepping around to face her, making it all but impossible to ignore him, "advice."

"On . . ."

"My mission, as well as another matter . . ." This last was said against her ear, which stirred to life tingles of excitement, all along her nerve endings.

However, she reminded herself that she was upset with this man. "Oh, yes," she said. "Your mission." Here was yet another justification for her to doubt this man, she thought. *His mission*, which was an esoteric task that, though steeped in legend and mystery, was impossible.

Yet, she had promised him that she would not pass judgment on him because of it, and she would keep her word. It didn't necessarily follow, however, that she believed him. Indeed, not.

After a slight pause, she continued. "Well, then," she said, all without glancing behind her, "I assume you and he have much to discuss. It would be ill of me to detain you in such a circumstance as this. Pray, feel free to leave me to humor him."

"We have already had our talk."

"Oh?"

"And so you see, I have much time . . . time to plead my circumstance to you in the hopes that you will listen to me."

"Mr. Lion, let it not be said that I will not listen to you. However, at the moment, I am awaiting the engagement of—"

"Miss Joselyn?"

Suzette turned her head to watch Nate Salsbury, Buffalo Bill's partner, approach them. He said, "Miss Joselyn, the musicians are ready for Irena's performance. Do you know where she is?"

"Why, yes, I do. She is by the entrance . . ." Suzette hesitated as she glanced in that direction now, but there was no sign of Irena. "Hmmm . . . She was there only a moment ago. Perhaps she has stepped outside."

"Thank you, I am sure she has," said Salsbury. "I shall look for her there." Salsbury tipped his hat and departed immediately.

"This is stunning regalia, Black Lion," said Annie Oakley, as she and her husband, Frank Butler, joined Suzette and Black Lion, leaving Suzette no choice but to turn around. Annie continued, "It looks to be ancient, and I have not seen anything like it in the show."

Frank smiled, and raised his glass in greeting, but remained silent. And it was up to Black Lion to answer. "It belonged to my father. It is his ceremonial shirt."

"Ceremonial?"

"It is the tradition of my people that, when one is to attend a celebration with others, one dresses in his ceremonial best."

Annie nodded. "Yes," she said, "and Miss Joselyn . . ."

"Pray, please call me Suzette."

Annie grinned. "Suzette, that was a spectacular performance this afternoon. It was a stroke of genius."

Suzette returned Annie's smile. "Thank you, but I'm afraid the congratulations should go to Mr. Lion, here, whose idea it was. Like many in the crew, I was as stunned as they were when he departed from the script."

"Indeed?" said Annie, and she gave Black Lion a considering glance.

"Miss Joselyn . . ." It was Nate Salsbury speaking again, as he rejoined their party. "I cannot find Irena anywhere, and we are ready for the entertainment to begin. The dignitaries from Denver are waiting. Please forgive me, but I know that you, too, have operatic experience. I do not suppose I could impose upon you to . . ."

"Oh, yes. Of course. I would be honored to sing in Irena's stead, if that is what you mean to ask. But tell me," said Suzette, "did you check her quarters? She might have retired there, perhaps to change clothes."

"She is not there."

"Indeed?" Suzette frowned. Where could Irena have gone? She glanced at Black Lion to ask for his favor in this regard, when he took the moment upon himself.

He said, "While you prepare your song, I will look for her."

"That would be most appreciated," Suzette acknowledged, slanting him a grudging yet genuine smile. Then, turning toward Salsbury, she said, "Would you escort me to the musicians?"

"I would be most happy to do so," said Salsbury, and presenting her with his arm, he said, "Shall we go?"

"Yes," agreed Suzette, and muttering a quiet "Would you excuse me" to Annie and Frank Butler, Suzette went in search of the lead musician.

"Ah, I see," said Jacques Marcelle, the leader of the trio of musicians, as well as its flautist. Besides himself, there were a clarinet player and a harpist. "You are to sing in your grandmother's place?"

"Yes," said Suzette. "I fear we cannot locate Irena at present, and since I have little knowledge of what she was to sing tonight, I would ask if you and your company know 'The Last Rose of Summer'?"

"*Oui*, mademoiselle. In what key would you like it?"

"B-flat, please."

Mr. marcelle nodded, and Suzette took her place on the very small stage.

"Are you ready?" asked Nate Salsbury.

"Yes." Suzette nodded.

"Good, then I will introduce you." And with hardly a pause, he began, "Ladies and gentlemen. It is my pleasure to introduce you tonight to Miss Suzette Joselyn, a lyric soprano from the London Opera House. She has kindly agreed to entertain us with a song. Let us welcome her. Miss Joselyn? . . ."

He gestured toward her, and Suzette, amid applause, smiled her thanks at Salsbury.

"Ladies and gentlemen," she began, "the song I am about to sing is an aria entitled 'The Last Rose of Summer,' from Friedrich von Flotow's opera *Martha*. Originally a poem by Thomas Moore, it was set to music by John Stevenson. In the opera, the main character, Harriet Durham, sings this beautiful Irish melody to her lover." Nodding to the other musicians, the first strains of the intro began.

She sang:

> "'Tis the last rose of summer,
> Left blooming alone;
> All her lovely companions
> Are faded and gone;
> No flower of her kindred,
> No rosebud is nigh,

> *To reflect back her blushes,*
> *Or give sigh for sigh."*

Not a sigh was to be heard from the spellbound audience. Suzette awaited the interlude, then continued . . .

Black Lion had taken a place toward the rear of the room, and with arms folded over his chest, he listened to Little Blue Eye's high, musical voice:

> *"I'll not leave thee, thou lone one!*
> *To pine on the stem;*
> *Since the lovely are sleeping,*
> *Go sleep thou with them.*
> *Thus kindly I'll scatter,*
> *Thy leaves o'er the bed,*
> *Where thy mates of the garden*
> *Lie scentless and dead."*

Watching her, listening to her, Black Lion felt as though some mythical force had borne him to another place and time, such was the power of her voice. And though she sang a melody with unfamiliar words, he stood enchanted.

It was the next verse of the song, when he at last caught her eye. Was it his imagination or, from that moment onward, did she sing only to him?

> *"So soon may I follow*
> *When friendships decay,*
> *And from Love's shining circle*
> *The gems drop away.*
> *When true hearts lie wither'd*
> *And fond ones are flown,*

> *Oh! who would inhabit*
> *This bleak world alone?"*

The final note was high, drawn out, and when at last, the music faded into nothing, it took the assembled crowd a moment to recover. At last, brilliant waves of applause greeted her, and the "Bravo! Bravo!" was shouted out amid further praise.

Suzette nodded, smiling and bowing, accepting her due gracefully. But before she left the platform completely, she lifted her gaze to glance out at *him*. The others around him faded. She didn't smile at him, but she didn't have to. He recognized the hunger that echoed deeply within her gaze.

He sincerely hoped it was for him. Having once known the sultry wonder of her affection, these last few days without her had been unbearable. Despite their troubles and the differences between them, Black Lion now harbored a knowledge deep in his soul.

He loved this woman. It was the wrong time for love, the wrong place, for he could not afford to give her the attention that a wife so thoroughly deserved.

Yet, there it was. He had found his life's partner. And as they stared at one another, he knew that their hearts were one. With time her anger would cool. For now, his realization was enough.

When she averted her gaze, Black Lion quietly left Buffalo Bill's welcome tent to keep his promise to his wife, and go in search of the Song Bird, Irena.

Suzette accepted the praise from an admirer graciously, beaming her pleasure. Yet when she glanced back to the spot where Black Lion had been, he was gone.

Disappointment flooded her. She had been looking

forward to speaking with him. True, she was certain her words to him would have been sarcastic, perhaps even antagonistic, for he still had much explaining to do before she would give him quarter.

Nevertheless, she had welcomed the opportunity to spar with him.

"Miss Joselyn." It was Buffalo Bill who had come up behind her. "This is the first time I have heard you sing. Does Irena know that she has a rival in you?"

Suzette laughed. "I could never compete with Irena, nor would I want to. She is an act all to herself."

"That she is. That she is, and the Wild West is grateful to have her." Cody leaned down close to her, and the scent of whiskey was heavy on his breath, as he said, "It would be my pleasure, Miss Joselyn, if you are willing, to show you exactly how wild our Western country can be . . ." He grinned inanely.

If it weren't for the fact that Cody was completely serious, Suzette might have greeted his offer with a short laugh. The suggestion did seem outrageous. Even more so because, since she had arrived here, Cody had paid her little heed, catering instead to his opera star, Irena.

However, she kept her own counsel, realizing that Cody *was* earnest, as well as drunk, and she chose her words carefully. "It is a fine offer, and I thank you . . ."

"Fine, fine." He grinned at her, and laid his hand on her shoulder.

"But," Suzette said, sidling out of his reach, "I already have a secret life with . . . someone else . . . and it is wild enough."

"You do? With who?"

She grinned at Cody, remained silent and offered her hand to him. "Mr. Cody, I thank you," she said, her voice and her intent firm. She turned away from him to stroll to the other side of the tent.

"Splendid, dear, splendid," came a compliment from one of the cowgirls.

"Thank you very much." Suzette smiled.

"That was beautiful, very beautiful," said Annie Oakley, as they met each other in passing. "I hope you will sing for us often."

"Thank you, I hope that I shall, as well," said Suzette, as she stepped out into the night.

The cold air felt marvelous in her lungs; it was clean and invigorating. Wistfully, she wished that Black Lion might find her standing here, if only so they could continue their argument.

What, she wondered, did that indicate about her? That she enjoyed being with him, even if they did nothing more than spit at each other. For a moment tonight, she had felt as if the two of them had connected, being to being. There had been no other people, no environment. Just him. Just her.

And she had found him . . . magnificent . . .

Magnificent? She pulled up her thoughts at once. Indeed, until she determined if the man were married to another or not, she would avoid *all* thought of him . . . if that were possible.

The prospect of avoidance was unreal, however, since she had promised a rendezvous with the man later this evening. Would she discover him to be truthful, after all?

Only time would tell. Until Irena reappeared, Suzette would have to take upon herself her grandmother's duties, here at the party. Hopefully Irena would return soon . . .

CHAPTER 18

The celebration party was still in full swing in the wee hours of the morning. Suzette had already sung three songs with one more planned, and at present she was slowly drifting outside in order to escape the stuffy atmosphere. But she had barely arrived outside when Black Lion found her, and announced that Irena was nowhere to be found.

"Once you leave the party," he said, "we will talk some more of this."

"Later? No, please, tell me now. What have you discovered?"

"*Hiya!* I think it best that I not speak of it yet."

"Why?"

"Because what I have to say will be upsetting to you, I believe, and you still have duties before you this night."

Suzette frowned. "Is it that bad, then?"

He didn't answer.

She looked at him sullenly. He had changed his

clothes, she noted. Though still wearing buckskin, his leggings, his shirt and his moccasins were tanned, scarcely decorated and appeared to be purely functional. His hair was parted in the middle and tied in back, as though he couldn't bother having it in his way. Over one shoulder was a blanket, strapped around the other shoulder was a rawhide bag that looked to hold many things. Indeed, she thought he looked as though he might have stepped straight out of the past.

However, she kept the observation to herself, and continued speaking, saying, "If it is bad news that you have, you really must tell me."

Again, he didn't comment; rather, he crossed his arms over his chest, and so serious, so stanch, an expression did he present her, he reminded her of an unmovable boulder.

Her frown deepened. "How can you do this? How can you seek me out and tell me that something has happened to her, and then not disclose what it is?"

Again, he didn't comment.

"Is she all right?"

"I believe she is well. I can say no more now. I will wait for you here until you can leave the party. At that time, we will talk. But not until then." His look at her was firm, strict, and unfortunately for her, it was becoming evident that on this matter, he was quite prepared to hold his ground.

Frustrated, she spun away from him. But before she left, she said, "Please stay here, for I will return shortly." And then she stepped back into the crowded room.

Winding a path through several groups of people, she at last approached the musicians, where she sought out the lead flautist, Marcelle. She said, "Monsieur, pray, is it too early for me to leave? I fear that Irena will not be in attendance at all tonight, and I am afraid that I am not used to these late hours."

Jacques Marcelle smiled at her kindly. "You should do as you think best, Mademoiselle. No one can accuse you of not having done your duty for your grandmother. You have already sung three songs for us tonight. And in truth, we ourselves will not be here much longer."

"Thank you very much," Suzette said. "It has been a pleasure singing with you this evening."

"It has been our pleasure."

Suzette grinned at the man, stepped away from him, and picking up the front of her dress, she turned to thread her way once more through the crowd. She found Black Lion where she had left him.

"Mr. Lion," she spoke up at once, "I am now free to leave. I would ask, however, that you accompany me to Irena's tent before we proceed to your lodge. It is so late, and I would like to change my clothes."

Black Lion nodded. "As you will," he said, and stepping away from the tent, he proceeded to lead the way toward Irena's tent.

"Where is Irena?" Suzette asked, as she followed him, holding up the front of her dress so that she could hurry to keep step with him.

"I cannot say yet," he said, "but as soon as you are able to sit, I will tell you everything I have discovered this night."

"Is it that bad, then?"

"Not bad," he answered at last, "but I think you will be upset."

She sighed. "Then let us hurry."

Suzette threw back the canvas flap of the tent and turned toward Black Lion. "Come," she said, inviting him to enter. "This is a good place for us to talk, and I fear I am too anxious to wait until we go to your lodge."

"Very well," he agreed, and he ducked inside. He waited until she had lit one of the gaslights and was seated, although he remained standing. Then, without further ado, he said, "Irena has left with the medicine man who accompanied me here tonight."

"The medicine man?"

"*Hau*."

"When will she be back?"

He shrugged. "I do not think she intends to come back."

Suzette drew her brows together. "How can this be? She has an obligation here—I believe she signed a contract. This is not something that she would ignore."

"Yet," he said, "she is gone with him, and my friend cannot remain long in this country. He was here for a night only, and it was his intention to rejoin our people, to return to the place of my birth."

"The place of your birth? The Sioux reservation?"

"The reservation is not where I was born," he said simply. "As you might recall, I am not Lakota by birth. The territory of my people is farther to the north."

"Yes," she said, "a question, please."

He nodded.

"By 'your people,' do you mean . . . your original tribe?"

"I do. We are called the Lost Clan, and we are part of the Blackfoot Confederation."

Her frown grew more pronounced. "I do not understand. I thought that your tribe did not exist in the real world, that . . ."

"They are real," he said, "they are simply entrapped in a place that is part of this universe yet not of this time."

She shook her head. "I truly do not understand. If we go to this place, will we find your tribe?"

"We will not," he affirmed.

"Then how can your friend, this medicine man, take my grandmother there?"

"I do not know, but he is a man of some spiritual power. If anyone could take her to our time, it would be he."

Suzette clenched her jaw. "But Irena is real, flesh and blood."

"That is so," he said, "as are my people. They are merely caught in a trap. That it is of their own making does not make it less a trap."

"But if she goes there," said Suzette, a cloud of apprehension marring her brow, "then she, too, would be enslaved there?"

"I do not know."

"She would not be able to return here?"

"Again," he said, "I do not know."

Truly alarmed now, a chill took hold of her, and she said, "I have a terrible thought, that I almost hate to ask, but . . . Since Irena is real, is of this world, and your people, at present, are not—at least not in this time that we exist in—would it kill her to go there?"

Again he shook his head. "You ask me questions that I cannot answer."

"Well, someone—and that must be you—should take the pains to answer them. We are discussing my grandmother!"

He nodded. "So we are. I am sorry, but I do not have the answers your seek."

"I am looking for a particular person—someone I met when I was in America many years ago. I have never forgotten him."

"And do you love this man?"

"I do."

In the stroke of an instant, Suzette understood what had happened. This man tonight was he—the man whom Irena had fallen in love with. It all fit.

"Do not be upset with me," Irena had said. It was only now that Suzette grasped the significance of those words. It was Irena's way of saying "good-bye."

Good-bye? Did Irena know that this man was not a man, that he was . . . But if not a man, then what was he? A ghost?

Shivers racked Suzette's body. If a ghost took a person to an unearthly place, would that other person not become a ghost, as well?

No, no, it could not be. This man Irena loved . . . he *had* to be a real man. What Black Lion was intimating couldn't be true.

But what if it were true? Were there not phenomena that we, as yet, did not understand?

That was it, then. Without another thought, Suzette knew what she had to do.

Lifting her gaze to meet that of Black Lion's, she said, "When do we leave?"

He nodded at her, as though he had expected her to say nothing else. "I am ready to depart at once. But first I ask you to consider that White Claw is a medicine man, and if he loves your grandmother, as I expect he does, he will not bring her to the Clan if it will harm her."

Suzette hesitated. "Can you swear to this? That no harm will come to Irena?"

"No man could make such a promise about another—"

"Then it's not good enough for me. This is my grandmother we are speaking of."

He nodded. "I understand. We can leave at once—as soon as you are ready—if it is in your mind to go after her."

"Very well. Wait here. It will take me little time to pack some clothes, some food and things for survival."

"You cannot take any of those."

"What?"

"Do you not recall," he said, "that not only is Irena obligated to stay here with the show, so, too, am I. Plus there are some people in this country who say that all Indians caught off the reservation should be exterminated."

Suzette gasped. "Surely not. You must exaggerate."

"I do not lie or stretch the truth. No, if we are to go, we will travel through country where there is no path, for we must go in such a way as to ensure we cannot be found. Not only by any white people who might see us, but by scouts the Long-haired Show Man might send against us."

She frowned. "Is that possible?"

"*Hau*, it is. But this way requires that you take nothing with you."

"Nothing?" She arched a brow. "But what about a change of clothes? Feminine articles that I need?"

"We will find these things that you require from the Earth. But you cannot go about the countryside in this dress you wear now. Have you something that does not tear easily and is comfortable? Also, we will travel on foot, so your shoes should be well-made."

"On foot?"

"There is no other way to scout. To go by horseback announces our presence."

"But we'll never catch them in time to save Irena."

"We have a chance to find them, for they will have to travel in the same way we do."

"Irena . . . walking hundreds of miles? And at her age?" Suzette turned a wide-eyed stare at him. "We really must find her soon. I will go change . . . quickly."

"*Waste*," he said, "it is good. But change only your clothes, not yourself." Though he said it seriously, and his expression was sober, there was still a light in his eye.

Suzette nodded, but she didn't smile. It would take much more than a pun to make her smile again.

Black Lion saw little to be gained in seeking to change Suzette's mind—not when her grandmother was missing. True, Black Lion believed that White Claw would do nothing to harm the Song Bird, Irena. But, were his and Suzette's places reversed, Black Lion knew he would leave nothing to chance; knew he would act as his wife did.

However, leaving the show behind them would not be without danger. Any journey ventured at this time of year would be hard on his wife, especially in her condition. Therefore, in addition to following White Claw and endeavoring to catch up with him and Irena, Black Lion must commit himself to keeping Little Blue Eyes and her babe safe.

There were other dangers, as well. Since both he and Irena had signed contracts with the show, it was possible that their absence would not go unnoticed, particularly when it could appear to the white men that both women had been stolen.

Alas, he could foresee many dangers, and many duties ahead of him on this trip. But it didn't also follow that their journey together was not to be without . . . pleasure.

They would be in constant company with each other. This he desired very much. It would allow him opportunity not only to come to know his wife better, but to also persuade her that he had married her true.

Perhaps, if he were lucky, there might even be other pleasures to be found. But he dare not think of that now. At present, it would be enough to consider that his wife might come to believe in him.

Suzette emerged in record time, dressed in a bicycle ensemble of deep green velveteen. It was the height of fashion, with bloomers resembling Turkish trousers disguising her legs so well that for the moment, her conscience was eased. Leather boots, which extended up over her calf muscles, would protect her legs and feet. A deep green velveteen jacket completed the apparel. Over her shoulder, she carried a purse that contained every feminine article she could have possibly crammed into it.

There were some things a woman couldn't do without.

Black Lion nodded at her in approval. "We must leave immediately," he said. "Already it is the darkest part of the night, and dawn awaits. If we are to make good time, we must go now."

She bobbed her head up and down. "I am ready."

"There is one other detail you should know. When on the trail, you must do as I say, without question, for if we are to travel without arousing suspicion, we must remain undetected, and not always will I be able to talk freely to explain myself. Do you think you can do this? Obey without question?"

"Yes, I think so," she said. "But you will keep in mind that I am with child."

"*Hau.* Always."

"Then I am ready."

"Waste. Will you turn out the light, then?" he asked, and no sooner had she done this than he took her in his arms, planting a kiss directly on her upturned lips.

She moaned, not able to help herself, the sound seeming to rouse him, for his hands roamed up and down her body, over and over again.

It was delicious, and she sighed, melting her body into his. She might have done more, as well, but she suddenly remembered that this man might have secrets from her as yet undisclosed.

No sooner had the thought materialized than she shimmied out, away from him, putting some distance between them. Swallowing hard, she said, "I fear we must set some limits between us, for there are still matters that are yet unsettled. Know this: As a guide, I put my trust in you, but as a husband, I have little faith. Indeed, until I am able to question Rabbit Leggings thoroughly on the matter, I would ask that you keep your distance from me."

Although it was evident he listened carefully to her, his jaw had jutted forward. "Then let us go to Rabbit Leggings now, and awaken her so that you may ask your questions of her."

"We have not the time to do that, and you know it."

"Then perhaps I should tell you," he said, taking a step toward her, "that I have been released from my fear that I must withhold myself from you."

"Oh? You have?" She took a step backward.

"*Hau*, I have. I can now be a good husband to you . . ."

His implication was clear, and though excitement burst along her nerve endings, seeming to come to pool, there, at the apex of her legs, she took another step away from him, if only in self-defense. And she said, "You make a rather vivid point, However, though the prospect is . . . enticing . . . we would lose time, and at present, time is precious."

"*Hau*," he said, "but before we go, I should warn you. We will be much alone, and it is my intention to lure you into my arms, and to make you wish to be my true wife."

She gulped, and said nothing. However, she took one more step back in retreat.

He must have recognized the effect he had created, for he grinned and reached out to flick a lock of her hair over her shoulder. Then he smiled, and said, "A man so loves a challenge."

She inhaled on a breath, took another step back, and said, "It is not a challenge."

But he simply smiled at her. "Now, about scouting. There are some rules that you must know and agree to."

"Oh?"

"*Hau*, it is so. Firstly, one does not walk, one crawls on one's stomach or knees and forearms, in your case on all fours."

"On all fours? You must be joking."

"I am not."

"For hundreds of miles?"

"Sometimes we can walk."

"Sometimes?"

"We must go without detection, and these are the ways it is done."

Closing her eyes, Suzette shook her head, and said, "Oh, Irena, when we at last find you, you and I will have to have a very long talk."

He grinned. "Are you ready?"

"I suppose that I am." She sighed.

"Then let us be away." And with no more to be said, he bent down, coming onto his stomach, and crawling along the floor of the tent in this fashion, he exited out the back of it. She followed him—trying to do as he did—into the cover of bushes and trees.

"Irena, my dear grandmother," she whispered to herself. "Just wait till I see you again. Just wait."

It didn't take long for Suzette to discover that scouting was, indeed, tiring. Her forearms and elbows, her knees and her calf and thigh muscles would never be the same. Nor would her bicycling outfit. Already the green velveteen was torn, and though she herself hadn't thought to do so, she had discovered that Black Lion would often backtrack, culling the ground for what, she didn't know. More often than not, he returned with remnants of her clothing.

When she had asked him about it, he had said, "Such cloth as this will indicate our path, and until we are well out of the range of the show's scouts, we must not leave a trail."

This was a concept she hadn't stopped to consider. She asked, "Do you think Cody will send scouts after us?"

"He might. Your grandmother was, after all, under contract, as was I . . ."

"Yes, of course," responded Suzette. "But isn't it hard to do—to not leave a trail?"

"That is why I am often returning to go back over our path, to erase the signs of our passage over our Mother the Earth."

Suzette tilted her head to the side. "Fascinating," she said. "It does take quite a bit of time, however. Not that I am complaining. I am happy for the break. But I do worry that we may not catch them with ample time."

"I believe we will find them."

"I am glad to hear that."

They had ceased their travel for a moment, and were at present encamped beneath a giant oak tree, which sat in a glen protecting a small stream. Reaching into the pouch he wore over his shoulder, Black Lion protracted from it a breakfast of dried meat and chokecherries. Luckily, the stream would provide a drink of cool, refreshing water, making their breakfast complete.

"We could go on a little farther," he said, "while the light is still dim, but I think not. We will rest."

Though Suzette was so tired she could have gone to sleep right there, she still objected, saying, "I thought we would not stop at all."

"We must rest during the day."

"Rest?" she asked, even while she lifted drowsy eyes to meet his. "Rest when Irena's life is in danger?"

"We do not know that her life is in danger," he corrected. "We rest because you are tired." With that said, he reached for her hand and brought her fingers to his lips. "You are with child. Do not forget this."

"How could I possibly forget it?"

"Also," he said, "if we are to find your grandmother we must not be caught ourselves. Therefore, we will proceed only during the evening hours, when our chances of being seen are slim. During the day, since we must stop anyway, we will rest."

"Yes, yes, but—rest during the day?"

"*Hau,*" he said, "I think we will erect a shelter here, since there is good cover, as well as water for food and for bathing."

"Could I not simply lie down beneath this tree?" She yawned.

"And be easily found?" He grimaced. "I think not. Come, you can help me with this, if only a little, for I will need many sticks and pine branches."

She sighed. "Oh, very well, if I must, I must."

In the end, she did help him to erect a shelter. Made of earth, leaves, pine boughs, branches and grass, once Black Lion had "landscaped" the earth around it, it fit so well into the scheme of things, it did literally disappear into the environment around them.

But by the time it was finished, Suzette was so fatigued that as soon as her bed of pine branches was laid out within that neat little lean-to, Suzette collapsed upon it.

At least her overexertion did one thing: It made for a very peaceful sleep, indeed.

CHAPTER 19

They had been on the move for four days. Traveling through each night, sometimes walking, but more often creeping over the landscape, they stopped each day before dawn to make camp and to erect another temporary shelter. Often, Suzette noted that their lean-tos were built around rocks, although once it had been nestled into a cliff. Each shelter was then carefully "landscaped" so that the eye could barely discern it from the natural environment. Her bed was often soft, made of pine branches when they could find them. However, if none were to be located, her bed then consisted of the blanket that Black Lion carried with him at all times.

There were times of intimacy, however, for when they did lay down to rest, the spaces were small, and Black Lion's presence filled each cozy hideaway. Always Suzette was more than aware of him, fretting over the accidental touch, the chaste looks that passed between them, their whispered words to each other.

He usually sat not more than a few feet from her, and like a sentinel, he always faced toward the entrance.

When she lay down to sleep, it was his woodsy scent that clung to the blanket beneath her head. It teased her, made her wish for things she should not dare to want.

Alas, she was weakening toward him. She even suspected he was aware of this, as well. However, much to her surprise, nothing happened.

Also, he never lay by her to go to sleep, and he was rarely with her when she awakened. He was always on watch, and although she assumed he rested at some time or another, she had never seen him do it. When she awoke, he was often sitting in the same position he had chosen when they had retired.

In truth, she wondered about his earlier promise. If he meant to lure her into his arms, he was going about it in an awfully odd fashion. He didn't touch her, he didn't make overtures, despite the fact that she was required to bathe each morning with him on guard. He didn't talk to her of lovemaking or their marriage, not even a gentle tease about it.

Indeed, he couldn't have been more of a gentleman. Problem was, she was hoping he would do something, make some move toward her that might indicate he still desired her, even if she rejected him.

But he did nothing. He was polite, considerate, concerned over her welfare, never pushing her too hard or too long. A few days back she had been so tired that she couldn't go on, and he had carried her. But even then, he had acted like a polite stranger.

Had he forgotten the dare he had issued her?

Possibly. There was certainly enough reason to think so. However, there were several times when she had caught him off guard, had found him watching her, and at those times, there could be no mistake that there, within his gaze, had been admiration, perhaps even hunger.

But at such times as these, he would lower his glance or look away from her. Was something wrong?

At present, she was sitting on a large log as she watched him draw pine branches next to their shelter. She said, "Do I smell funny?"

He glanced at her as if she might have been speaking Greek. But all he said was, "You smell fine." He continued to set branches around their rock shelter.

"Is my figure already becoming too plump?"

"Plump?" he answered, not looking up from his work. "A pregnant woman is not plump, she is simply with child. It would be very hard on her child, if she did not grow to accommodate him."

"Then I am, aren't I? Is that what you're saying?"

He frowned, as if sensing that here was a dangerous topic for any man. But at least the conversation had one desired effect: He stopped his work to gaze at her.

After some deliberation, he said, "Are you finding the trail too hard for you?"

"No."

Again, frowning, he turned toward her. He said, "Then where is this conversation tending?"

She gave him an innocent look. "It's not *tending* anywhere. All I ask is for you to answer my question and tell me if you find me too . . . chubby."

He blew out a breath, and jerked his head slightly to the left. "You are not pudgy and you are not chubby. You are simply pregnant."

"Mr. Lion, you are talking all around this and not getting to the point."

"*Hiya*, what point?"

"I am trying to make the case that since I am becoming bigger, you do not find me to be so pretty."

To his credit, he looked taken aback. "Have I said anything to make you think this?"

"No, but you do not have to. Your actions speak for you."

"My actions? Have I not been considerate to you?"

"Yes, you have."

"And have I not been taking care of you, despite our journey?"

"Yes, you have done very well in that regard. It's only that . . ." She sighed. "I suppose the matter is irrelevant, so . . . please ignore it. Pretend I said nothing."

If she hadn't had his attention before, she certainly had it now. He took his measure of her . . . slowly. By this time, the two lines between his brows had cut deep grooves. However, he said not a word.

She glanced away from him.

At last, he commented, "Why would you think this of me?" And when she didn't answer, he went on to say, "Perhaps you should finish what you were saying."

"Oh, very well, if you must know," she said, sighing, "you seem to treat me as though I am as attractive as a sack of potatoes."

"But I—" He stopped, and a look of cognizance gradually came over his face. After a while, he said, completely deadpan, "Actually, I have always found potatoes quite appealing, and a sack of them would be almost more than any man could resist."

"Meaning that you think I am now ugly."

"Meaning that I find you beautiful . . . and appealing."

"Then why do you . . . are you not . . ."

"Why am I not making love to you at every chance I have?"

She gave him a sheepish glance. "Well, you did tell me that you intended to lure me to your . . . The truth is, I hardly feel lured."

"Indeed?"

"I fear it is true. You are very polite, very considerate of me, very . . ."

". . . understanding?" It was his turn to sigh. "You are trying to find and help your grandmother. I would aid you in your search, since your condition hardly makes this easy for you."

"Yes, but—"

"And there are other dangers here as well; animals, the countryside, scouts who are out looking for us. Do not doubt me, I have every intention of luring you to my sleeping robes, but I would do so at a safe distance from the white man's scouts."

"Oh."

He came down onto his knees before her, so that his face and hers were level, and he said, "Besides, I have seen how tired you are when we stop to rest. I would not add to your troubles."

"Oh. That's nice of you, but you still haven't answered my question . . ."

"Have I not?" he asked, picking up her hand, pressing it within his own. And without any further encouragement, he said, "Then let me be clear on this: I think you are the most beautiful woman of my acquaintance, and I am grateful every moment of every day that I had the presence of mind to propose to you the first moment I ever saw you. I intend to keep you as my wife. I always have."

She leaned in toward him, and he reached up to smooth the backs of his fingers over her cheek. He said, "You brighten my day."

"Indeed? Hmmmm . . ." she moaned, as he slid his fingers down over her neck. She shut her eyes, sighing again, and said, ". . . more . . ."

"More of what?" he asked, his voice low and husky. "More talking, or more of this?" His lips captured hers.

"I think I like . . . the last one . . ." she whispered, ". . . best."

Even before the words had left her mouth completely, Black Lion had raised up onto his knees and was folding her into a deeper embrace, when he said, "Then you forgive me for what Rabbit Leggings said?"

"No," she said, "but it does not matter right now. I seem to . . . need this."

"I, too," he agreed, nestling her head against his shoulder. "I, too."

He picked her up from where she sat on the log, and held her closely in his arms, much as a man might hold his bride. Carrying her to the shelter, he kicked back the pine branches that served as their doorway, and gently set her inside.

The lodge was small, it smelled of earth and pine and trees, and they would have barely been able to sit upright within it. Yet it was a haven. Fragrant boughs and his robe served as their bed, and as he set her upon its softness, he followed her down to the mat.

She didn't have time to think, for he immediately pressed his lips over hers, nudging her mouth open, so his tongue could dance with hers. He smelled of earth and wind and pure fresh air, and when she responded with everything in her, a growl escaped from his throat, the sound of it sending shivers of yearning over her skin.

Oh, to be closer to him, to feel his strength next to her. She pressed herself toward him, but it still wasn't enough. No matter how near she set herself to him, it didn't seem close enough. She moaned at the inadequacy, not certain what she could do to attain the intimacy she craved.

At last, a thought occurred to her, and she said, "I think we are both wearing too many clothes."

"Too many?" He frowned at her, and said, "Do you not recall what happened the last time you complained of my shirt and asked me to take it off?"

"Yes, I do remember," she answered without so much as a smile.

She noted the exact moment when realization dawned on him.

He said, "Ah," and in his haste to remove his shirt, he practically tore the thing off him, throwing it to the side.

Immediately her gaze was caught and held by the view of a very male, very muscular chest. How would his skin feel against her fingertips? she wondered. As she reached out to touch him, she noticed at once the differences in their skin texture and tones.

Hers was light against his. Too light, she thought. Indeed, at that moment, she believed his skin was the handsomer of the two by far.

His muscles were hard as she spread her fingertips over him, and she yearned to feel the texture of his chest against her own. Immediately, she sat up, and intent on making this a reality, she hugged him, nestling her head in the crook of his neck.

But it still wasn't as close as she had hoped, perhaps because she was fully clothed.

At once, she applied herself to the task of taking off her own clothes, and though she was daintier and slower at the act of stripping than he had been, the buttons on her jacket came undone easily, and she shrugged out of it. However, there were layers of other clothing beneath.

He was frowning at them. "Why do you wear so many garments?" he asked.

"'Tis the style, I fear. But the clothes do keep a body warm."

"Perhaps. Yet, so many of them hinder free movement."

"And are a bother to remove, as well." She smiled up at him.

He grinned back at her. "It is true, I think."

Together they set to work over the buttons of her blouse, and she thought she had never seen a more delighted look come to a man's face, when he discovered that she had set out on this trip without a corset.

"It was just too much of a bother," she explained.

"I am glad of that bother," he responded back, as he slid the straps of her chemise down over her arms and off. At once, the undergarment dropped to her waist, revealing her femininity to his hungry gaze.

And he did admire her.

After a moment, he said, "You realize that if we go farther than this, neither one of us will be able to stop, until . . ."

She didn't comment.

He continued, "I say this as a warning, so that if you object to what we do, you should tell me while I still have the will to stop."

"I appreciate that," she said. "And I should stop, but . . ."

He lifted an eyebrow. "But?"

"I . . . want you."

His reaction to her simple statement was a groan—a sound much too sensuous for her peace of mind. He lay her back against their fragrant pine mat and set to work kneading her soft and exposed feminine mounds, his lips following where his hands led. First he adored one breast with kiss upon kiss, then the other. Then, while his lips paid tribute to her, his fingers were already working over the buttons on her trousers.

At last it was done and he came up over her to press another hot, wet kiss against her lips. She gloried in his fresh taste, musky and masculine, and in response she surged upward, determined to feel as much of his skin against her as she could. He acquiesced with no protest, and as soon as his flesh met hers, her pulse kicked into double time. So stirred was she by him, she forgot to think.

Back and forth, up and down, chest to chest, they reveled against each other, dancing to a rhythm of their own. He growled softly in her ear, saying, "It feels so good."

"Hmmmm," she mumbled, unable to utter anything intelligently.

"Are you ready for more?"

"Please," she begged.

Coming up onto his knees at her side, he reached down to urge her trousers and pantalettes down over her thighs, her calves, her feet. And while the cooler air assailed the lower part of her body, she was dismayed to see that he still wore breechcloth and leggings.

"You are almost fully clothed," she commented.

"*Hau*, that I am. Soon, I will lay naked with you, but for now, I would admire you."

And admire he did. His gaze touched her everywhere. "You are a beautiful sight for any one man," he said, and reaching out for her hand, he held it within both of his own, kissing each and every one of her fingers. Briefly, he shut his eyes, rubbing her fingers against his cheek. Then he added aloud, "*Canto'kignaka.*"

She smiled. "What did you say?"

He hesitated, and his response was not the one she expected, for she had anticipated that he would do no more than translate. However, he sighed. "My words mean that I have placed you in my heart," he replied. "Perhaps it is too soon for me to tell you this, but I fear that . . . I love you."

Her smile faded, even as her gaze clung to his. "You love me?"

He nodded. "Though I am uncertain that now is the right time to tell you, mayhap it is best that you know."

But she was still caught up in the wonder of his confession, and she said again, "You love me?"

"*Hau*," he said. "In truth, I may have loved you from the first moment I ever saw you. I cannot be certain of that, but it is possible. What I do know with surety is that I love you now . . . and no matter what happens to me or to us, once I give my love, it is forever."

"I . . . I . . ." she stammered, knowing she should say something back to him. But what? So unexpected was his declaration, she was momentarily stunned. In due time, she said, "What do you mean by no matter what happens? You don't expect anything bad to happen to you, do you?"

"A man never knows," he answered, "and I am on a quest with an enemy I little understand and little know."

"Yes," she said, "your quest with . . . the one you call the Thunderer."

"*Hau, hau.*"

"Well, I have this to say to that. You had better not let anything happen to you. I have only just found you."

He grinned at her. "Does that mean that you like me a little?"

"I suspect it may be true," she agreed, "since here I am, naked before you."

"So you are." He smiled at her devilishly. "It is good that you remind me of this."

She laughed slightly. Then, coming up into a seated position, she threw her arms around his neck and hugged him. Simply hugged him.

"I am not certain what I feel," she told him honestly.

"I desire your lovemaking very much, but I still hesitate to trust you. However, I can say that I have admired you from afar, I wish for your touch, I melt when you look at me and I get excited at the mere mention of your name."

His grin became more pronounced. "It is so?"

"Indeed."

"I am glad to hear it," he whispered against her ear, and he nudged her back onto their mat. He then began to kiss her there, behind her ear, then over to her neck, to her cheek, to her lips, back down to her neck, to her chest, to each breast. She fidgeted beneath his ministrations, and closing her eyes, she offered herself to him as though she were a banquet.

He seemed only too willing to relish her, and his fingers slid reverently over her breasts, and his kisses ranged ever lower . . . down to her stomach, her naval. On her own, her legs parted in invitation, and he accepted. With the fingers of one hand he aroused her, and with every touch her nerve endings erupted, as though set afire.

She squirmed beneath him, seeking the pleasure she knew he could give her. So when he at last found her most secret place, there between her legs, she sighed in relief.

Then he was taking her on an erotic journey, his tongue and his lips providing her with the means. Fiery and wet, his kisses made love to her.

"Spread your legs farther," he whispered.

She did so at once.

An exquisite pleasure was building up within her. Slowly at first, it raged within her, and then with more and more impetus it spread, until she was lost to his expertise. She twisted beneath him, if only to experience the feeling more fully. And then it happened, and she was tripping over the edge of an emotional and highly charged precipice. As pleasure burst free within her, another very intimate discovery exploded within her thoughts.

She loved this man. She loved him dearly. How this had happened, she wasn't quite certain. Yet, she could not deny it. Nor did she even wish to. She simply loved him.

Should she tell him? Should she confess her heart's deepest secrets?

No, she decided. Not yet. For now, it was enough that he was here with her. She would savor the moment, for in truth, she was uncertain if this might be all she would ever have of him . . .

"It seems to me," said the beautiful woman of his dreams, her voice as soft as a whisper, "that thus far our lovemaking has been a very one-sided affair. And unless you have once again taken matters into your own hands . . ."

He laughed, not knowing if she might share in his joke. Somehow, however, he thought not. In his opinion, she might be too innocent to know that her words could be taken literally.

She said, "What is funny?"

Black Lion came up onto his forearms over her, and he grinned up at this woman, to whom he had given his heart so thoroughly. "At some later time," he said, "I will tell you about the workings of a man, and how a man might sometimes literally take matters into his own hands."

Though she was too innocent to understand his meaning, she smiled up at him.

"But tell me, are you suggesting what I think you are?" he asked, and if his voice were a little seductive, he could not very well be blamed for it. While he had brought her to the peak of her pleasure, he had yet to meet his.

"Yes," she said, "I am." She glanced down at him. "I believe, however, that you still have on too many clothes for where my thoughts tend."

He glanced downward. "So I do," he agreed, and as he sat up, he began to tug at the strings that held his breechcloth and leggings in place. He said, "This is, indeed, a lucky day for me."

Her laugh was soft, feminine, completely sensual, and he felt himself stir to life more vigorously than ever.

At last he had untied the strings that held up his breechcloth and leggings, and the soft buckskin fell gently onto the blanket of their mat.

He then came down to lay over her, and using his forearms, he kept himself from leaning into her.

She glanced down at him, then quickly back up at him, and with eyes slightly rounded, she said, "I know I said this once before, but . . . you are big."

This time he did laugh. "Only at times like this," he said. "Come, it might be easier for you if I were to lie down by your side."

She nodded, and she scooted over to make room for him. She said, "May I . . . may I touch . . . you . . . there?"

Ah, how he enjoyed this. He said, "It is my hope that you will."

"Oh."

His grin was one of complete happiness, as he brought his weight to the side of her, aware that he was finding more and more reason to love this woman.

Then she touched him, and his seed practically burst from him.

"Should I kiss you like you have done to me?"

"I would be most honored."

She didn't appear to need further inducement, for she began to make love to him at once, running her fingertips over his face, his neck, down to his chest. He groaned with appreciation, pleased to observe that the sounds he made seemed to give her confidence.

Onward and downward she proceeded. Now it was his turn to squirm, for even this simple action nearly drove him over the edge.

But then she was scooting lower, her breasts touching him in so many intimate places. He sucked in his breath, hoping for control. And then she touched him there, first with her fingers, then with her tongue. He moaned, jerking upward involuntarily.

Oh, how he would love nothing more than to bury himself into the soft warmth that was hers. But of course, given her condition, he could not.

Odd, how, no sooner had the thought occurred to him, than she was taking the whole of him into her mouth, running her tongue gently up and down his shaft. At that moment, he forgot all about burying himself within her. This was quite enough.

In fact . . . all at once, he pulled himself out of her mouth and emptied his seed against her abdomen.

His spirit soared, for at that moment, he realized a very deep secret. Only a woman genuinely in love with a man would perform such a duty.

She loved him.

She didn't have to tell him, she might never tell him. It was enough to simply know. And like a crazy man, he couldn't keep himself from smiling.

"Hmmmm," he said, as he rolled to her side, keeping her well within his arms. "Hmmmm," he said again, "I have only this to say to you, my wife. *Cante' kiyusa.*"

"Oh? What does that mean?"

"It means that for good or for ill, I hold you in my heart. I give you my love, and I hope that in the future I will earn yours."

She didn't respond, but then, he hadn't expected her to.

CHAPTER 20

Lightning crashed above her, around her, the acrid scent lending the air the sickening odor of poisonous gas. She stood defenseless in the middle of the prairie. Thunder sounded from all directions. It cracked the eardrums, it tested one's courage, and she cowered before its power. A man—or was he a god, for he was half blue, half gray—stepped toward her.

He was laughing. "I will kill him," said the god.

"No!"

The god laughed. "I have bested better than he."

"No!" she cried again.

"Go back from whence you came. You are not wanted here; you do not belong here."

Lifting her chin, she said, "I belong with my husband. I always will. It is you who is out of place. Go!"

"I belong everywhere," *said the god,* "for I am the Thunderer."

She could think of nothing to retaliate, since this was obviously the truth; she did the only thing she could. She yelled out, "Why do you wish me to go?"

The Thunderer said simply, "Because you are a danger to me."

"I? I?" she asked again. "How can I be a danger to you? You, who are a god?"

The Thunderer laughed. "You will have to discover that for yourself. Or perhaps I should kill you, first."

He lifted his hand to do so . . .

Suzette gasped and sat up as though shot from a gun. She was alone.

Where was Black Lion? Was he all right? Was he in danger?

Sunlight streamed into their shelter from between the cracks in the branches. Her pulse was racing, and she inhaled pine-scented air on a deep breath, calming herself.

Glancing around the environment, she took stock of where she was. She was not out in the open, she was not confronting the Thunderer, she was in a shelter. There was no storm here, and no reason to be concerned.

The dream had seemed very real. *But it's only a dream*, she told herself.

Still, her emotions were running rampant, urging her to do something—to leave here to find Black Lion, if only to ease her mind that he was all right . . .

As if she had conjured him up by her thoughts, Black Lion appeared at the entrance of their shelter, squeezing in through the tight entryway. Seeing her sitting up, and alert, he said, *"Hau,* it is good that you are awake, for this day is a pretty one and . . ." He frowned at her. "Is something wrong?"

She sighed. "No, nothing is wrong. It is only that I am happy to see you."

"Happy?" His look at her was doubtful.

"Yes, I am happy," she defended, then she sighed. "But I am hungry. Have you any pemmican or water or something else to eat?"

He nodded and reached for the food, which he always kept in a rawhide bag. He gave her a handful, a prize that she gladly accepted.

"Hmmm, this is good. Did you make this?"

"*Hiya*, no. Rabbit Leggings made it."

"Ah, Rabbit Leggings, again."

"She is the wife of my friend, my *kola*, Two Bears."

"Two Bears? But I thought that *you* were Two Bears. Are you not also known by this name?"

"So I am, when I am with the Wild West Show. But I am known there as Two Bears only because I took his place with the show. It was Two Bears who was under contract there, not I."

"Indeed?"

"My friend was too ill to make the journey with the show over the water. He asked me to go in his place and pretend to be he. It is the only reason I have been allowed to remain with the show. People think I am Two Bears, and that I am married. And those who are from my tribe, the Hunkpapa Lakota, and know the truth keep their silence."

"Indeed," she repeated, though she was certain her look at him was most likely one of caution. She continued, "Then what you are saying is that Rabbit Leggings is married to Two Bears, but that person is not you?"

"*Hau. Hau.*"

"And you expect me to believe this?"

"I do."

She exhaled slowly, cleared her brow and said, "I do not understand what magic it is that you hold over me, but I am inclined to believe you. Come, sit here beside me. I have had a bad dream, and I think I should tell you it, since you were a part of it."

He did as she asked, and having seated himself beside her, he offered her more pemmican. Then he said, "I will listen to this dream, for dreams can be *wakan*, holy."

"Truly?"

He nodded. "It is rare, however, that a woman would have a dream that is *wakan*, though it does happen occasionally."

"Then it is only for the men of your tribe to experience this?"

"*Hau, hau.* This is so, but perhaps it is only so because a woman rarely seeks to dream, whereas a man must."

"He must?"

"*Hau.* Since men go to war and their lives are often at stake, a man will seek to have an advantage over his enemies. He will sacrifice and attend to ritual in order to experience a sacred dream, for these tell him how to have power over his enemies. Most often an animal or some other form of life will take pity on the one who has sacrificed so much, and will offer the power of his species to the man."

"Then a god, himself, rarely speaks to one who is having a dream?"

"Again, it is rare, but it does happen. Have you had a spirit dream?"

"I . . . I cannot tell, though I seriously question it. Without doubt I have had many a bad dream in my time, and I am certain that is all this is. Still, it involved you, and I was afraid, and—"

"Eat first," he said, interrupting her. "If it is a spirit dream that you have had, let us honor it in the right way and speak of it in a council. To do otherwise could cause the dream to lose its power, or to recoil upon you."

"But it is not for myself that I worry."

"I understand," he said, "but let us say no more about it until we have eaten."

She swallowed the pemmican he offered, and asked, "Where have you been?"

"I have been backtracking to see if we are being followed."

"And are we?"

"We are."

"Pray, that is bad news! I would have thought they would have given up after a few days."

"Perhaps most men might. But I think it is the Long-haired Show Man, himself, who follows us, and he is a scout of some merit. Perhaps he, too, favored your grandmother."

"I would like to think so, but it is a well-known fact that Mr. Cody has a fancy for opera singers as a rule. Perhaps he objects to losing two at the same time."

"Maybe this is so," said Black Lion, "but this does not alter the fact that he is following us, and I must keep his progress well within my sights."

"Oh, yes, of course," she said, then taking another bite of jerky, she asked, "Did you sleep well?"

He didn't answer; rather, he tore off a bit of jerky with his teeth.

She frowned at him. "You do sleep, do you not?"

"I rest," he said, taking hold of another piece of dried meat.

"Yes, so you have said, but there is a difference between resting and actual sleep. Do you *sleep*?" she persisted.

He didn't answer at once. Instead, he continued chewing over his meal as though it were particularly tough. At last, however, he said, "Once we are away from the danger that the Long-haired Show Man presents, I will sleep more."

"In other words," she said, "you do not."

He didn't answer.

"Do you stay with me, remaining awake, while I slumber, then?"

"Sometimes I do," he answered after a time. "Other times I backtrack to erase our trail and to spy on the men tracking us. There are four of them. Soon, I hope that they will give up their search."

"I, too. And when that happens?"

He glanced up at her, sending her a most endearing leer. "Then we might engage in more of this morning's pleasantries."

As his glance raked over her, she was suddenly reminded that she was still quite naked.

He fingered the blanket that she was using to cover herself, pushing it down her arms. He said, "Perhaps before our council, there is time for another matter of importance. And since the white man's scouts are a good distance from us . . . Have you had enough to eat?"

She smiled. "Of food," she replied, raising her gaze up to meet his.

He considered her look momentarily, then he stole a kiss from her upturned lips. "But," he whispered against her mouth, "you are hungry for something else?"

"I think you must be able to see my thoughts."

He grinned at her, as he pulled the blanket from around her completely, and setting it beneath her, urged her back onto it. "Or perhaps," he said, "you see mine."

Whatever was the truth of the matter, it was of little concern to either of them, since it appeared that they were both hungry for the same thing, Truth to tell, it was several hours before they were anywhere near ready to attend to the council.

Physically satiated, and lying with his wife in his arms, Black Lion's glance danced off the sunlight pouring through the cracks in their ceiling. His spirits soared, and he realized that he had never felt such joy.

Without doubt, the carnal release was satisfying, but when such delight was coupled with the fact of love, the fulfillment turned from mundane to extraordinary, unlike anything he had ever known.

Love had to be the cause of such joy. Like an exquisite piece of music, love made the erotic as delicate and flawless as a fine-tuned melody. Never, he thought, had he loved a person more.

Yet, he wondered if the two of them could make a happy life together. There were so many circumstances against them: culture, mind-set, daily ritual, not to mention the prejudice that would surround them always. Could they find happiness in such an environment?

Glancing at her now, he watched her sleep, memorizing the look of her dark eyelashes against the dainty flush of her skin, noticing as well the rhythmic rise and fall of her breast. Her long, dark hair was spread out over his arm, and her full lips begged for a kiss, but he dared not partake. His duty was to scout and to protect, and he still had much work to do this day. If they were to hold a council, he must ensure that the white men were still a full day's journey away.

With one more loving look at her, he left their shelter to attend to his duty.

* * *

It was late afternoon when Black Lion returned to their tiny haven. Expecting to find his wife asleep, he was pleasantly surprised to discover that she was awake and dressed. He smiled at her, slid into their dwarfish housing, and said, "I am happy to see you."

She returned his greeting in much the same manner, then said, "I have been worried about you. I assume you went to scout on those men who are following us?"

"I did."

"And are we still at a safe distance?"

"We are," he affirmed, as he crawled toward her, taking a position next to her. "And now we have some leisure, I think, to hold that council, unless you object."

When she indicated that she had no disagreement, he produced his pipe from within the parchment bag that he carried, and he said, "Is this your first Indian council?"

"It is."

"*Waste.* Then let me explain the ritual, so that you do not wonder about some of the ceremonies. First, the Red Man does not hold council without the pipe, for this is the way that we communicate with the Great Spirit."

When she nodded, Black Lion continued, saying, "Once the pipe is lit, we ask that the Divine Ones listen to our words, and so we offer the sacred smoke to the Sky, to the Earth, to the Four Winds and to the Great Spirit, hoping that each one in their turn will hear our words. We use *piiksiistsimaan.* This is the Blackfeet word for the sacred substance that we smoke. It is not tobacco as the white man raises it, but rather a mixture of tobacco with bearberry, red-willow bark and the leaves of the sumac. It is a sacred substance used only in ceremony."

Again, she nodded.

"Are you ready to begin?"

"Yes," she said, "I am."

"*Waste*," he responded, then he lit the sacred mixture in the red-stoned pipe. Once the proper respect was shown to the sacredness of their council, he took several puffs from the pipe. Then he offered the pipe to Suzette.

Suzette accepted the sacred article from him. "You want me to smoke?"

He nodded. "*Hau*. You . . . smoke . . ."

She did as he instructed, coughing a little with the first puff. He gazed at her with some concern, but mostly with admiration, for it was endearing to watch her, even though it was obvious that this was her first smoke.

But she said not a word. Instead, she returned the pipe to him.

Accepting it back from her, Black Lion began their council, and he repeated, "We smoke the sacred tobacco, offering our prayers to the Creator and to our Mother the Earth so that They may hear what we say. In accepting the pipe, you should know that one commits himself to a sacred oath, one that promises that what is said in this council is the truth, and no alteration. Once the pipe is smoked, no lies must ever fill the air where a council is held, for one is speaking before the Creator, and to lie would be as to curse oneself. Do you understand?"

Suzette nodded.

"*Waste*," he said. "It is good."

Thus speaking, Black Lion went on to say, "Now is the time for us to discuss your dream. It might be a sacred dream or it could be an ordinary one. Let us determine which it is. Can you tell me of it?"

"Yes," said Suzette. "But first, Black Lion, I am urged to tell you that I fear that you are in danger."

"That is true," he said, nodding. "I am in danger. We are in a country that is hostile to any Indian."

"No," she said, "I do not fear that you are in jeopardy from Buffalo Bill, his scouts or other white people. Rather, if my dream is to be considered, I believe you could be in peril from a mystical being, a god."

"The Thunderer?"

She nodded.

This surprised him, though he tried to keep the look of astonishment hidden from her. As he had said to her before, it was rare enough for a woman to dream as the men did. But to dream of the Thunderer . . .

If this were true, he thought, hers was no ordinary dream. Such a vision was also dangerous . . . for its beholder, since to dream of the Thunderer was to become a *Heyoka*, a backward person.

A *Heyoka* did everything topsy-turvy; he washed in sand, was dirtied by water, spoke the opposite of what he meant. He even walked backward. Indeed, to an Indian heart, to dream of the Thunderer was an occurence no man dare ignore, lest he be struck dead.

But Black Lion said none of his thoughts to her. After all, maybe he jumped ahead of himself. Perhaps it had been no more than a simple nightmare.

He nodded toward her, and said, "Go on, tell me of this vision."

"It was frightening at first," she began, "for there was lightning striking all around me . . ."

"But it did not touch you?"

"No. Instead, the Thunderer confronted me in a human form. That is, he looked as men look, but his skin was black and gray. And he threatened you. He told me that he was going to kill you, and he told me to leave here."

"The Thunderer said that? He told you to leave here?"

"Yes."

"And did you say anything back to him?"

"I did. I said that it was my place to stay here with my husband, and that I belonged here, that I would always belong here. I am afraid that what I said angered him."

Black Lion nodded, and though he was pleased that she desired to stay with him, he also knew he could not allow her to remain here if this truly was a sacred dream. To hold a vision of the Thunderer was the most sacred of all dreams, but it also carried the most penalties. Sudden death was one of them.

After due consideration, he said, "I am honored that you would seek to remain here with me, and that you would tell the Thunder Being this."

"Yes," she said. "In truth, it came as a surprise to me, too."

"And yet, I would urge you to do as the Thunderer has said. Though I am not a medicine man, I do know that to dream of the Thunderer is filled with danger."

She frowned. "Why do you say that?"

"Because it is true."

"Is it? I'm not certain I believe that. Besides, perhaps it was not really a dream," she said.

"Not a dream?"

"What I mean to say is that the dream was so real that when I awoke, I thought he had truly been there. I know it's nonsense, but . . ."

"All things are possible," interrupted Black Lion. "You may have met him in this world—perhaps you met spirit to spirit."

"Perhaps. But I don't believe in such things."

Black Lion nodded. "You do not have to believe in such things for them to happen. Therefore, I think it wise not to take chances. You should leave this country, as he told you to do. If you do not, this dream could cause your death. You could be struck down by lightning."

She looked as though the thought might have impressed itself upon her, because she remained silent for several moments. But then she said, "Even if I did believe, I cannot leave here. I told him that I would not, therefore I cannot."

"But—"

"Please understand, it is not that I am being fearless or obstinate. It is that I truly cannot go."

"You must—"

"Shhh. There is more," she interrupted. "He means to kill you, he told me so. And for some reason I cannot fathom, he is afraid of *me*."

Black Lion remained silent. What could he say, when words failed him? The Thunderer? Afraid of her?

"Besides," she continued, "let's pretend for a moment that you are right, and that the Thunderer does exist. I doubt seriously that he is demanding that I leave here for my own good. He was greatly antagonistic to me, and I fear it would be unwise of me to follow the orders of someone with such animosity."

Black Lion shook his head. "But—"

"There's also something else. He said that I was a danger to him. How can *I* be a danger to him, unless . . . While you were gone, I thought much about this, and I believe that my danger to him is that somehow I might be able to help you free your people. And if this is so, how could I, in all conscience, leave?"

Black Lion frowned, but he remained silent. In truth, he was afraid to speak, for he feared that his voice might fail him. Did she realize what she was saying? Did she know that she was aligning herself with him, with his people, and that to do so was dangerous?

After a time, he said, "It is good of you to think of this, but they are not your people. And even if they were, you are not bound to help them."

"Am I not?" she countered. "Are you not my friend? Are you not my husband? Have you not helped me when no one else could or would? If I were to leave, would it not be an act of cowardice? I would be deserting someone in a time of need, someone who has shown me nothing but kindness."

He swallowed, but otherwise he remained silent.

"No," she went on to say, "I will stay. I must stay. For you, for Irena, for my child."

His voice continued to plague him, but after a long pause, he was finally able to say, "Think wisely, my wife. It is for your child that you must go."

"I am uncertain I agree," she said. "If I walk away from you, when I could stay and help, how could I ever think well of myself? To seek my own safety when someone dear to me is in danger? How could I live with myself?"

"But—"

"And if I do not think well of myself," she continued, "how could I raise my child to value a life of honor and integrity, when clearly, I have not?"

Black Lion swallowed, hard. An intense silence filled their tiny shelter. When at last he did speak, he said, "Courage can take many forms, and a man sometimes forgets that a woman, too, can show great fortitude. Therefore, much as I disagree with you, I must honor you, for it is not my place to spurn an act of valor. So I will honor your decision. But be aware that if you stay here, I will guard you more closely than I have ever done in the past, because if something happened to you, I would not want to live in this world. Without you, my heart would be heavy. Know that if one of us must die, it will be me."

"No one is going to die," she said. Then, with more conviction, "No one. In my dream, when I was talking back to the Thunderer, I little understood why I was holding my ground and refusing to do as he asked. But now I think I know. It is because I love you, and if I can help you, I will."

She loved him. She had actually said it. She loved him.

Despite the solemnness of their conversation, and the danger that now hung over them, she had declared her love, and a feeling of utter happiness surged through him.

Picking up her hand, Black Lion kissed each one of her fingers, before he said, "And I love you."

"Do you?" She raised an eyebrow, as though she might doubt the truth of his words.

"I do."

She smiled at him happily, but then went on to say, "I have one more question. Why do you think," she asked, "that the Thunderer believes I am a danger to him? Would he only be trying to confuse me, or is there a reason?"

"*Hau*, there is a reason, I think," said Black Lion. "It is my opinion that he believes you know the song."

"The song? What song?"

"Perhaps I should have confided this to you before now, but since we are speaking openly, let me confess the deepest secret of my soul. In order to end the curse for my people, I seek a sacred song."

"Indeed? A sacred song? Yes, yes, I remember that once when you sang me a song the night we wed . . ." She cleared her throat. "Is that the same one?"

"*Hiya*, no, it is not. I can never sing *the* sacred song until it is presented to me by another, at which time I must raise my voice, and chant along with that person, and not omit a word, or make a mistake. If I can do this, the song itself will pierce through the hatred that the Thunderer bears for myself and my people. The song will melt the barriers between us, and place love in the Thunderer's heart. If I can find this song, it will save my people."

His words were solemn, yet he smiled ever so slightly at her. "My spirit protector has shown me this song. It is a white man's melody. Yet, besides its theme and words, I know nothing of it."

"A white man's song? . . . Well, now I see the danger that I present to your enemy, for I know many white man songs."

"I am certain that you do, and, in truth, it has been a hope of mine that either you or your grandmother might sing the sacred melody at some occasion when I am in your presence, for I will recognize it at once."

"But why wait for us to originate it? If you could hum a few bars, I could—"

"I cannot do that. Until the time the song is presented to me, to sing the melody to anyone who may not know it would end my chance to help my people forever. And though you might remember many songs, if you do not have knowledge of this particular one . . ."

"I understand." A look of cognizance came over her gradually. "Excuse me for asking again, but it is definitely a white man's song?"

"It is."

"Is there any reason to keep me from singing as we travel?"

"*Hiya*, there is none, except our safety."

"Then perhaps I will start serenading you a little more often."

"*Waste*," he said. "That would indeed be good."

They shared a quiet smile, and shortly thereafter, Black Lion ended their counsel. He would have said more, but he didn't know how to voice his fears.

And he was afraid for her. But all he could do at this

moment was wait, and watch and try to protect. Though she may not believe there was any danger, he knew differently.

At least, he thought, they had settled one matter between them: They loved each other, and this was, indeed, more valuable to him than even his own life.

CHAPTER 21

Though Suzette longed to sing as often as possible, Black Lion would not allow her to hum, croon or even speak until it was safe to do so. These times of safety were rare, but usually ocurred in the early morning, when they were settling down to rest.

However, once she did start singing, Black Lion listened to her intently. Oftentimes, her melodies had the effect of lulling him to sleep, a circumstance she favored. But alas, as soon as she stopped serenading him, he usually awakened.

Before too long, however, her worries increased. Prior to the onset of this journey, she had considered her musical repertoire vast, but she was slowly exhausting her mental library.

Already she had sung all the arias that she knew by Wagner, Mozart and Offenbach, as well as a few pieces by the more contemporary composers. Was it possible that she might soon run through the works that she knew by heart? Worse, what if the sacred song were one that she didn't know?

That thought led to another concern. What if she made a mistake and left out a word or note? Hadn't Black Lion made it clear that the song must be sung without fault?

Indeed, it was one thing to perform music when the chance of error held no penalty. It was quite another to sing when the stakes were so high. Could she do it?

She had once thought to voice her considerations to Black Lion, but she had hesitated too long. In truth, he seemed so happy in the knowledge that she was trying to help, that she hated to disappoint him. And as is so often the case, the more she could have spoken out, but remained silent, the more difficult a thing it was to do. As it was, her confidence now lagged.

Perhaps Irena could help. Indeed, Suzette's grandmother was much more experienced than she was in these kinds of things. Perhaps if Suzette and Black Lion could overtake White Claw and Irena this terrible burden would be lifted off of her shoulders.

On this thought, Suzette said, "Do you suppose we might catch up to Irena and White Claw before it is too late?"

At present, they had stopped to rest and nourish themselves with a supper of dried meat and water. Black Lion had lit a small fire for warmth, but it did little good. It was evening, it was cold, and the wind chilled her to the bone. Black Lion had scooped out a place for them in the center of some scrub bushes, but it was still necessary for them to sit close together, for the extra body heat as well as for the simple pleasure of being close.

She rubbed her hands together, blowing on them from time to time—trying to bring life back to the their stiffness. Her toes complained of the cold, her face felt permanently frozen, and though Black Lion usually rubbed her hands and feet when they stopped for a rest, Suzette was beginning to wonder if she would ever be warm again.

At last, Black Lion spoke, saying, "I think our chances are good that we will find them before there is the danger of White Claw taking Irena to the Clan—if, indeed, there is any danger in him doing so. He and your grandmother are at best a day ahead of us, and they are traveling slowly."

She sighed. "I am glad to hear it. I have been thinking lately. It seems to me that Irena could help. She knows more arias than I do. If you will let me take her into our trust, I think that . . ."

Black Lion was nodding. He said, "Perhaps we will do this when we find them."

He offered Suzette a piece of jerky and she accepted it. "Good," she said. "How long have we been on the trail now?"

"Six days," he said.

"Six days. Can that possibly be true? It feels to me as if it has been a lifetime."

He said nothing to this, though he scooted closer to her, bringing with him more of his warmth.

After a moment, she asked, "Have you thought that we might freeze?"

"I will not let you freeze."

"Can you be that certain of it?"

He bobbed his head up and down. "*Hau*. I have survived winters that are colder than this."

"I wish I could be so certain." She leaned in toward him, placing her cold hands on his warm chest, and bless him, he didn't complain. "Have you noticed how dark it is tonight?"

"I have," he replied. "It is because there is no moon to guide us."

"Ah," she agreed, "and no stars." She gestured toward the sky.

"*Hau*," he said, "no stars. There is cloud cover."

She placed her head against his shoulder and they fell into a comfortable silence.

For the first time since they had set up their camp, Suzette noticed how quiet the world was around them. Perhaps it was because there was snow on the ground that muffled all sound, or perhaps on moonless nights such as this, no predators roamed the Plains.

"Do you know," she continued after a moment, "I fear that my bicycling outfit will never be the same. Do you see?" She held up a hand. "There are tears all along my elbows, all the way to the shoulder of my jacket, and my knees—"

Crash!

Lightning struck suddenly, frighteningly, and so loudly that Suzette jumped farther into Black Lion's arms. Involuntarily, she screamed.

"Shhh," he soothed.

"Black Lion, what is this?" she asked, whispering and trembling at the same time. "This is the dead of winter. How can there be a lightning storm?"

"This is no storm," he replied with certainty. Then, through gritted teeth, he added, "It is my enemy."

"The Thunderer?"

"The same."

"But . . ." How could she explain that even though she had dreamed of the Thunder Being, even though she and Black Lion had talked through her uncertainty, she still did not completely believe his story of vengeful gods and ancient curses?

But, what if she were wrong? What if the Thunderer did exist?

"Do you think he has come for me?" she asked. "Is it

because I have failed to do as he demanded?" She threw her arms around Black Lion's neck and hugged him with all her might.

"Do not worry," he soothed, though there was anger in his voice. "If the Thunderer had it in his mind to come for you, you would not now be telling me of it. Now, shh, quiet." He placed his finger over her lips.

Suzette obeyed, though she little understood why. If the Thunderer were a god, and if he knew they were here, why mask their presence?

Another strike of lightning, as close to them as the last had been, wiped out further thought and had her cowering into Black Lion's embrace. He petted her hair in response, as though to ease her fears. Then he whispered in her ear, "I will go and meet this enemy of mine."

"No!" She practically spit out the word.

"I must. You know I must."

"But it may not be the Thunderer. It may simply be an act of nature."

He just smiled at her.

"If you go," she said, "then I will come with you."

"You will not come with me. You will stay here."

"But if he is real, and if he is here because of me . . ."

"He is here because I am here, not because of you or anything you have done."

"But I . . . I . . ."

"You know that this is true. You must stay here. I will meet him, but do not fear for me too much. If he meant to kill me, he would have done so already. I think his intention is only to taunt me."

Suzette backed up from within Black Lion's arms, putting a few inches between them.

"Please stay here . . . stay hidden . . ."

"I cannot."

"Then stay alive. Stay alive. That's all I ask." Another crash sounded around them, this one leaving a crackling noise behind it, as though it had lit a fire. And though Suzette would have gladly crawled back into Black Lion's arms at that moment, she knew she couldn't.

For a moment, they stared at one another. Then Black Lion set her away from him, took her head into his hands, and while pressing his forehead against hers, he said, "No matter what happens. Stay here. Hide. Do not follow me. Do you promise?"

"Must I?"

"You must. If I am to confront my enemy, and keep my wits about me, I cannot worry about you."

"Very well. I will stay here."

He nodded, then said, "I will always love you." And springing up to his feet, he was gone.

Within moments, she heard Black Lion striding across the clearing, to the spot where the lightning had last crashed. He came to a position, stopped, and she heard him say, "I am here."

Suzette watched as Black Lion raised his arms into the air, heard him say, "If you wish to speak to me, Thunder Being, I dare you to face me, man-to-man."

Suzette could hear a rumble in the skies, then a sound much like laughter rang out.

No sooner had it started than another crash of lightning hit the ground, causing the mud, snow and dirt to fly in all directions. Suzette cowered within the bushes, witnessing at the same time that Black Lion jumped involuntarily. But he did not retreat. Instead, regaining his balance, he paced forward, toward the spot where the ground had been ripped apart.

"Are you afraid to meet me?" he challenged, while she listened and wondered what she could do. "Are you afraid to confront me with nothing more than human prowess? It is well known that a god can kill a man, for it takes no courage. But can a god—as a man—kill another man? I dare you to discover this, my enemy. Meet me face-to-face, and we will see who is the better."

Was he crazy?

More laughter, this time terrible and loud, rang out through the wintry air, and she forgot whatever else she had been thinking, for it was the same voice that had visited her in her dreams—and the Thunderer was saying, "You are puny, human. I could kill you in an instant."

"We all know that you could. Yet it would take no valor and be without honor," countered Black Lion. "But come, meet me one against one, and we shall see who is the better," he dared. "Come and meet me."

Then it happened. Gray clouds dropped to the ground, while miniature whirlwinds spun fast and furiously, without advancing anywhere. And then, from within those whirlwinds, a man stepped forward.

Suzette pinched herself to be sure she was awake. The Thunderer's image was exactly as she remembered it to be. He was a man, yet not. His coloring was, as she had noted from her dream, blue and gray, like those of the angry clouds from which he came.

The Thunderer was pacing toward Black Lion, and Black Lion was speaking to him, saying, "Why do you hate us so much? Have we not paid enough for our past misdeed?"

"*Never!*" cried the Thunderer. "Those who have gone before you have been clever of late, I admit; they are free and have freed the bands of their clans, while my children, who committed no wrong in any of this, are dead. Yours is the last of the Clan still entrapped. Know this. It is my intention to keep you entrapped forever."

"Ah, and now we know. But," reasoned Black Lion, "as the wise ones have said, all things must come to an end, even curses and your hatred. Look at you! How can you live with such animosity? How can you bear it? No, your children would not have wished this for you, I think."

"Would they not?" challenged the Thunderer. "Though I have their images in stone, their spirits haunt me. And were they here, they would demand I seek retribution for their deaths. I know it! *Haiya*, I will not rest until I see a fitting punishment for this evil that your people have done to me."

"Is not an eternal life in the mist punishment enough?" countered Black Lion.

"Nay! Never! Had I the strength, I would put a hex on you that would be a hundred times more powerful."

"If that is how you see it, then come and kill me now," Black Lion summoned. "You can end this thing. Come, let us do battle, for I would show you kindness, and if we are lucky, the victor may yet free his own people."

"*Haiya!* You know I cannot battle with you and give you the chance to show me kindness. But . . ." The Thunderer paused. Then he laughed again, sending shivers up and down Suzette's spine. "But I can kill those close to you. There is one here who hides in the bushes."

"*Hiya!* You will never get to her, for I protect her. You would have to kill me first."

"*Aa*, yes," said the Thunderer, "I can see this is so. And there is little I can do about it, for I cannot disobey the Creator and kill you . . . yet. But there are others that are dear to you. Ah"—he pointed southward—"I see your friends now. There is a show there."

"My friends have done nothing to you," cried Black Lion. "They are not part of this."

"Are they not?" said the Thunderer. "Did they not make the mistake of seeking to be friends with you?"

"*Hiya!* Do battle with me now. I am prepared to fend off your advances. Or do you lack the courage and must place your anger upon innocents?"

But the Thunderer's only reaction to this challenge was another misplaced laugh.

"Three days," roared the Thunderer. "That is all the time you have to save them. Three days."

"*Hiya!*"

But further protest was useless. Stepping into the spin of a whirling cloud, the Thunderer retreated, then disappeared, back into the darkened night above them. The clouds began to move, and, indeed, they traveled south.

"*Hiya! Hiya! Hiya!*" Black Lion shouted to the heavens, and then, "Damn!" he shouted in English. "Come back!"

But there was no answer.

"*Hiya!*" he cried again, then as though he spoke to another, he said, "If he can, he will kill my friends. We must go back to the show, and in a hurry if we are to be there in three days. You and the Song Bird must return as well. How far away from us are you?"

Who was Black Lion talking to?

And then she saw him, White Claw, the medicine man. He stood there, next to Black Lion. But where had he come from? Or had he been there all along? Did that mean that Irena was here, too? . . .

"Irena?" Suzette stood up from her hiding spot and took a few awkward steps forward. "Irena? Is Irena here, as well?" She paced toward Black Lion.

"Your grandmother is not with us here," said Black Lion.

Suzette glanced around the clearing, but no one else was to be seen. "I thought I saw White Claw."

"So you did," said Black Lion. "But in spirit form only. White Claw's physical body is not here."

"In spirit only?" She frowned.

"Did you hear?" Black Lion asked.

"I did."

"Then you understand that we must leave to go south. I must get to my friends quickly."

"Yes, but—"

"I think that if we do not rest, if we travel as quickly as we can, we can get there in time to warn them. Tell me, if I give you the money I have made from the show, do you think you might be able to buy a horse in the next town we come to?"

She nodded. "I probably could, but—"

"Then come, we have no time to lose." He made a move to leave.

"But Irena . . ."

"White Claw also knows the danger and is changing his course to come south."

Again, Black Lion made a move to leave, but she pulled him back. "What exactly is the danger?"

"It is this: I am the last champion for my people and the Thunderer knows it," he said with little hesitation. "There are no longer any boys left in my band of the tribe who could follow me. Therefore, because I am the last, if I miss this chance to lift the curse, my people are doomed forever."

"But I don't understand," she said, frowning at him. "In going south to your friends, aren't you putting your life in danger? What good is that going to do your people if you die?"

"None. However, I have no choice."

"But if you are truly concerned about your people . . ."

"Then you choose for me. Who do you think should

die? My friends here, or my people who are still enslaved?"

"No one should die, particularly you. But if I were to
choose, I think I would . . ." She shook her head. "Oh,
go. I can see that you must. But when you get there,
show the Thunderer kindness instead of animosity."

"I will if I am able. Come," he said as he turned
away, "let us go and purchase a horse, for only in this
way can we arrive at the show quickly enough."

"Yes, all right," she nodded. "How far away is the
next town?"

"It is close. Half a day's walk perhaps."

She slanted him a frown. "We will walk during the
day? Then you no longer worry about being found by
a posse?"

"It is a worry, yes, but it can no longer be helped."

"Yes, yes, of course." Her expression stilled. "I assume we leave at once."

"We do. Come and gather your things."

"What things?" she asked, as she swung her purse
over her shoulder.

But he didn't answer. And without any further delay,
they set out for the next town.

CHAPTER 22

Their "rush" turned out to be a slower pace than anything Suzette would have imagined, given their circumstances. This was most likely due to her condition, she supposed, with Black Lion still treating her as delicately as he was able.

His thoughtfulness and his care did endear him to her. Still, she worried for him. She had offered to travel faster, stating that she thought it would probably not harm the child to do so.

"We will not take the chance," Black Lion had replied. "The Thunderer knows I come. And we are making this journey as fast as we can."

Indeed, they had taken to traversing over the Plains by day and night, stopping only long enough to provide their horse with a rest, and Suzette with the nutrition needed to keep her healthy. Interestingly, not a single person accosted them. In truth, they met with no one at all.

Perhaps this was partially due to the dark and dreary conditions that haunted their travel. Murky clouds lingered overhead, and thunder wailed in the heavens regardless of the hour of the day.

Black Lion was driven, and she was certain that were she not with him, Black Lion would have rushed over the prairie with no regard for himself or his health. Perhaps, she thought, it was to his advantage that she did accompany him. At least she liked to think this was so, for when the time came for a confrontation with the Thunderer, it would serve him well to be rested.

At present, with her body situated before him in a side-saddle style, she was essentially sitting in his lap, and thus was spared the jolting influence of the trail. Often she found herself sleeping in Black Lion's arms, particularly during the evening hours.

Now that they traveled by horseback, the trip south to Colorado seemed to be much shorter than the journey north. Or maybe her perception was tainted because she feared what they might find at the end of their trip. And she did fear it.

"We are almost there," Black Lion said to her on this, their third day of travel. He had nudged her awake with a tap on her shoulder and a kiss on her neck.

She opened her eyes to a roll of thunder, which raged through the sky above them. Squirming in her seat, she tried to attain a position of some comfort. However, there was very little to be found.

"Do you know what time of day it is?"

"It is early morning. The sun has yet to make an appearance in the sky."

"And will it appear?"

"I would like to think that it will, but it is doubtful. The farther south we travel, the more desperate the storm clouds appear on the horizon."

"I suppose it is to be expected, since we are openly defying the one who rules the storms," she said, glancing forward. She wondered at herself. Had she now begun to believe that a god could, indeed, take human form? Or was there some other explanation for what she was certain she had experienced? A reason she couldn't fathom? She said, "When do you think we will come within sight of the show?"

"Perhaps when the sun reaches the high point in the sky."

She nodded, then translated, "At noon, then."

Scowling, she turned her face toward his, and said, "Besides warning your friends, have you considered what we might say to Mr. Cody about our disappearance?"

Again, he shrugged. "I will tell him the truth, that I left to find my friend and the Song Bird . . . if he asks."

"Of course he will ask. I will let him know also that I begged you to go with me, in case he worries that you stole me. I have thought that perhaps this is why the scouts were so persistent—they may believe that you took me from the show by force. I know that before we left, there was certainly plenty of gossip about us."

"Perhaps," he said.

"Do you think the Thunderer has caused any harm to the show yet?"

"I do not believe that he has," said Black Lion as he leaned down to speak in her ear. "If he harmed my friends, I would know it deep in my soul. That this has not happened causes me to believe he waits for me only. Perhaps he manipulates me so that he might kill me in a more public place. Or maybe he watches for my arrival before he wreaks his vengeance upon my friends. Either way, it matters not. He awaits me."

"Us," she said. "He waits for us."

Black Lion didn't answer. But then, she hadn't expected him to. With another glance at the threatening sky above them, Suzette tightened her arms around Black Lion's neck and stared off into the horizon.

The day was still overcast, cloudy and cold, though there was no snow on the ground, due perhaps to a winter thaw that promised spring, but did not deliver. The air was frigid and stationary, even though overhead the clouds continued to shift. Suzette and Black Lion had come at last to within a few miles of the Wild West Show. They had at present traversed to the bottom of a large rise in the land, beyond which, nestled into an immense valley, was the Wild West Show. Suzette could hear the faint refrains from the Wild West band, as well as smell the scent of the smoke that always accompanied the show. Wrapped as she was in Black Lion's arms, the warmth of his body gave her a feeling of security that was, she knew, nonexistent.

Her stomach twisted with dread. What awaited the two of them down there?

Whatever it was, Suzette feared that it was nothing good for either of them. Voicing her thoughts, she said, "Black Lion, I do not like this. There may be so much trouble that . . . Alas, I fear for you personally. There is prejudice there, and I am afraid that people may act against you first, and ask questions later."

"I am aware of this," he said to her. "However, there is no choice but for me to go forward. My friends are in trouble, my enemy awaits. What would you suggest? Running away? You know I cannot do that."

"No, not running away, but perhaps I could go down there first—before you, if only to ensure that you might be able to proceed without harm."

He scoffed. "Are you suggesting that I hide behind a woman's skirt?"

"No, only that . . . I could make the others understand the particulars of our situation first."

He pulled a face. "If I were to let you do that, I would be committing a most cowardly act. No, we will go there together."

She sighed. "Very well. Then let us form a different plan in case there is trouble."

"The plan we have is a good one, and I see no reason to change it," he said. Then he raised an eyebrow at her, as though a thought suddenly occurred to him. "Do you intend to alter it?"

"Well, yes, actually I do. I understand you need to find your friends and warn them, but what I still don't understand is why you are demanding that I go to Irena's tent instead of remaining with you."

"I would have you be safe."

"But will I be safe there? What if the Thunderer comes to Irena's tent and you are not there with me? Has he not already threatened me in my dreams?"

"*Hau*, but I am the one that the Thunderer wishes to harm, not you."

She shook her head at him. "I don't know. It is a mistake, I think. The danger is not in being with you, for, as you say, you will be there to protect me. The danger, I feel, is in being alone."

He frowned.

It was a small reaction, but it was enough that she pressed her point. "I do believe that I could be of help. The Thunderer fears me. Therefore, there must be some danger from me. Pray, keep me with you."

Again, he frowned. "If I agree to this, do you promise that you will not deliberately antagonize the Thunderer? That you will stay out of the way, regardless of what he does to me?"

"I . . . I . . . How can you ask such a thing of me?"

"Easily."

Above them, lightning flashed in the sky, the rumble of thunder following.

She said, "I cannot promise you that. And you cannot ask it of me. You have no right to send me away, either. I am a part of this. He came to me in my dreams . . ."

When Black Lion remained mute, she sighed. Speaking to this man when his mind was set was like endeavoring to talk sense into a stubborn bull. But she was not so easily persuaded either. "I am safe only as long as I am with you. Perhaps you should revise your plans, for this is how it will be. I will remain with you." She folded her arms across her chest.

He drew in a deep breath, sighed, then pointed forward. "There," he said, "can you see it?"

Their horse had climbed to the top of the rise, and in the valley below, stretched out across the Plains, were the rambling structures that made up the Wild West Show. Fences, barns, tents, tepees, canvas-covered bleachers and an enormous arena met her gaze.

At present, it appeared as if the show were engaged in the segment of the program called "Cowboy Fun," for she could see, down there in the arena, the tiny figures of the cowboys riding the wild, bucking horses.

As she watched, she saw also that a cabin was being set up center stage, in preparation most likely for the "Attack upon a Settler's Cabin" scene. On the outer perimeter of the arena, several Indians were on standby, waiting behind the scenic backdrop for their cues.

As the cowboys retreated and the pioneers took center stage, the Indians began to creep up to the cabin.

"You and I did that scene once," she commented.

"I remember it well," he replied. "How much easier it would be if I could, like my ancestors, steal you and put you in my tepee and keep you there."

She shook her head. "I would still object, and you, I fear, would be required to listen to me complain."

It seemed impossible that, though their situation was desperate, he grinned at her and said, "There are times when I think you are as stubborn as a wild pony."

"Who is it calling who stubborn?"

He arched a brow at her, winked, then reined in their horse to make its way down the natural rise in the prairie. He said, "I see little evidence of the Thunderer down there. I am glad."

No sooner had he spoken the words, than with a crash, a bolt of lightning struck a barn in the valley and set it afire. Immediately, she heard a call to arms, and she watched as men poured out of the arena to gather at the barn. Screams and the neighing of the horses could be heard even from this distance. And it was strange, for only a moment earlier the air had been frigid and still, but now the winds had kicked up, and the tiny, spinning clouds were everywhere.

As they watched, the fire spread to another building. Then came several lightning bolts all at once, one close to the arena, causing the performers in the show to seek cover. Another building was set ablaze.

Already Black Lion was lowering her to the ground. "I must go down there at once. Look yonder. Do you see those whirlwinds? Already they are touching down within the arena. He means to harm those people. I know you want me to take you with me, but you must see that I cannot. I have to hurry and if you were with me, I might do damage to your child because of this. You must stay here."

She nodded. "Very well. I understand," she said. "Go! And Black Lion, don't you dare take chances, and don't you dare forget that I love you."

Placing a hand alongside her face, he bent down for a quick kiss. "How could I ever forget?"

He didn't give her time to answer. Instead, straightening away, he was gone.

Black Lion whipped the horse into a full run over the prairie. There were people everywhere, as well as smoke and noise. Indeed, so much commotion was spinning out of control before him that no one took any special notice of him.

Glancing desperately into the arena and around it, Black Lion at last found Two Bears in the middle of the arena. His friend was caught up on the roof of one of the burning buildings. Worse, he was trapped from all sides.

Where were the rest of the men? Were they concentrating on the fires to the buildings, letting this one burn out of control?

Sprinting into the arena, Black Lion urged his horse up close to the settler's cabin. Out of the corner of his eye, he saw a whirlwind descending and touching down within the arena. That the cloud was gray and blue was not a good sign. He had to work fast.

"*Kola!*" Black Lion called out to Two Bears. There were screams everywhere, from the players as well as the audience, and Black Lion feared his friend might not hear him above the din. "*Ito*, come," he called out again, "I am here at the side of this cabin. *Kola, ito!* Leap through the flames and jump down onto my pony. Now! Do it now! Hurry, before the roof collapses and kills you!"

Rising up, Two Bears ran in the direction of Black Lion's voice.

"Easy, girl," Black Lion coaxed his pony. "It is almost done."

On the edge of the roof now, Two Bears took a flying leap through the fire and vaulted down, and except for catching his ankle, it was a perfect jump.

Two Bears was panting as he said, "*Kola!* My friend, when did you return?"

"There is no time to explain," said Black Lion. Swinging his leg over the horse, he jumped to the ground. "Take this pony," he shouted. "On the plains to the north, I left my wife to fend for herself. Go to her now and see to her. Stay with her. Defend her if you must."

"*Hokake! Kola!*" Saluting each other with a quick, fast grip on each other's arms, the two men straightened up, and while Two Bears kicked the horse in its flanks, Black Lion watched him speed out of the arena.

But only for a moment. He turned quickly to see what had become of that cloud. His worst fear was realized. It was, indeed, the Thunderer. But the god had spun away from him, and Black Lion could only watch helplessly as the Thunderer flicked his wrist and shot lightning toward the log cabin. The whole structure turned to a blaze.

Were there people within?

"*Hokake!*" Rushing toward the cabin, Black Lion kicked open the door. Indeed, there was a white woman in that small, little room, one of the show's actresses, who, instead of fleeing the cabin, like she should have done, was cowering inside. Black Lion motioned her to come out, but she seemed to lack the courage. She appeared to be frozen in place. Black Lion darted inside, picked her up and dashed outside with her.

"Go! Leave here at once!" he said, setting her back on her feet. She needed no further urging, and with a quick "thank you," she charged out of the arena as fast as she could.

Again, Black Lion turned to confront the Thunderer, but the god had turned his attention to the canvas-covered bleachers.

There were thousands of people there unable to leave fast enough.

It did occur to Black Lion that he might show this half man, half god kindness, understanding. But even as the thought took hold of him, he watched as the Thunderer struck one of the Indians on the sidelines. The man fell dead.

That was enough.

Shouting out his battle cry, Black Lion leaped forward, hurling himself into the blue and gray mass that was the Thunderer. Lightning crashed and thunder bellowed above them, yet Black Lion was so intent, he did not notice it.

Man and god rolled over and over in the dirt and grass, first one on top, then the other. The Thunderer produced a knife. Black Lion followed suit.

Neither was supposed to kill the other, or so the Creator had decreed, so long ago. But there were some things a man had to do.

The Thunderer threw a jab with his knife. Black Lion ducked, grabbed hold of his enemy around the waist and pulled with all of his strength.

The mighty Thunderer toppled, but only for a moment. Gaining his feet, the Thunderer lunged forward, and thrust out again with his knife, and it would have been a fatal stab had it met its mark, but Black Lion parried it by hitting out at the Thunderer's arm. The Thunderer went down again.

He was vulnerable and exposed. Now was Black Lion's time to strike, and he very well might have plunged his knife into his enemy's chest, when . . .

"No!"

Black Lion recognized that voice. It was his wife.

What was she doing here? Distracted, he dropped his concentration. It was a fatal mistake.

The Thunderer seized advantage, coming up over Black Lion, and taking hold of his own knife, he plunged it deep into Black Lion's body.

CHAPTER 23

Standing alone on the prairie, Suzette's intuition would not be ignored. As she watched Black Lion ride away, she knew she couldn't stay here. She was needed there, with him. Somehow, in some way, she had to be there.

Since access to a horse was all but impossible, she picked up the edge of her skirt, and stepped quickly toward the show.

Smoke filled the already cloudy and gray sky; it pervaded her lungs, and she could only imagine that those souls breathing the air down there were likely to choke. Voices, screams, shouts echoed through the air, and the urgency that filled the heavens prompted her to hurry.

In the distance, a rider broke free from the complex, and even as she watched, he was speeding toward her. Was it Black Lion, who had come back for her? Did he realize he needed her after all?

Her spirits rose.

But as the rider pulled closer into view, she realized it was not Black Lion.

A man pulled in rein as he drew near her, and he

said, "I am Two Bears. Your husband has asked me to look after you."

She nodded. "Good," she said. "Could you give me a ride? I need to be down there."

Two Bears looked doubtful. "I do not believe that my friend asked me to bring you to him."

"And yet, I must go there. If you will not take me, then I'll go on my own."

He looked uncertain. He hesitated. And she said, "He would have taken me with him, had he not needed to rush."

At last Two Bears nodded. "*Hau. Waste.* I will do it. Come closer." She did so, and Two Bears, reaching down, pulled her up behind him onto the pony.

"What is happening down there?" she asked, as they set out over the prairie. "I have heard screams and shouting, I can see the fires, and there is so much smoke in the air."

"It is the Thunderer, my *kola*'s enemy. He is come here in the flesh, and he is angry. He tried to kill me. My friend, your husband, saved me. But that is all that I know with certainty. Your husband, my *kola*, asked me to ride out to you and take care of you."

"Yes," she said, bobbing her head up and down.

It seemed to take forever to get there, and when they did at last arrive, the air was so heavy with debris and smoke that it was hard to see, let alone breathe and know what to do.

"Where is he?" she asked.

"He is in the arena with the Thunderer."

"Please take me there, quickly."

Two Bears did as asked, and heading through the entrance, he delivered her into the arena. As he helped her down from the horse, he said, "You should know that Rabbit Leggings is my wife. She is not married to your husband."

Suzette smiled at the man, and she said, "I know."

And that's when she saw him. Her stomach turned and twisted, and she grabbed hold of her belly as though in protection. Could this be true? Were her eyes really seeing her husband engaged in a struggle with a man who appeared a god? She pinched herself.

Indeed, she was awake.

Had her husband lost his mind?

She had to do something, but what? The men slashed out at each other, both waving knifes. And Suzette realized that if she did nothing, she would lose Black Lion.

"No!" she cried out. Unfortunately, it was the exact wrong thing to do.

Black Lion hesitated. It gave the Thunderer the chance he had been waiting for. As though looking at a play in slow motion, Suzette watched in horor as the Thunderer plunged his knife deeply into Black Lion's body.

"No!" she cried again. "No!"

But Black Lion wasn't dead. He sat up, desperately motioning for her to run away, but the Thunderer knocked him down again, and drew back his arm, lifting that knife high into the air. He was ready to strike.

She had to do something to help, but what?

And that's when she knew what she was perhaps destined to do.

Without thinking further, she began to sing, shyly, tentatively at first, treading ever so slowly forward toward the two enemies. She sang:

> "O mio babbino caro,
> mi piace è bello, bello;

> vo'andare in Porta Rossa
> a comperar l'anello!
> Sì, sì, ci voglio andare!
> e se l'amassi indarno,
> andrei sul Ponte Vecchio,
> ma per buttarmi in Arno!
> Mi struggo e mi tormento!
> O Dio, vorrei, morir!"

It was a well-known aria, written by the composer Puccini. In the opera a rich man's daughter pleads with her father to allow her to marry the man of her choice. And though Suzette doubted that this was *the* song her husband sought, what difference did it make? At least her actions were having an effect, the Thunderer had stopped, was listening to her, though he still held the knife high in the air.

And so she continued to sing in the three-four time of the aria:

> "O mio babbino caro,
> mi piace è bello, bello;
> vo'andare in Porta Rossa
> a comperar l'anello!
> Sì, sì, ci voglio andare!
> e se l'amassi indarno,
> andrei sul Ponte Vecchio,
> ma per buttarmi in Arno!
> Mi struggo e mi tormento!
> O Dio, vorrei, morir!"

Somewhere amid the song, another voice had started to harmonize along with hers. Cound it be? Yes, it was Irena. Irena was here, raising her voice along with Suzette, as though to give Suzette confidence. Glancing quickly behind her, Suzette met her grandmother's gaze, and for a moment, her spirits lifted. Looking forward again, Suzette saw that the two men seemed to be held in suspension. Thus, there was only one thing to do, and that was to continue. The aria had only the one verse, and she began to repeat it, only this time, Cody's Wild West band had arranged themselves back in the arena. And though slow to start, they began to play along with her. Stepping right up to the two men, Suzette came down onto her knees beside Black Lion. He was bleeding from the hip, but he sat up in recognition of her. And so she sang, the pleading in the song perfect, for it fit the pleading in her heart:

> "O mio babbino caro,
> mi piace è bello, bello;
> vo'andare in Porta Rossa
> a comperar l'anello!
> Sì, sì, ci voglio andare!
> e se l'amassi indarno,
> andrei sul Ponte Vecchio,
> ma per buttarmi in Arno!
> Mi struggo e mi tormento!
> O Dio, vorrei, morir!"

Midway through the song, another voice joined hers. It was low, it was male. It was Black Lion singing every word along with her as though he had been born Italian.

Reaching out, she touched Black Lion's face, running her fingers slowly down his cheek, to his breast. It was the only way she knew to demonstrate her love for him. How she loved this man, and if it were destined that she were to lose him, she would have him know of her devotion.

Glancing up at the Thunderer, she saw the hatred still

etched within his gaze. But still, he did nothing, and it
gave her hope. With full accompaniment now, she sang
the song once again:

> "O mio babbino caro,
> mi piace è bello, bello;
> vo'andare in Porta Rossa,
> a comperar l'anello!
> Sì, sì, ci voglio andare!
> e se l'amassi indarno,
> andrei sul Ponte Vecchio,
> ma per buttarmi in Arno!
> Mi struggo e mi tormento!
> O Dio, vorrei, morir!"

Suzette stumbled toward the god, and reaching out to
him, fell to her knees and grabbed hold of his hand.
Placing her face against that hand, she sang out the
song's last refrain, pleading:

> "Babbo, pietà, pietà!" *Daddy, have pity, have pity!*
> "Babbo, pietà, pietà!" *Daddy, have pity, have pity!*

The music ended. Suzette by this time was unable to
hold back the tears, and not another sound could be
heard within the arena.

The Thunderer's arm, which had been holding the
knife, came down as though now that the music had
stopped, he was at liberty to kill her. It was obvious that
he would do it.

"No!" cried Black Lion, throwing himself in front of
his wife. "No! She is with child."

It was difficult to know what went through the
Thunderer's mind. But as he gazed first at one of them,
and then at the other, his features changed. He glanced

at her stomach, then into her eyes. And as she stared back at him, she watched as the hatred seemed to drift away.

His arm dropped to hang limply at his side, and shaking his head so very slightly, the Thunderer let the knife fall to the ground.

He said in that booming voice of his, "*Go!* Both of you! I grant him his life. I grant you life. And I will not do to you as has been done to me. I will not kill your child. Go!"

Suzette gasped aloud, and sitting back, she at last let the tears fall freely.

But the spectacle wasn't over. The clouds above them parted, and a single beam of light, fell directly into the arena. And there, within that light, were four figures, all of them half bird, half human. And Suzette didn't need to be told that it was the Thunderer's children. Moreover, they were laughing and singing as though all these thousands of years had never happened.

"*Father!*" they cried out one after another. "*Father!*"

And Suzette, gazing up into the Thunderer's face, thought she had never seen a man more on the verge of tears.

He called out, "My children! You are alive! You are alive!"

And that was when the impossible happened: The Thunderer did, indeed, cry.

Meanwhile, the audience, who had witnessed the entire affair, at last came alive, as though they, too, had been held in suspended animation. Amid the "bravos" and the applause, as though this had been a performance like none other, they came to their feet in a standing ovation.

But there was to be no repeat performance this day. Instead, a better thing had happened. Because of a song and a child, there was now less hatred in the world.

CHAPTER 24

Suzette looked up. A crowd of people, all of them American Indian, surrounded them. But she recognized none of these people. Who were they?

"It is done. These are my people," said Black Lion, as though he read her thoughts. Though his injury did not permit him freedom of movement, he pulled Suzette into his arms. And there were tears in his eyes as he said, "The curse is gone. I can hardly believe it. My people are free at last."

He was crying. She was crying, and they embraced as White Claw and Irena joined them. Irena took Suzette's hand in her own, while White Claw said, "Grandson, you are injured. Come, I will attend to you."

"*Aa*, yes," said Black Lion in the language of the Blackfeet. "And I will welcome your attention, Grandfather, but first let me cast my eyes upon my people, for I have not seen them in many years. My father, my mother . . ." He held out his arms toward them.

Two people stepped forward to join them. But though

the American Indian might have disdained a public show of affection, they, too, joined the embrace.

"We are proud of you, my son," said a man that Suzette thought must be Black Lion's father.

"My son . . ." said Black Lion's mother, simply.

"It is time," said White Claw. "Let us take you to your lodge where I can attend to your wound."

The two men helped Black Lion to his feet, and it was only then that Suzette realized there was blood staining the front of her bicycling suit. Her tears spilled down upon it to join his blood.

Blood and tears, and yet so much happiness.

As they trailed behind the men, Irena hugged Suzette and didn't let go, even when they entered into the Indian encampment. Buffalo Bill detained them for a moment along the way.

"Welcome back, ladies," he said. "I am happy to see you, though I do admit you both gave us quite a chase. However, I hear that you also furnished us with a show unlike any other this afternoon."

Irena answered, grinning up at him. "Yes, indeed, we did," she said, "although I am afraid that the show was a one time only performance."

"Then you are not back to stay?" asked Cody.

"I will honor my contract with you," said Irena, "but then I must follow my heart. Indeed, the reason I came here was to find the love of my life. And at last I have found him."

Cody nodded, and for a moment, he looked sad. However, he recovered swiftly enough.

"Nice to have you back, as well, Miss Joselyn," he said, his glance taking in Suzette's ragged appearance.

She smiled and said, "My pleasure, Mr. Cody, though actually, my name is Mrs. Black Lion."

"Mrs.? Mrs.? Black Lion?"

"Yes, indeed," said Suzette. "When you have a moment, ask your chaplain about it."

Glancing from one of them to the other, Buffalo Bill pulled his hat off his head, rubbed his arm against his forehead, shook his head, and said, "Well, I wish you women happiness." Suddenly, he grinned at them both, and sauntered away.

"He's really not such a bad person, is he?" Suzette commented, watching his departing figure.

"No, indeed," said Irena. "But he does seem to have a penchant for the opera stars, does he not?"

Suzette laughed. "I do believe that he does."

Later that night, White Claw held a council consisting of himself, Irena, Suzette and Black Lion, as well as Black Lion's father and mother. As the day had worn on, Suzette had been given the opportunity to change clothes, as had Irena. At present, they were both comfortably seated around the lodge fire in Black Lion's tepee.

Black Lion's wound had been dressed, and he, too, was wearing his best buckskin. He was also looking quite dear, and fortunately, quite well. As was traditional, the men were seated on the left, the women on the right, with White Claw at the head of the council toward the very back of the lodge.

Lighting the pipe again with buffalo dung, White Claw presided over the ceremony, ensuring that the pipe was properly presented to the Sky, to the Earth, to the Four Winds and was passed to each person in the council, including the women.

When it was done, and the pipe was returned to him,

he began, saying, "I have called us together so that I can answer any questions that you might have. As you know, all our people are freed from the mist at last. It is done. But I fear you may still have questions. We will start first with your wife, Black Lion, for without her quick thinking, the curse might never have been broken."

Suzette, never one to back away from praise in the past, found herself blushing and averting her gaze.

"Have you any questions, Little Blue Eyes, wife of Black Lion?"

Suzette hesitated momentarily, then said, "I do have one question."

White Claw nodded.

"What are your intentions toward my grandmother?"

So unexpected was the inquiry, White Claw smiled. "Are you speaking of my wife, the one we know as the Song Bird?"

"Your . . . wife? . . . Irena, you didn't tell me," Suzette accused.

"There has been so little time, Suzie. And there's been much to do, preparations, and . . ."

"Well, congratulations to you both!" said Suzette.

Irena smiled, while White Claw said, "We are very happy to have your good wishes. Have you any other questions?"

"Actually, yes, I do. It is apparent that the song melted the Thunderer's heart, is that correct?"

White Claw nodded.

"Then if his heart had melted, why did he start to kill me?"

"He has lived too long with hatred, I fear. But when your husband informed him of your condition, not only did the curse end for our people, but for him, as well."

"But who brought the children back to life?"

"That is a very good question, and indeed, it requires

a good answer. Our people committed a wrong all those years ago, yes, but the Thunderer was not, himself, innocent. He, too, killed many people, and his heart has ever since been filled with hatred. What he failed to realize is that he, too, must sacrifice, for every life taken is precious. When he threw down his knife, refusing to kill you, he sacrificed a thing of some worth to him. He forfeited his hatred. And as he saved your child's life, so, too, did the Creator save his children. It has come full circle."

Suzette nodded. "Yes. I see."

"Do you have any other questions?"

"No, none that I can think of now."

White Claw nodded. "Then we will ask our champion, Black Lion, have you any questions?"

"I do," spoke up Black Lion. "It is this: The Creator gave us the clue to show kindness and decency to our enemies. To help them. And yet, even as I ended the curse, I did not help my enemy. I understand that the song melted the Thunderer's heart. Was it that which freed my people? For I failed in my resolve to show kindness."

"This is another good question. Indeed, it was not the song that freed your people, though it helped because it started the disintegration of the Thunderer's hatred. Yet, this is something I have little understood, for, upon the curse being lifted, each champion has voiced much the same thing to me. Each hero has, without fail, told me that he thought he was doing wrong, and that he was sacrificing his chance to help his people by *not* showing kindness to the enemy. I have pondered this deeply. I have asked the Creator, and at last I understand. It was not enough to simply be kind to an enemy, to sacrifice oneself for one's people and to have only their welfare at heart. The people themselves had to sacrifice, to give up everything for the curse to end. And this was the crux of the matter. You, as their champion, were 'the people.' When you sacrificed their plight, it was you, as the people, who sacrificed everything. Doing one's duty, keeping only the tribe and its welfare in one's heart, could never break the curse. Do you see?"

Black Lion looked confused, while White Claw went on to explain:

"You, as your people's champion, represented your band of the Clan. To the Creator you *were* the people. Therefore, thinking only of the Clan's welfare and putting your people before all else was, to the Creator, selfish. Indeed, each hero who broke the curse eventually sacrificed everything, and I think it safe to say that without love such sacrifice would never have happened. *Haiya!* It is this that broke the curse . . . it was love. And perhaps we should always remember this: It was love that had the power to conquer a curse thousands of years old."

Black Lion nodded.

"Have you any other questions?"

"Only one other."

"*Aa*, yes, what is it?"

"Will my wife and I be able to find happiness in this world, when there is so much prejudice?"

White Claw grinned. "*Aa*," he said, "you will find much happiness, indeed. Your people need you. Your people need your wife. As it has been before, so it will be. Your lives will be filled with love, honor, and perhaps also with music."

EPILOGUE

The Wild West Show, Colorado Territory

The baby's cry split through the air. Black Lion, who had been pacing in front of the tent that he and his wife now called their home, stopped and grinned.

Flinging back the tent's flap, he rushed into the white man's tepee, not stopping until he reached the chamber the two of them called their bedroom. He was greeted by Irena's and Rabbit Leggings's delighted smiles.

"It's a boy," said Irena. "A fine-looking, beautiful boy."

"A son, my son," said Black Lion, grinning inanely. "And my wife?"

"She is doing well. For this being her first baby, it was a quick birth. I think she is blessed. But she is also missing her husband, I believe. The doctor will allow you a few moments with her, I am certain."

Black Lion needed no further inducement. Coming around the Japanese partition, his gaze sought her out at once, and he was pleased to see that his wife looked healthy, if a bit tired. And in her arms was the babe.

"Black Lion," she said, as soon as she looked up to see him. "Come closer and meet your son."

Black Lion did as asked, and knelt down beside her bed. The baby was wrapped in a soft blanket. His skin was red, his hair was black and his eyes were a clear blue.

"He is beautiful," said Black Lion. "Almost as beautiful as my wife."

She grinned. "How you flatter me. I am certain I am quite a mess."

"You are the most beautiful woman of my acquaintance, and I will hear no argument saying differently. Black Lion offered his finger to the babe, who took it immediately.

"I have been thinking of names," she said.

"Oh? Have you a name for him already?"

"If you agree, I would like to christen him after my father, John Carl Black Lion."

"It is a good name," said Black Lion. "A very good name, indeed."

He raised his gaze to hers, and she smiled at him. "I love you so much," she said. "And I have never been so happy."

"And I love you. You, my wife, you hold my heart, will always hold my heart." He kissed her then, knowing with certainty that whatever the future would hold for them, they would always have each other.

NOTE TO THE READER

In writing this book, I tried to stay as historically accurate as possible. The scenes that I have described in the Wild West Show were scenes inspired directly from Buffalo Bill's original program. There are many pictures of these genuine acts, as well as a few movies that were made of them. I did, however, take two liberties that I thought I would mention.

Buffalo Bill generally opened his shows with the American Indians riding first into the arena. I altered the sequence to have the Indians enter the arena last. My reasoning is that "he who is last on the program is often the most important." While this is not always the case, having the Indians enter last into the arena worked well within the story line of the book.

One other liberty that I seized upon concerns the song "O mio babbino caro" by Puccini. The aria is from the opera *Gianni Schicchi*. My friend, Caroline Veach, a tremendous musician, helped me find this song. When she and her husband heard the story line of the book, they both suggested this song and loaned me the DVD

Andre Rieu, Live in Dublin. This is probably one of the most moving and beautiful songs and performances I have ever heard or seen, and it inspired the ending so greatly that I left the song in the story. However, the aria was first premiered in 1918 and my story takes place in 1892. I hope you will pretend along with me that this song was in existence during the time period of this story.

Thank you.

Karen Kay

GLOSSARY

Because there are some words and ideas in my story that may be foreign to the reader, I've provided a glossary for your ease in reading. Please note that wherever possible, in the story itself, I have placed the English translation after the world used.

Aa—A Blackfeet word meaning "yes."

Band—In most North American Indian tribes, a band refers to a smaller unit within a tribe—the people of which are mostly related. These people hunt together and camp together. Often the different tribal bands meet together in the summer and/or fall to socialize and celebrate. The Hunkpapa are a band of the Lakota Sioux tribe. Sitting Bull was a member of the Hunkpapa band of the Lakota Sioux.

Ece—A Lakota word that means to be surprised, usually with indignation.

Eya—A Lakota word meaning "well, then . . ." or "also, too . . ."

Grandfather/Grandson—These terms of endearment were exchanged between the young and their elders. For a youngster to call a man "grandfather" or an elder to call a boy "grandson" does not necessarily denote a direct blood relationship. Thus, any elder could be called "grandfather" by any of the young people of the tribe. And vice versa.

Hannia—A Blackfeet word that is used as we might say, "really!"

Hau/Han—A Lakota word meaning "yes." Men say "hau," women say "han." Often today men and women in greeting will say, "Hau, hau," which would mean "hello."

Hepela—Surprise of joy at greeting a friend.

Heyoka—A Heyoka in Lakota society is a backward person. This person would have dreamed of the Thunder Being in order to become a Heyoka. Heyokas did everything backward. They spoke the opposite of what they meant, washed in sand, became dirty in water, slept with blankets in summer and none in winter. They walked backward and did everything backward. To dream of the Thunderer in this manner was one of the most sacred of all dreams, yet one that was dreaded most, for if one who had been given this dream disobeyed it, he did so at risk of sudden death from a lightning strike. A good movie that demonstrates a Heyoka is the movie *Little Big Man* starring Dustin Hoffman.

Hiya—A Lakota word meaning "no."

Ho—A Lakota expression meaning "well, then . . ."

Kola—A Lakota word meaning "friend." At this time

kola meant a special kind of friend—usually friendship between males. These friends would hunt together, war together and would pledge to give their lives for one another. Such pledges were a sacred oath.

Medicine—Medicine refers to the great mystery or to something mysterious or powerful. To have medicine meant that one had obtained a certain power, usually through dreams or some deed. Thus for one to say that another "had medicine" was a compliment, meaning that the person had some kind of spiritual power.

Nacece—A Lakota word meaning "perhaps."

Sacred Song—The American Indian owns different songs. These songs may be passed down from relative to relative or simply given to one by another. They may also be given to one by the spiritual forces of nature or by the birds and animals. But one did not sing a song without the owner's permission to do so.

Sece—Another Lakota word meaning "perhaps."

Spirit Protector—A spirit protector was usually an animal, or in some cases, a being, who would take pity on a man who was undertaking a vision quest. This animal or being would give his power to the man for life, provided the man held firm to what the protector instructed him to do. As I have said in this book, the Creator takes no sides, and so a man would plead with the forces of nature for aid in his life, particularly if he were going to war or were to be engaged in another activity that might hold some danger.

Tula—A Lakota word meaning "to be surprised."

Wakan—A Lakota word meaning "holy," or "sacred."

Waste—A Lakota word meaning "good."

Winkte—A Lakota word for a person who is a hermaphrodite, a person who is both male and female.

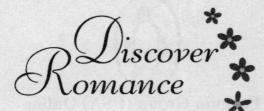